PETER C
CAN LAD

REGINALD Evelyn Peter Southouse Cheyney (1896-1951) was
born in Whitechapel in the East End of London. After serving
as a lieutenant during the First World War, he worked as
a police reporter and freelance investigator until he found
success with his first Lemmy Caution novel. In his lifetime
Cheyney was a prolific and wildly successful author, selling, in
1946 alone, over 1.5 million copies of his books. His work was
also enormously popular in France, and inspired Jean-Luc
Godard's character of the same name in his dystopian sci-fi
film *Alphaville*. The master of British noir, in Lemmy Caution
Peter Cheyney created the blueprint for the tough-talking,
hard-drinking pulp fiction detective.

PETER CHEYNEY

CAN LADIES KILL?

DEAN STREET PRESS

Published by Dean Street Press 2022

All Rights Reserved

First published in 1938

Cover by DSP

ISBN 978 1 914150 91 3

www.deanstreetpress.co.uk

CHAPTER ONE
FREEZE-OUT FOR A DAME

I AM standin' lookin' at this house and I think that if ever I get any dough I will settle down an' get myself a dump like this.

Because it has got what they call atmosphere. It is standin' back off the roadway on the side of a little green slope. There is a white thicket fence separatin' it from the road an' there are flower beds and ornamental bits edged out with white stones all over the place. Through the gate there is a flight of wide steps linkin' a sorta terrace path that runs up to the front door.

Me—I reckon I would like a rest. Travellin' by airplane is all very well but it sorta gets you tired. But then I've found that anythin' gets me tired. Even "G" men get tired, but maybe they told you about that.

Walkin' up the path to the porch I get wonderin' what this Marella Thorensen is goin' to be like. I'm sorry that we never got any picture of this dame because if I see a picture of a dame I sorta get ideas about her. But as I'll be seein' her in a minute maybe the picture don't matter.

This is a funny sorta job. You've seen the letter that this dame wrote to the Director at Washington. She says it's mysterious. I looked this word up in the dictionary, an' it says that mysterious means enigmatical, so I look up enigmatical an' it says that means beyond human comprehension. Well, it ain't beyond my comprehension.

Work it out for yourself. If this dame writes a letter to the Director of the Federal Bureau and suggests in it that there's some sorta funny business goin' on that he oughta know about, well it looks like there is some sorta hey-hey breakin' around these parts. O.K. Well if that's so it looks a bit screwy to me that she don't go an' tell her husband about it. After all if you've been married to a guy for ten years he's the guy you go to. So what?

But then ladies do funny things. But who am I to tell you that? I reckon you knew that for yourself. Dames are a lot more definite than people think. It's guys who are the romantic cusses. I've known plenty dames who was very practical, like one in Cincinnati.

She was a religious dame this baby, an' she stabbed her second husband with a screwdriver just because he wouldn't go to church of a Sunday, which shows you that women can get tough too.

These ruminations have brought me to the front porch. There is a pretty ornamental bell-push, and when I work it I hear a musical bell ring somewhere in the house. I stand there waitin'.

It's four o'clock an' there is a bit of a breeze blowin' up. I think maybe there is goin' to be some rain. Nobody don't take any notice of the bell so I push it again. Five or six minutes go by. I take a stroll around the side of the house. It's a swell place, not too big or too small. A path goes around to the right an' behind the house I can see a well-kept lawn with a little Chinese pagoda stuck in the far corner.

In the centre of the back of the house are two French windows givin' out on to the lawn, an' I can see that one of 'em is open. I walk up. When I get to the French window I can see that whoever was comin' in or goin' out last time they was in such a hurry that they had to bust the handle off, which is a funny thing to do to a glass window.

I stick my head inside an' look inta a long low room. It's full of nice furniture, an' all sorts of pretty knick-knacks. There ain't nobody there. I go in an' do a spot of coughin' just to let anybody know that I'm around. Nothin' happens.

On the right of the room in a corner is a door, I walk over to this, open it an' go out inta a passage. I cough some more but I might be a consumptive for all anybody cares. I walk along the passage an' come to the hallway behind the front porch. There is a table on the right with a brass tray on it with some mail.

Under the table up against the wall where it has slipped down off the tray I see a telegraph form. I pick it up an' read it. It is a telegram from the Director to Mrs. Marella Thorensen tellin' her that Special Agent L. H. Caution will be contactin' her between four an' five to-night.

Well, where is she? I turn around an' I call out Mrs. Thorensen. All I get is the air. I walk back along the passage an' up to a wide flight of stairs away down on the left. I go up. On the first floor

I turn around into another passage with the banister rail on the right where it turns and two or three white door rooms on the left.

Facing me at the end of the passage is a door an' it is open, an' lyin' on the floor is a woman's silk scarf. I walk along and stick my head in the door. It is a woman's bedroom an' it looks very nice to me. It also looks as if some one has been havin' a spot of hey-hey around here because all the things on the dressin' table between the two windows that look out towards the front of the house are on the floor. A big lounge chair has been overturned an' there is a towel lyin' curled up like a snake right in the middle of the blue carpet. I think that maybe Mrs. Thorensen has been in a bad temper about somethin'.

I go downstairs again, walk along the passage an' start doin' a little investigatin'. I go all over the place but I can't find anybody. When I get into the kitchen I see a note stuck up against a tea canister on the table. This note is addressed to *"Nellie"* an' it says:

"Don't worry about dinner. I shall not be back until nine to-night."

It looks to me like Nellie has taken time out too.

I go out of the place the way I came in an' shut the French window. I go back to where I have parked the hired car, get into it an' light a cigarette. I reckon that if this dame is not goin' to be back till nine o'clock to-night I might as well go over to San Francisco an' have a word with O'Halloran. Maybe he can wise me up to something.

I am just goin' to start the engine when I see a car come around the corner way down the road an' pull up outside the Villa Rosalito. A dame gets out. She is a slim sorta baby with a nice walk, an' she is wearin' a funny little hat an' has got black hair. I reckon she is goin' to pay a call on Mrs. Thorensen.

I start the engine an' drive off, but because I am a curious cuss, as I go past the car outside the villa, I take the number. Way up at the end of the pathway I can see this dame pushin' the bell-push. I reckon she'll be disappointed.

I make San Francisco by five-thirty. I put the car in a garage an' go along to the Sir Francis Drake Hotel which is a dump where

I have stayed before. I check in, take a drink an' a shower an' do a little quiet thinkin'.

Maybe you are thinkin' along the same lines as I am, an' anyhow you gotta agree that it looks durn silly for this dame Marella Thorensen to write letters askin' for "G" men to be sent along an' then, when she gets a wire to say that I am comin', to scram outa the house an' leave a note for the cook sayin' that she won't be back till nine o'clock. At the back of my head there is a big idea that there is somethin' screwy goin' on around here.

I get a hunch. I call through to the Hall of Justice, an' ask if O'Halloran is there. I get right through to him. "Hey, Terry," I tell him, "listen. Are you doin' some heavy sleuthin' or have you got enough time on your hands to come around to the Sir Francis Drake an' talk to Lemmy Caution?"

He says sure an' he will come around.

Terence O'Halloran, who is a Police Lieutenant in 'Frisco, has been a buddy of mine since I got him a beat poundin' job in this man's city a long whiles ago. This guy can also drink more whisky than any cop I ever knew, an' in spite of the fact that his face is as homely as a mountain gorge he sometimes has brains. Pretty soon he comes around an' I order up a bottle of Irish whisky, an' start workin' the pump handle on him.

"Looky, Terry," I tell him, "this is sorta unofficial, see, because right now this business is not a police department job, but maybe you know something about Mrs. Marella Thorensen, an' if so you can spill it."

I tell him about the letter this dame has wrote to the Bureau of Investigation, an' how I came out to contact her.

"I'm goin' back there to the Rosalito dump at nine o'clock," I say, "an' I thought that maybe I could fill in the time gettin' the low down on this babe an' her husband."

"There ain't much to tell, Lemmy," he says. "I don't think I've seen the dame in years. She's easy to look at an' she only comes into 'Frisco once in a blue moon. But her husband is a fly baby. I reckon this guy Aylmar Thorensen knows his groceries all right, an' I'll tell you why.

"Six years ago this palooka is just another attorney. He gets an industrial case here an' there but he don't amount to anything much, an' then all of a sudden he gets himself appointed as attorney for a guy called Lee Sam. Ho Lee Sam is in the money. He's got a silk business in California an' four factories on the other side of the slot. But like all Chinks he hasta go on makin' some more, so he starts musclin' around in the number rackets, and pin table takes in Chinatown an' gets himself tied up with a guy called Jack Rocca who come here outa Chicago an' who has got a record as long as the Golden Gate bridge.

"One way an' another it looks like these two are goin' to get themselves in bad with the Hall of Justice, but this guy Thorensen is always there with bells on just when things are lookin' not so hot. If it wasn't for him keepin' Lee Sam's nose clean I reckon that Chink woulda been in plenty trouble—money or no money."

I nod. "An' I suppose Lee Sam pays plenty to keep a legal eye on the proceedin's?" I ask him.

"Right," he says. "An' has Thorensen done himself good. That guy has got himself two cars an' a swell house out at Burlingame an' an apartment on Nob Hill. He's a clever guy that Thorensen, but maybe some of these guys are so clever that in the long run they double-cross themselves."

He lights himself a cigarette.

"Say, Lemmy," he says, "what's this dame Marella Thorensen tryin' to do to you Federal guys?"

"Search me," I tell him, "I wouldn't know, but I reckon I'm goin' to find out. This dame leaves a note for the cook sayin' she'll be back by nine o'clock so I'm bustin' outa here at about a quarter to nine. When I've seen this dame maybe I'll know what I'm talkin' about. In the meantime," I go on, "supposin' we eat."

I ring down to the desk an' I order a dinner, an' we sit an' eat an' talk about old times before prohibition when men was men, an' women was glad of it.

At half-past eight Terry scrams. He has got to go back to the Hall of Justice on some job, an' at a quarter to nine I start thinkin' about gettin' the car an' goin' back to have my little talk with Marella Thorensen.

I am just walkin' outa the room when the telephone bell rings. It is O'Halloran.

"Hey, Lemmy," he says, "what do you know about this? You remember I was telling you about this guy Lee Sam. Well, he's just been through here on the telephone. He says he's worried. I'll tell you why. This guy's daughter has been over in Shanghai, see, on a holiday or something. O.K. Well this afternoon she rings him up. She's just got in at Alameda across the Bay on the China Clipper from Shanghai. Well Lee Sam is plenty surprised at this because he didn't know anything about this dame coming back, and he says so what? She tells him that she's had a letter from Marella Thorensen saying that she's got to see her and fixing that she'll be in at the Villa Rosalito this afternoon.

"Lee Sam's daughter says that she is taking a car right away and going out to the Villa Rosalito at Burlingame, that she reckons to be there in about half an hour and that she ought to be home at the Lee Sam place on Nob Hill at six o'clock.

"O.K. Well, she ain't appeared and the old boy is getting scared. He is wonderin' what's happened to her. He's gettin' all the more scared because he's been ringing the Villa Rosalito on the telephone and he can't get any reply. It looks like there ain't anybody there. I thought I'd let you know and if you're goin' out like you said maybe you can tell me what's goin' on around there. Then I'll let the Chink know."

I do a spot of thinkin'.

"O.K. Terry," I tell him. "But you do somethin' for me, will you? There ain't any need to get excited about this Lee Sam girl yet. Maybe I've gotta idea about that. Stick around. I reckon I'll be back here somewhere about eleven o'clock to-night. You blow in. Maybe I'll have somethin' to tell you."

"Right," he says, "I'll ring this old palooka an' tell him we'll get in touch with him later." He hangs up.

It looks like this business is gettin' a bit more mysterious, because it looks to me now that the dame who got outa the car that I saw outside the Villa Rosalito musta been the Lee Sam girl, an' I wonder where she has got to, because she musta found out pretty good an' quick that there wasn't anybody in the place.

I go down an' around to the garage where I have left the car, an' I drive good an' quick out to Burlingame. There is a mist comin' down—one of them blanket mists that blow down over the San Francisco district from the Sacramento River, an' I aim to get out there whilst I can see.

I pull up outside the Villa Rosalito, walk up the long terraced path to the front door an' start playin' tunes on the bell. Nothing happens. I had an idea it wouldn't. I walk around the side, round to the back an' get through the French window like I did before. I notice it is open an' when I came out I closed it, so maybe the Chinese girl went in this way.

I switch the lights on an' take a look all round the place. There just ain't anybody there. Finally I go inta the kitchen. When I get there I see the note that was propped up against the tea canister is gone an' I wonder if Nellie the cook has been back. If she has, where is this baby?

I go back to the hall an' I grab the telephone. I ring through to O'Halloran an' ask this guy if he's got any news. He says yes, that he has been on to Lee Sam an' the girl's cashed in all right. She got in just after nine o'clock. She's been stickin' around seein' friends. I ask him if he has said anythin' to this Lee Sam about Mrs. Thorensen not bein' out at the Villa Rosalito, an' he says he ain't said a word, that there didn't seem any call to say anything, but that the daughter would know that anyway.

I then tell him that I'm comin' straight back to the Sir Francis Drake Hotel, and as it is good an' foggy I reckon to be back there about eleven o'clock, an' that maybe he would like to meet me at the dump an' drink a little more whisky. He says O.K. he will go any place to drink whisky.

I go outside, start the car up an' drive back. The mist has come down like a blanket an' there is a thin drizzlin' rain. It's a miserable sorta night. It's not so easy to drive an' it is quarter after eleven before I get back.

Upstairs in my room I find O'Halloran. He has finished the bottle I ordered when I was there before so I get another one up an' we have a drink.

"Look, Terry," I tell him. "I'm gettin' plenty leg-work on this job. Right now I'm takin' a run up to this Lee Sam's place. I wanta have a word with that daughter of his. I reckon I wanta know where Marella Thorensen is."

He puts his glass down. "Why don't you call her husband?" he says. "He's got an apartment up on Nob Hill. Maybe she's out there."

"Yeah, an' maybe she ain't," I tell him. "If this dame wanted to talk to her husband about this business that she wants to talk to me about, she'd have done it before. Right now I don't wanta disturb this guy Aylmar Thorensen. I just wanta talk to this Chinese dame, but if you wanta be a good guy I'll tell you what you can do. Stick around here an' go on drinkin' whisky. Maybe I'll want you to do somethin' for me. If I do I'll call you through from Lee Sam's place."

"O.K. Lemmy," he says. "Me—I'm happy. I've got my feet up an' I'm drinking whisky. What can a guy ask more than that?"

I leave him reachin' for the bottle.

I jump a cable car up the hill an' get dropped off somewhere around this Vale Down House where Lee Sam lives. As I walk up to it I see a lighted window stickin' outa the mist. The house is one helluva big place standin' in its own grounds with a high sorta wall around it an' big ornamental gates. It looks like this Chinaman has got plenty dough.

I go through the gates, walk along the drive an' ring the bell. A slit-eyed palooka in a butler's coat opens the door. I tell him that I am a Federal Officer an' that I would like to have a few words with Miss Lee Sam, an' he shows me inta some sittin' room that is filled with some swell Chinese furniture, an' tells me to park myself.

About five minutes later a guy comes inta the room, an' I reckon that this will be Lee Sam. He is a fine old benevolent lookin' guy with white whiskers an' a Chinese pigtail, which not many of 'em wear these days. He is wearin' Chinese clothes an' looks like he'd stepped out of a picture on a willow pattern plate. He has got a nice quiet sorta face, bland an' smilin', an' he speaks good English except that he can't sound his "r's."

"You want see Miss Lee Sam?" he says. "Can I help. Velly solly I disturb Police Department unnecessarily. Daughter is quite safe. She was driving alound seeing fliends."

He smiles. "Young people velly thoughtless," he says.

"Fine, Lee Sam," I tell him, "an' I'm glad your daughter's O.K., but I wanta have a word with her, see? I wanta see her about something else."

He looks a little bit surprised, but he don't say anythin', he just sorta shrugs his shoulders, turns around an' walks outa the room. I sit down again an' light myself a cigarette, an' in a coupla minutes the door opens an' a dame walks in. An' what a dame!

I tell you she's got everything. She is tall, slight an' supple, but that don't mean she's thin. She has the right sorta curves. I tell you that dame's figure would have made a first-class mannequin jump in the lake out of envy. Her hair is as black as night but her eyes are turquoise blue. If I didn't know that this dame was Lee Sam's daughter I'd never have guessed she was Chinese in a million years. I woulda thought she was just a super American lovely.

She is wearing a black silk Chinese coat an' trousers worked over with gold dragons. The coat is buttoned high to her neck an' a pair of black satin shoes with diamond buckles set off her feet swell. Her skin is dead white an' her lips are parted in a little smile as if she sorta thought she liked you but wasn't quite certain. Her teeth are pearly an' even, an' she has got about twenty thousand smackers' worth of diamond necklace around her neck an' another ten grands' worth on her fingers in rings.

If this is what dames look like in China then I am wise to why so many palookas are tryin' to be missionaries.

She stops right in front of where I am sittin' an' looks down at me. "Good night to you," she says. "You wish to speak to me?"

I get up. "Just a few questions, Miss Lee Sam," I tell her. "My name's Caution. I'm a Federal Officer. I suppose you don't know where Mrs. Thorensen is?"

She looks surprised. "Marella was at home when I saw her last. I arrived there at four-forty-five. There was no one there. I waited a little while and then she returned. That would be five o'clock or a little after."

"O.K." I say, "an' then what did you do?"

"We sat an' talked."

She is lookin' at me with the same half smile, sorta old-fashioned, if you know what I mean.

"An' how long was you sittin' there talkin'?" I ask her.

She shrugs her shoulders. "For a long time," she says. "Until about seven o'clock or maybe later. I left there at about twenty minutes to eight."

"An' you left her there?"

She nods her head.

"If that's so, Miss Lee Sam, can you explain why it was that your father couldn't get any answer on the telephone when he called through after he'd got worried about you?"

She is still smilin'. She looks to me like a very swell-lookin' school teacher bein' patient with a kid.

"I can tell you that, Mr. Caution," she says. "When we were talking Marella took the telephone receiver off the hook so that we should not be disturbed. Then afterwards we went up to her room and I expect she forgot to put it back again."

I think a minute. I remember that when I went out there the second time an' rang O'Halloran from there the telephone receiver was *on* the hook all right.

"That's possible," I say. "An' why did you go out there in such a helluva hurry directly you got in on the China Clipper?"

She smiles a bit more.

"She wanted me to," she answers. "She wrote to me in Shanghai. She told me to go to her very urgently because she was in trouble. She write me by air mail on the first of this month. She said I was to come to be with her on the 10th at latest. She is my friend," she says, "so I came."

I grin. "Lady," I tell her, "I wish you was so friendly with me that you'd fly four thousand miles if I wrote you a letter. Was that the only reason?"

"That is enough reason, Mr. Caution," she says. "If I loved you I would fly four thousand miles to you if you asked it."

I reckon that I oughta keep my mind on the business in hand, so I don't say anything to this crack.

"Maybe you've got the letter that Mrs. Thorensen wrote you askin' you to come over?" I say.

She shakes her head. "No," she says, "I destroyed it. I saw no reason to keep it."

"What's you first name Miss Lee Sam?" I ask her.

"Berenice," she says.

She looks at me an' her eyes are like a deep stream in the summer. I tell you this baby is no pushover. She has got poise an' calm an' the whole works an' her brain is as snappy as a whip.

"Don't you think it a nice name, Mr. Caution?" she says.

"So your mother was American?" I shoot at her.

"Yes," she says. "How did you know?"

"Your father can't pronounce 'r's'" I tell her. "So he wouldn't have christened you Berenice."

"You are very much more clever than you look, Mr. Caution," she says. "And you are right about my father. He pronounces it 'Belenice'; but he has another name for me. It is Chinese. It means 'Very Deep and Very Beautiful Stream.' Do you like that Mr. Caution?"

"Lady," I tell her, "you're beautiful all right an' I think you're plenty deep."

She starts smilin' again an' turns around as the old guy comes inta the room. He comes over to me.

"Gentleman to spleak to you," he says. "Telephone in hall outside."

I go out after him. I leave her standin' there smilin'. It is O'Halloran.

"Listen, you beautiful brute," he says. "I been amusin' myself doin' a little telephonin' around this town an' here's a flash for you. Half an hour ago some cops from the Harbour patrol find a body floatin' around the New York Dock. They sent it along to the morgue. It's a dame. I ain't been around there because I hate leavin' this whisky, but here's a rough description. Height about five feet five: weight estimated at 120 to 130 lbs. Blonde an' bobbed hair. Does that mean anything to you?"

"O.K. Terry," I tell him. "Just stick around an' I'll take in the morgue personally. I'll be seein' you."

The old guy has disappeared. I go back inta the room. She is still standin' there where I left her.

"Listen, lady," I tell her. "There's just one thing more. What clothes was Mrs. Thorensen wearin' when you saw her?"

"She was wearin' a blue suit with an oyster coloured crepe-de-chine shirt," she says. "She had on grey silk stockings and black patent court shoes."

"Any rings?"

"Yes, a diamond and ruby betrothal ring, and a diamond set wedding ring, and a single ruby ring on her little finger. She always wore those."

"Thanks a lot," I tell her. "I'll be seein' you some more Very Deep an' Very Beautiful Stream," I crack at her, "an' mind you don't run out to the sea while I'm away."

I scram.

I jump a cab that is wanderin' an' I go down the hill. I pay off the cab at Kearney an' walk along past the Hall of Justice to the morgue. This is a long low dump lyin' beside the hall on the other side of a little roadway.

It has started to rain like hell an' in spite of the mist it is sorta close an' heavy. Away down the street I can just see the blue lamp outside the morgue.

Just along by the entrance I can see a dame. She's got no slicker an' no hat an' no umbrella; she is just standin' there lookin' as if she was lost an' likin' it.

"Hey, sister, don't you know it's rainin'?" I tell her as I walk past. "What's the matter? Has some guy stood you up?"

She looks at me sorta fresh, but there is a scared look in her eye. "On your way, sailor," she says. "Maybe I like rain; it sets my hair."

As I turn inta the entrance I am thinkin' that all dames are nuts anyhow. I go up the entrance steps an' push the door open. Inside on the right of the hallway is the office. I go in there. There ain't anybody in it; but there is a bell for the attendant on the desk.

I push it. Then I wait around for a few minutes. Nothin' happens. I push the bell again. After a bit the door on the other side of the counter opens an' the attendant comes in. He is in his shirt sleeves an' his uniform cap is about two sizes too small for him. I start wonderin' why it is that they always give these morgue guys caps that are too small.

"An' what can I do for you?" he says.

I show him my badge. "There was a dame brought in here to-night by the Harbour squad," I tell him. "I wanta have a look at her."

"O.K." he says. "This way."

He opens up the flap in the counter an' I go through. Then I follow him across the office an' along a passage an' down some stairs. As we go down the air gets plenty cold. We go through an iron door at the bottom an' he switches on the light. Then he gives a sorta gasp an' points with his finger.

"Well, can you beat that?" he says. "Look. To-night just after they brought this dame in the freezin' apparatus down here goes wrong an' I have to telephone through for a whole lot of ice to keep this place cold, because we got eight stiffs down here. One ice block was put on that iron shelf above the tray they laid that dame on an' look what's happened to it."

I look. Right along the sides of the walls are what looks like white japanned filin' cabinets, an' the trays they lay the bodies on come outa these on rollers. Way down at the end of the morgue is a white tray out with a dame's body on it, an' a block of ice about three feet square has slipped off the shelf from above the tray right on the face of this dame. It wasn't no sight for babies, I'm tellin' you.

I go along an' look at it. It is dressed in a blue suit with patent court shoes, an' I can see that the shirt was oyster silk—that is before the ice slipped. I look at the left hand. There is a diamond and ruby ring on the third finger an' a weddin' ring set with diamonds next to it. On the little finger is a big single ruby ring.

"O.K. buddy," I say. "That's all I wanted to know."

I scram. I walk back to the Sir Francis Drake an' go to my room. Terry is there drinkin' whisky an' playin' solitaire. I give myself a drink.

"What's eatin' you, Lemmy?" he says. "You been to the morgue?"

"Yeah," I tell him, "but that ain't what's worryin' me right now. I just got a funny idea. Listen, Terry, you tell me how the freezin' apparatus at the morgue can go wrong?"

"It can't," he says. "Not unless the electricity for the whole city goes wrong with it."

"O.K." I say. "This is where you an' me go out an' get busy."

He looks up. "How come?" he says.

"Look, Terry," I tell him. "When I go down to the morgue I see a dame standin' outside in the rain just for nothin' at all. Inside I see that the attendant's hat don't fit him. Also he tells me that the freezin' has gone wrong an' that they have had to get ice in, an' shows me how one block has slipped an' wiped out the face of the dame that was Marella Thorensen. Like a big sap I fell for it."

"For what?" he says.

"Just this," I tell him. "We're goin' out to find what they did with the real morgue attendant, the one they got outa the way while they brought that ice block in an' smacked it on the face of that corpse. The guy I saw down there was a phoney. That's why his hat didn't fit him."

I put on my hat.

"I'm layin' you six to four that we find the real guy down there in one of the trays," I say. "The girl outside was the look out. When I got in they was fixin' the job an' the others got out the back way while one smart guy came back into the office when I rang the bell an' played me for a sucker while they was doin' it."

Terry sorta sighs an' heaves himself up. We go down in the lift an' grab a cab outside.

When we get down to the morgue office there ain't anybody there at all. We go through the office an' along the passage and down the stairs to the corpse room. I switch on the light an' light a cigarette an' then we start pullin' out the trays with the stiffs on.

We found the morgue attendant all right. He was in number five tray. His eyes are wide open an' lookin' sorta surprised.

Which he was entitled to be because somebody has shot this guy three times.

O'Halloran finishes the bottle.

"Ain't it like life?" he says. "Anyhow this dame Marella hadta die sometime. Why couldn't she get herself a piece of pneumonia or somethin' normal instead of havin' herself put outa circulation by some gun guy thereby causin' plenty trouble for all concerned?" He hiccups so hard he nearly ricks his neck.

"What I wanta know, Lemmy," he says, "is why some bozos haveta smash this dame's pan. It don't make sense to me. An' look at the risk they was runnin'. It's just sorta ridiculous. Here is the morgue stuck right next to the Hall of Justice. There is about seven cops on night shift who mighta strolled inta the morgue office any time to pass the time of day with Gluck. I don't get the idea at all."

"I get it plenty," I tell him, an' as I say this Brendy comes in.

Brendy is the Precinct Captain. He is a nice guy an' plays along very sweet with anybody who don't rub him the wrong way. He is a bit sore about bein' got up over all this besuzuz.

"Well, you guys," he says, "we got that identification sewn up all right. I had Thorensen down an' it nearly made him sick. I don't reckon I've ever seen a guy look so green around the trap. It's Marella Thorensen, an' if somebody will proceed to give me some sorta low-down on all this ice block stuff I'll be very pleased to listen to 'em."

He grabs himself off a glass an' gives himself a snifter.

"Also," he goes on, "I wants know just what we are goin' to do about these killin's. This job starts off as a Federal Investigation inta some sorta low-down that Marella Thorensen says she has got about Federal offences around here. O.K. Well, now the situation has changed plenty. There's two bump-offs in my precinct, an' that's a matter for me an' the Chief of Police. How're we goin' to play it, Lemmy?"

"Look fellers," I tell 'em. "Let's take this thing easy, shall we? Brendy, you don't know that you got two bump-offs. You're only certain that you got one. You know that Gluck, the morgue attendant, was murdered, but you don't know that Marella Thorensen was, an' that's why somebody put that act on with the ice block."

They get interested.

"Here's how I see this thing," I tell 'em. "The doctor says that Marella Thorensen was dead before she was chucked inta the drink. O.K. He knows this because there ain't any water in the lungs. So she died before she went inta the water, didn't she, an' at the present moment there ain't any medical examiner who can say just how she did die. Well I'm goin' to make a coupla guesses.

"Here's the way I reckon they played it. Somebody shoots Marella through the head, an' the next thing is to get rid of the body, so they take it along down to the wharf an' slam it over the edge.

"Now you tell me something, Brendy. How was it that the Harbour Squad found Marella floatin'?"

"Some guy calls through on the telephone to the Squad Office," he says. "Some guy says he has seen a stiff floatin' around the Little Basin, an' then he hangs up. The Squad go out an' look around an' they find her."

"All right," I say, "an' then the Squad pick her up an' stick her in a patrol wagon an' send her along to the morgue, an' that's that.

"Now you guys have gotta admit that there is something screwy about that call. If the guy who called through was a legitimate guy he is goin' to say who he is, ain't he? But he don't. He just hangs up an' scrams. So it looks to me as if he called through just so that Marella Thorensen should be found, an' what does that mean. Well, it means that somebody wanted the world to know that she was dead, see?"

They nod.

"O.K." says O'Halloran, "so what?"

"Well, if you guys are goin' to accept that, maybe you will accept this as well: What reason would some guy have for bumpin' Marella, throwin' her in the ditch an' then callin' through so's the Harbour Squad will find her an' get her identified? Well it looks to me as if the reason might be this one: This dame Marella Thorensen has sent a letter to the Bureau of Investigation to say that she is goin' to spill the beans on the 10th January—to the operative who is sent down. Well now, if somebody kills this dame to-night an' we all find out that it is her, then the Federal operative knows durn well that he ain't goin' to take any statement from Mrs. Marella Thorensen, don't he? So what does he do? He reckons that the two deaths—Marella's an' Gluck's—are just the business of the local Police Department, so he scrams back to Washington, don't he?"

"That sounds like sense to me," says Brendy.

"It is sense, an' it's just what I ain't goin' to do," I tell 'em. "I reckon that if these guys took all that trouble to let us know that Marella was dead then they done it because they wanted me to pack up on this job, an' the reason they would want me to pack up is because I might find out from somewhere else just what she wanted to talk about, an' that's why I'm goin' to stick around."

"O.K.," says Brendy, "an' supposin' for the sake of argument that that is right too, we still ain't got any further with this ice business, hey Terry?"

Terry shakes his head. "Me—I just cannot understand about that," he says.

I grin. "I reckon it's simple," I tell 'em. "Look, here's how I figure it. This guy who has shot Marella Thorensen an' had her chucked in the harbour has either called through himself or got some guy to call through to the Harbour Squad so's they'll find her an' so's we'll know she's dead, like I told you before.

"O.K. When all this business is over an' the body has been sent down to the morgue, this guy suddenly gets a very funny idea. He remembers that the probability is that the bullet he shot this dame with is still in her head an' he particularly don't want the medical examiner to find that bullet. Now you guys know as well as I do just why he wouldn't want that bullet found."

They both look up. They're gettin' interested.

"Sure I know," says Brendy. "He don't want that bullet found because we can identify the gun that fired it from the bullet itself. That means to say that Marella was bumped by a guy who has already ironed out somebody around here, and whose gun has been identified once before by a bullet taken out of a corpse."

"Swell, brother," I tell him, "you're gettin' warm. That bein' so what does he do? He knows durn well that if that bullet is found we'll know who killed Marella an' we'll also know who it was who was so keen to get her outa the way so's we shouldn't find out about this letter she wrote.

"So he takes a chance. He loads some ice blocks on a truck, he gets down to the morgue, he gets Gluck downstairs on some pretence inta the corpse room an' bumps him. Then he opens the back door an' the other guys come in with the ice blocks. They drop one of 'em on Marella's face an' they get the bullet. They're just finishin' off when they hear the bell ring in the office upstairs. That's me. I've just arrived. So one of 'em—a guy with a nerve—grabs off Gluck's cap, takes off his coat an' comes up an' does that act with me.

"When he hears that I'm a Federal Officer who's come around to have a look at the stiff that's just been brought in, he gets a bit of a shock, but his nerve is still workin' so he pulls that story on me about the freezin' apparatus havin' gone wring, an' I fall for it."

They look at each other.

"Lemmy, I reckon you're right," says Terry. "It looks like that's the low-down."

"Maybe," I tell 'em, "an' if it is we still got a clue. Maybe we can still find this guy an' d'ya see how?"

"Sure I do," says Brendy. "All we gotta do is to go through the Police records an' make a list of every guy whose gun has been matched up by the ballistics department with a bullet that has been taken outa some stiff during the last year or so. Then I reckon the guy we're lookin' for is somewhere on that list."

"O.K. Brendy," I say. "Maybe you'll do that for me. Another thing is this," I say, "you guys have gotta realise that this Marella Thorensen killin' is tied up like I said with a letter she wrote to the Director of the Bureau. O.K. We don't wanta play these two killin's separately. Let's make this one job. I reckon we can all help each other. What do you say, Brendy?"

"That's O.K. by me," he says. "Lemmy, I don't mind playin' around with you. I'll speak to the Chief in the mornin' an' get his O.K. on it. Where do we go from there?" he says.

I light myself a cigarette. "You tell me about Thorensen, Brendy," I say. "What happened when you got him down to the morgue to-night?"

"He wasn't lookin' so good," says Brendy. "He comes down an' I tell him that maybe we've got a bit of bad news for him. I tell him that a Federal officer was trying to find his wife this afternoon an' couldn't, that a body has been found by the Harbour Squad, an' we'd like him to have a look at it. I tell him that maybe he'd better prepare himself for a shock.

"He don't say anything very much. He just says O.K. So I take him down to the corpse room and I show him Marella. He just looks at it like he was poleaxed, then he nods his head an' he says 'that's her all right,' an' that's that. Then he went back home, and," Brendy goes on, gettin' up, "I reckon I'm going home too. I can do with spot of sleep all right. I wish guys wouldn't kill each other so much around here."

"O.K. Brendy," I say, "but tell me somethin'. Who's the guy on duty at the Precinct Office? Is he an intelligent guy?"

Brendy looks at O'Halloran an' grins.

"Terry's on to-night," he says. "I don't know whether he's intelligent or not."

"I'll chance it," I tell him. "Look, Terry," I say, "it's a quarter to two now. I'm goin' to buy myself a cab an' I'm goin' up to see Thorensen. I reckon he won't expect to be seein' anybody before to-morrow. I wanta talk to that guy.

"Well, let's suppose that I'm with him until three o'clock. Here's what I want you to do. At a quarter to three you ring up Lee Sam at his place an' tell him that you're sendin' up a squad car to pick him an' his daughter up; that you want 'em to come down pronto. You get 'em down to the Precinct Office an' you keep 'em down there askin' 'em a lotta phoney questions until about four o'clock. Then you can let 'em go an' it'll give me time to do what I wanta do."

"An' what are you going to do?" says Brendy.

"This," I tell him. "Thorensen is livin' at the Chase Apartments on Nob Hill. That's about five minutes walk from Lee Sam's house. You boys have told me that all the servants in the Lee Sam place are China boys an' they ain't particularly brainy. O.K. When I leave Thorensen I'm goin' round to the Lee Sam dump. There won't be anybody there because by that time Terry here will have got the old man and the girl down at the Precinct. I wanta give that dame's apartments the once-over. I wanta take a look round. I think maybe I might find somethin'."

They look at me again.

"What's the idea?" says Brendy.

"Well, work it out for yourself. You guys tell me Berenice Lee Sam pulls in here this afternoon on the China Clipper. She goes straight off to see Marella Thorensen, because she says that Marella Thorensen wrote her askin' her to come up urgent, but what she don't know is that when she arrives I'm just leavin' the place an' Marella ain't there.

"Berenice says Marella turned up soon afterwards. She also says that Lee Sam couldn't get through to the house on the telephone because Marella left the receiver off the hook so's they shouldn't be disturbed, but when I went back to the Villa Rosalito for the second time, the receiver was on the hook all right.

"I got an idea that Marella Thorensen never went back to that place. I got an idea that she ain't been to that place since she went out earlier in the day, because somebody knew that when Marella went home she was goin' to see me an' they'd made up their minds that she just wasn't goin' to do that thing.

"O.K. Well Berenice either knew that somebody was going to bump Marella or she didn't. If she didn't know an' Marella didn't come back what does she wanta tell me a bundle of lies for about the conversation she had with Marella; about telephones bein' taken off receiver hooks?

"The second thing is, if she did know, what did she wanta go there at all for? Well there might be an answer to that. Maybe Marella had some evidence stuck away at the Villa—some documents or papers of some sort—an' maybe that was what Berenice was after. It looks to me like there was some rough housin' around at the Villa Rosalito this afternoon. Some guy had smashed the lock on the French window at the back anyway. There was a scarf lyin' on the floor in the bedroom an' the dressin' table was disarranged.

"An' there is another little thing: When I went over that dump the first time there was a note in the kitchen addressed to Nellie, saying that Marella would not be back until nine o'clock and tellin' her not to worry about dinner. When I go back afterwards that note is gone. Now if Marella had written that note for Nellie to read when she come in she wouldn't take it away, would she? But somebody snatched it, didn't they? So don't it look to you like that note was just a fake? Don't it look like a signal for somebody who was comin' to that house. Well, who was it went to the house? It was Berenice Lee Sam, wasn't it?"

Brendy lights himself a cigar.

"You know, Lemmy," he says, "you're buildin' up a sweet case against this Lee Sam girl."

"Maybe I am an' maybe I ain't," I tell him, "but there was somethin' durn screwy goin' on around that dump this afternoon. If the Lee Sam dame went to that place to find some papers or somethin' that incriminated somebody maybe she hasn't been able to get rid of 'em yet. Maybe they're still in her apartment, an' I'm goin' to have a look. So you get her an' the old man down at the Precinct like I told you.

"An' listen, Terry," I go on, "there is another thing you might do about this dame Nellie. Get on to the night duty man at Burlingame. Ask this guy if he knows who this Nellie is. I reckon everybody will know Mrs. Thorensen's cook. Get him to send an officer round to wake this baby up an' ask her just what arrangements was made with Mrs. Thorensen to-day about what time she was comin' in an' ask this guy to give you a call through an' let you know what he's found out. Maybe Nellie can tell us something."

"O.K." says Terry, "I'll look after it an' let you know, Lemmy. What time do you expect to be back here?"

"Me—I oughta be back here by four-thirty o'clock," I say, "but you needn't bother to ring me through then because when I come back I'm goin' to bed. I wanta see this guy Thorensen to-night because I always like to talk to guys in the middle of the night—their brains ain't workin' so well."

Brendy yawns. "O.K. babies," he says. "Me, I'm goin' home to read a detective story so's to get my mind off all this stuff."

"Oh yeah," says Terry, "I know them stories. They're the ones you haveta put paper covers on so's you wife can't see the pictures on the front. Is she still ridin' you Brendy boy?"

"You shut your trap," says Brendy. "My old woman's swell. She says to me the other mornin' when she wakes up that she has just dreamed that some guy blasted her down with a Tommy gun. Say do you guys believe dreams come true?" he says sorta hopeful.

"It's practically certain," says O'Halloran. "I usta buy meat pies at some eat-house in California, an' every time I eat a couple these pies I usta dream about dames. They was swell dames too with plenty curves. It practically broke me up when they closed the dump down. Well, so long, Lemmy," he goes on. "I'll get the Berenice baby an' her pa down at the Precinct like you said."

"Yeah," says Brendy, "an' just keep the party clean, willya? You be careful with that dame an' don't get tellin' her about what you usta do when you was poundin' a beat. Maybe she don't like that sorta story."

"O.K." says O'Halloran. "You're the boss. Should I tell her about my operation?"

They scram.

I meet Thorensen in the hallway of the Chase Apartments. Outside I have seen that there is a big roadster waitin' with plenty baggage on it. As I go in I see this guy comin' towards the entrance along the passage. I grin to myself because it looks to me like I have caught this bozo in the act of takin' a run out powder.

I go up to him. "Are you Thorensen?" I ask him, an' when he says yes I tell him who I am an' what I am. He don't look very pleased to hear it.

He is a big guy. His body is sorta pear shaped—slidin' shoulders that even tailor's paddin' won't disguise—an' a round belly that sticks out. His face is heavy an' jowly an' he looks plenty worried. His eyes are deep an' far-seein'—clever eyes—an' his skin is a funny lead colour. I don't like him very much.

"Goin' some place?" I ask him. "I s'pose you're comin' back for your wife's funeral? I wanta have a little talk to you, Thorensen," I go on. "There's one or two little things I wanta ask you."

"I haven't a great deal of time," he says, sorta surly. "This very unfortunate accident to my wife must not delay the plans for the transfer of my business to Los Angeles, which I had planned some time before this awful thing happened. But naturally I want to help in any way I can. I want to know how this accident occurred, but I must leave fairly soon, so perhaps you will make your interview as short as possible, Mr. Caution."

"So you think that your wife's death was an accident?" I ask him, while we are walkin' along the corridor.

He stops an' turns around to me while he is openin' the door. As he pushes it open he says: "What else should it be? I imagine Marella fell into the dock, although what she was doing in the neighbourhood of the harbour is more than I can figure out."

We go inside. The apartment is swell. This guy knows how to look after himself. I look around to see if there is a picture of Marella Thorensen anywhere, but I can't see one. I reckon that a guy who ain't got a picture of his wife around ain't very fond of her.

Thorensen motions me to a chair an' points to a liquor stand that is near me. I shake my head, but he goes over an' mixes himself a stiff one. His hand is tremblin' a bit an' he looks to me as if he has got the jitters.

"Looky, Thorensen," I tell him, "you're a lawyer an' you don't need any advice from me. But I reckon that the best thing you can do is to kick in with all you know, because that way it's goin' to be easier for you."

I tell him about the letter that his wife wrote, an' why I checked in at Burlingame to see her. He says he don't know anything about it; that he didn't know that she wrote the letter an' that if he hadn't known that she was a sensible woman he woulda thought that she had gone plain nuts.

"Listen, Caution," he says. "I'm goin' to tell you how things were and then you can draw your own conclusions. Marella knew that I was leaving San Francisco to-night. She knew that I was going to make Los Angeles my headquarters and that although I should be running a branch office here I should be living there.

"We didn't hit it off very well. We'd been practically strangers to each other for some time. I used to go out to Burlingame at the week-end now and again merely for the sake of appearances. But the idea of a divorce didn't appeal to her for some reason or other.

"When I told her about my idea of moving my head office over to Los Angeles she was only mildly interested. She said that it wouldn't make any difference to her anyway and that she'd probably see about as much of me as she did now.

"But what happened out at the Villa Rosalito to-day; why she wrote that letter to the Bureau of Investigation, why after having written it she wasn't there to see you, and why she came into San Francisco to-night, I don't know, and that's the whole truth. I can't understand a thing about it."

"O.K." I say. "Well, if you don't know anything, you can't spill it, can you?"

I think I will give this guy his head an' let him scram. We can always keep a tail on him if we want to.

"All right, Thorensen," I say, "you can go. You might drop in at the Hall of Justice on your way an' leave your Los Angeles address with the night precinct officer. If we want you we'll let you know."

I turn around to him quick. "So you're closin' down your connection with Lee Sam?" I say. "You're walkin' out on the guy who put you on your feet. Is that the clever thing?"

He smiles. "I have many other interests, many other clients, Mr. Caution," he says, "and my office here is quite able to handle Mr. Lee Sam's affairs."

"O.K." I tell him. "Good-night, Thorensen."

"Good-night," he says.

I scram. I leave him standin' there in front of the fireplace, with the glass in his hand lookin' worried. His big belly seems to be saggin' more than it was before an' his eyes are sorta tired.

I reckon this Thorensen is a lousy liar.

I decide to do a spot of housebreakin'. I figure that it won't get me any place to go ringin' the front door bell at Lee Sam's dump, an' that I might just as well be clever.

Away around the back of the house is an iron gate leading to a garage, an' I get over this easy. I go along in the dark past the garage which is standin' away from the house, an' come up to the house the back way. I find a shoulder high window leadin' to some pantry or somethin' an' I bust it open.

In three minutes I am inside the house standin' in the hallway outside the room where I spoke to Lee Sam an' Berenice earlier on.

I look at my wrist watch. It is five minutes to three, so I reckon I got plenty time to look around.

I go up the wide stairway an' along a passage at the top. I want to find where Berenice has her rooms. I try two or three doors along the passage openin' 'em nice an' quiet so's not to arouse anybody who might be inside, but they are all empty. When I go inta the end room I know it is hers.

There is a bit of moonlight an' I can see lyin' across the bed the black an' gold suit she was wearin' when I spoke to her. The room is a big one an' after I have pulled the curtains over the big windows I switch on the light an' look around.

It is certainly a swell dump. All the furniture is white an' the rugs an' trimmin's about the place musta cost plenty. On the right hand side of the room is an openin' inta another room. This openin' is bigger than a door an' has got a Chinese silk rope fringe hangin' down.

I am just walkin' across to this openin' when lyin' on a chair near a dressin' table I see a handbag an' a pair of gauntlet drivin' gloves an' I get the idea that Berenice mighta been usin' these when she drove out to the Villa Rosalito in the afternoon.

I grab the bag, open it an' start lookin' through. Inside is a jade an' diamond cigarette case, a .22 automatic pistol with an ivory butt, a billfold, a little bottle of perfume an' some loose change. There ain't anything else.

I put the bag back on the chair an' in doin' so I knock one of the gauntlet gloves off the chair. Something falls out of the glove an' when I stoop down an' pick it up do I get a kick or do I. Because in my hand I have got a letter that I can see was written by Marella Thorensen to her husband, an' it says:

This is to tell you that I am more glad than ever that you are leaving San Francisco. Since I last talked to you I have discovered exactly what has been going on between you and Berenice Lee

Sam. It seems that the old story about the wife being the last to know is true in this case, because although I have thought you pretty bad I never thought you'd go as far as that.

I suppose that's how you originally got the Lee Sam business.

I'm not going to stand for this. I'm not going to discuss it with you because that wouldn't do any good anyhow, but I'm going to have a show-down with the Lee Sam girl, and if she won't listen to reason I'll make her.

I don't mind being the neglected wife so long as too many people don't know about it. But I'm certainly not going to have a situation like this under my nose and do nothing about it—and I don't mean divorce either!

Marella.

I stand there with the letter in my hand, listenin' hard, because I wanta get outa this dump without anybody bein' wise to the fact that I have been here.

Before I found the letter I didn't give a continental if any of Lee Sam's people had found me nosin' around but now I have a peek at this letter I reckon I wanta scram outa here an' do some quiet thinkin'.

This letter ties the job up. It is certain as shootin' that Marella Thorensen had found out that her husband had been playin' around with Berenice Lee Sam, an' that the urgent letter askin' Berenice to go out to the Villa Rosalito was written so that Marella could have a show-down with Berenice an' tell her plenty.

An' all that would be a swell motive for Berenice wantin' Marella outa the way. After all guys like Lee Sam are very hot on their daughters behavin' themselves an' I reckon that Berenice knew that if her old man found out what the shemozzle with Marella was there would be plenty trouble. An' that was the reason why the receiver was off the hook at the Villa. *Berenice took it off.* She took it off so that if Lee Sam came through in the middle of the show-down Marella—who was all steamed up—shouldn't blow the works to the old guy over the wire.

I reckon that Berenice just stuck around until Marella came back. Then Marella asks Berenice to go upstairs to her bedroom to have this pow-wow. Berenice lets Marella go up the stairs first an' flips the telephone receiver off the hook as she passes it.

Then the two dames have a show-down an' the things on the dressin' table get disarranged, an' the scarf gets thrown down on to the floor. I reckon Marella was in one helluva temper an' was just chuckin' things around because she felt that way.

When Berenice leaves she puts the receiver back on the hook on her way along the passage to the front door, but what I wanta know is what Marella was doin' then if she was doin' anything at all?

Was she doin' anything? Or was she bumped? Did Berenice get busy with the .22 automatic an' after givin' Marella the heat pull her inta her car an' drive her over to the harbour while the fog was on an chuck her in?

I open the handbag again an' pull out the gun. It is fully loaded. I smell it an' it smells clean, as if it hadn't been used lately, but this don't mean a thing because there has been plenty time to clean the gun.

I put the gun back an' close the handbag. I put the letter back in the glove where I found it an' I make everything look like it was before I got nosin' around. I switch off the lights an' pull back the curtains. I ease out inta the corridor an' gumshoe along an' down the stairs an' out by the pantry the same way as I come in.

I go walkin' down the hill thinkin' plenty. The mist is clearin' off an' the rain has stopped. Way down in front of me are the lights twinklin' an' San Francisco is lookin' almost like the swell place the guide books make it out to be.

I'm plenty puzzled with this business. I don't get it at all. I can't get the proper slant on anythin'. I'm rememberin' that my job is to get next to the stuff that Marella wanted to tell me. After all she wouldn't write to the Bureau just because she'd found out about Aylmar and Berenice.

I am next to the note to Nellie all right. That was a phoney. It wasn't left for Nellie; it was left for somebody else *an' that* somebody else was me. It was left so that I shouldn't stick around waitin' for Marella because it said she wouldn't be back till nine o'clock. So it was written by somebody who knew that I was comin' along; somebody who had read the telegram from the Director that I found in the hall behind the table, an' as Berenice hadn't arrived when I found the note to Nellie it musta been somebody else, an' at first pop that somebody would look to be Thorensen wouldn't it?

But the idea would be wrong because I know that Thorensen hadn't been outa his office in 'Frisco all day—so what the hell!

I am just crossin' the first intersection on the cable car road when a Chevrolet comes around the corner. It slides around pretty fast with the tyres squealin' like hell. Some guy stick out his head an' takes a shot at me an' my hat goes off. I drop flat just as a couple other hellions open up on me an' I can hear the lead ricketting off the sidewalk alongside me.

I let go a hell of a groan an' lay out flat. The car runs up the hill an' slows down for the next corner. Somewhere down the hill I can hear a cop blow his whistle.

I roll over, unlimber the Luger from under my arm an' open up on the Chevrolet. I am firin' for the tyres an' I reckon I musta got one because when it goes around the corner it skids like hell.

I run up the hill, keepin' to the wall of the house on my left. When I get to the right hand turnin' I can see the car twenty thirty yards down the roadway slowin' down. I try a couple more shots an' one goes through the rear window. I hear the glass smash.

The car stops dead. Three guys jump out an' start runnin' like they meant it. One of these palookas turns around an' fires twice, but he couldn't see anything to fire at because I am in the shadow.

I loose off three more shells after these gun-babies, but don't do any good. Away down the roadway I can hear their feet runnin' on the sidewalk. O.K. Let 'em go!

I ease up, put the gun away an' light myself a cigarette. Then I walk over to the car an' look through the window.

There is a dame lyin' huddled up in the corner of the car I open the door an' switch the top light on, an' do I get a thrill?

Because the dame in the corner is the doll who was waitin' outside the morgue in the rain when I went down to take a look at what was left of Marella; the doll who was look-out for the boys who bust Marella's face with the ice block.

An' there are guys who say that life ain't sweet!

CHAPTER THREE
TALK BLONDIE!

"LOOK, bozo," she says, "what the hell's the use of your pullin' all them acts on me. I ain't talkin' because I don't know nothin', an' if I knew anythin' I still wouldn't squeal to no copper, an' where do we go from there?"

I look at this doll across the table. We are in some eats factory down on Fisherman's Wharf, an' this dame is as fresh as when I started workin' on her.

"You're breakin' my heart, Toots," I tell her. "I reckon you're a tough sorta doll too. I reckon that if you was to make up your mind that you wouldn't talk—well, that would be that now, wouldn't it?"

I take a large bite of hamburger an' relax. I sit there watchin' her.

This dame has got somethin'. One time, I reckon she was as pretty as they come, but she has nearly peroxided herself out of existence an' her hair is so brittle from bleachin' that it looks like her father was a glassblower. She has got big blue eyes that look at you sorta innocent . . . but these eyes know plenty—got me?

She reminds me of a dame that I met up with in Akron years ago. This dame had gotta guy that I got sent up for a fifteen year stretch, an' after they had stuck the bozo in the can she writes me a note an' says she wants to thank me for savin' her from marryin' a mobster an' will I come around because she wants to thank me personally an' that maybe I would like to take a look at her etchings.

Well, I will try anything once an' I am also partial to art, so I get myself all dolled up an' I go around to some flop house where this dame is hangin' out.

After she has told me I am one helluva guy she gives me a couple drinks of some stuff that woulda burned the skin off an armour plated crocodile, after which she proceeds to show me a trick with a knife. It was lucky all right that when she tried to stick it inta me she hit the top button on my vest otherwise I would be playin' a harp right now an' not even interested in the blonde that I am lookin' at.

I look across the table at this baby. I think she looks plenty wise an' I think too that she has got something extra over the ordinary moll that gets around with a tough mob. There is intelligence in the way she looks, an' she moves her hands an' fingers in the way a dame who has got brains moves 'em. I reckon she is saucy—an' tough.

"O.K., Toots," I tell her. "Now let's get down to cases. I been pretty nice to you, ain't I? Why I ain't even pinched you yet when I got a first class accessory-to-attempted-murder charge against you. I'm tryin' to play along with you nice an' easy an' you won't give. Why don't you get wise, sister?"

"Listen, Mister," she cracks. "You ain't got nothin' on me, see? The fact that I was in that car don't prove a thing, see? I was unconscious when you found me, an' for all you know I mighta been unconscious all the time. I don't know anything about them guys who tried to rub you out. I don't even know 'em an' if I was to see 'em they'd all be like strangers to me. Besides you ain't the first guy who's staked me to coffee an' a couple hamburgers. Them guys just offered to give me a ride that's all."

She takes a nice dainty sip of coffee an' smiles over the cup at me.

"Now we're all set, big boy, ain't we?" she says. "You go ahead an' make your pinch. I been pinched before but they've always hadta let me out some time."

"All right, sweetheart," I tell her. "You have it your way. Me . . . I ain't pinchin' you. You just finish your coffee an' let's get down to the morgue."

She tautens up a bit. "How come the morgue?" she says.

"I'll tellya, honeybunch. I got this thing all doped out. Do you think that I don't know why you was in that car with them rod-merchants. You bet I do. They didn't know me, see? But you did. You was the doll who was look-out outside the morgue to-night an' you knew I was the guy who went in. So somebody thinks I'd be safer outa the way. So they arrange to give me the heat."

I take another bite of hamburger.

"Now who would be keen on givin' me the heat?" I ask her. "Well, I'll take a guess an' I'll lay six to four against bein' wrong. The guy who wanted me outa the way was the guy who put that act on in the morgue to-night. The guy who took me down to the corpse room. The guy who handed me that hooey about the ice. He's scared because he knows that I'll know him next time I see him, see, sister? So he gets three rod-men to tail on after me after I leave the Francis Drake to-night an' give me the heat when possible, an' he sends you along with 'em because you'll know I'm me an' there won't be any mistake."

She looks at me an' gives me a big wink. "Ain't you the little Sherlock Holmes?" she says. "So what, Gorgeous?"

"Oh nothin'," I tell her. "But I figured this way. I figured you are a tough baby an' that you ain't goin' to talk because you ain't afraid of bein' pinched. So I ain't goin' to pinch you. No, Toots, I got somethin' better for you."

She looks interested.

"Such as what, fly cop?" she says.

"Well," I tell her, "I reckon that you an' me meet down at the morgue an' that you might like to spend a night down there. There's a bunch of stiffs laid out on the trays, but you won't even see them. They're under cover. But there's one stiff who ain't. I mean Marella. Marella is still out on view. An' she ain't at all pretty because by the time that your friends was through with her any beauty she mighta had was sorta spoiled."

I get up. "Come on, tough baby," I tell her. "I'm goin' to lock up in the corpse room down at the morgue. Then I'm goin' up to the office to smoke cigarettes an' drink coffee until such time as you start screamin'. When you've screamed good an' plenty maybe I'll come down an' make a deal with you, the deal bein' that I'll let you out when you've talked. An' if you don't talk you can stay along there with Marella. Maybe she'll be tough with you. An' I reckon that to-morrow mornin' you won't haveta worry about peroxide any more. I reckon your hair'll be white for the rest of your natural."

She looks at me. Her eyes are glassy.

"Jeez," she says. "Would you do that to a girl?"

"Try me," I tell her. "I don't like tough babies. Come on, Toots. Let's get goin'."

She starts cryin'. "I couldn't stand for that," she whimpers. "I tellya I couldn't stand for it. Gimme some more coffee an' I'll think a little an' maybe do a little talkin'."

"Like hell you will," I tell her. "You're goin' to talk plenty or you're goin' down to the corpse room."

I call the wop an' order more coffee.

"Listen, Toots," I tell her. "You talk an' you give me the lot. Don't give me any hooey. Don't pull any fast ones. Because if you do an' I get the idea that you're bein' clever I'll lock you up with Marella, an' you can scream the roof off but you'll stay there till they bury the dame."

She asks for a cigarette so I give her one. She sits there for a minute smokin', lookin' sorta sad.

"I never reckoned I'd talk to coppers," she says, "but it looks as if I've gotta."

She leans across the table. "Look, Mister," she says, "I'm comin' clean, an' this is the truth. I don't believe that the guy who sent me on this job knows anythin' about all this business you've been talkin' about. Here's the way it is.

"I get around with a guy called Joe Mitzler. He's straight enough, see, but he's just a tough egg."

"Just a minute, Lovely," I tell her. "How didya meet up with this Joe Mitzler?"

She looks down at the table. She looks sorta sad. She gets that expression in her face that a dame always gets when she is goin' to hand you a bundle of first-class boloney straight off the ice.

"Joe picked me up in a dump in Chinatown here in 'Frisco," she says. "I used to get around with a travellin' burlesque show. I was a good girl an' I was tryin' to get my brother through college, but I threw out with the manager. He thought that handin' me a pay envelope every week entitled him to be put on the free list for everything, an', believe it or not, I ain't that sorta girl. So he fired me an' the show goes off an' leaves me kickin' around here like a stranded mackerel on the beach at Wiki-Kiki."

She looks up at me sorta coy.

"I ain't tellin' you that I couldn't fall for a guy," she says. "I can fall plenty. I could fall for you," she goes on, "because you're big an' you got brains an' nobody can hand you a lotta dope because you know all the answers."

She lets go a sigh so big that I was waitin' to hear her brassière strings bust. Then she goes on:

"I get a job in this place in Chinatown," she says, "servin' drinks an' generally makin' myself useful an' singin' a hot number now an' again. But the same sorta thing is happenin' all the time. Guys make a play for me an' when I don't like a guy I am just as likely to smack him one on the kisser as not.

"Just when I am sick of playin' along like this, an' wonderin' how long I can last out, this Joe Mitzler comes along. He treats me a bit better than the rest, an' finally he spills me a long spiel about bein' fond of me, so I give up an' play along with him, an' what would you have done?"

I give her a hot lingerin' look that I got from a picture of Clark Gable in a movie magazine.

"Me—I would still be fightin' for my honour," I tell her, "but go on honeybunch, tell me what happened after you told Joe that you was only a little woman an' that you just couldn't struggle against him any longer an' that you hoped for your dear old mother's sake that he would give you a fair deal an' not just give you the big bum's rush an' then leave you with nothin' but a phoney century bill an' a pain in the place where your heart usta be."

She looks up at me like she was hurt.

"You can laugh," she says, "but that's how it was.

"O.K. Well, to-night some guys come along an' they see Mitzler an' they say that they wanta have a little talk with some feller who is gettin' a bit fresh, meanin' you I suppose, an' will Mitzler let me go along with them so's I can show 'em who he is because I know him, havin' seen this guy once before.

"One of these guys slips Mitzler a fifty bill, so he tells me to get goin' an' play along with these fellers an' point this guy out that they wanta meet, an' of course," she goes on, "Mitzler don't know an' I don't know that these guys are aimin' to rub you out. O.K. We get inta a cab an' they take me along to some garage where they put me in the Chevrolet, an' when I get in I can see that they have all got a gun with them an' I don't feel so good, but what was a girl to do. I reckon if I'd started anything they'd just as soon given me the heat myself as not.

"We go around an' we stick down that side street, near the entrance of the Sir Francis Drake Hotel, an' when you go up to the Lee Sam house, one of these guys says he reckons you'll come out the same way as you went in, so we wait down the street round a corner. But they leave one of these fellers opposite the house so's he can signal when you come out.

"O.K. When he sees you come out this feller runs back to the Chevrolet an' gets in. They go after you an' they put on that shootin' act, an' they thought they'd got you. That's all I know, an' believe it or not it's the truth."

"O.K. sister," I tell her, "I believe you. Why shouldn't I? But you tell me somethin'. Where do I find this side-kicker of yours, this Mitzler guy?"

"He's around," she says. "We live in a dump off California; he'll be there now."

I ask her for the number of this house an' she gives it to me.

"All right, sweetheart," I say, "maybe I'll go an' see this friend of yours."

"Just a minute," she says, "there's one little thing I'd like to tell you. Maybe if you get around to Mitzler's place you might get sorta tough with him; you might make him talk, see? O.K. Well, what's goin' to happen to me. Don't you think that these guys who tried to get you will get after me pretty good an' quick?"

She looks at me sorta pathetic.

"I reckon they'll make me look like mincemeat in twenty-four hours," she said. "That's what I'm goin' to get for talkin' to you."

"It just shows you, kid, don't it?" I say. "You should always keep good company, an' not get mixed up with mobsters. Anyhow," I go on, "I've gotta idea about you. Let's get goin'."

I pay the check an' we go outside. We wait around there for two three minutes until a cab comes up.

"Listen, baby," I say.

I look at my watch. It is four fifteen.

"Me—I'm goin' around to see this friend of yours, this Joe Mitzler, an' maybe you're right when you think that these bozos will get out after you if they think that it was you that spilled the beans to me, so I've got a big idea."

I feel in my pocket. I take out my roll an' peel off five five-dollar bills.

"Here you are, baby," I tell her. "Here's a quarter of a century for you. Now take my tip. You get down to the bus stop an' buy yourself a nice ticket that's goin' to get you way outa San Francisco before these guys start lookin' for you. I reckon you've got enough dough to get out an' to keep goin' for a bit."

"Say, mister," she says, "are you swell? I bet there ain't many coppers would do a thing like this. I think you're tops."

I grin at her. "That's O.K. by me," I say. "Maybe I'm a little angel but people don't know it. So long, blondie."

I get inta the cab an' tell the guy to drive to California Street, but when he has got round the corner I tell him to stop. I tell him to wait until this dame has passed the end of the street, to let her get well ahead an' then follow quietly after her. Me—I know dames. From the side street I can see blondie walkin' along but she ain't walkin' towards the bus stop. Two three minutes afterwards a cab comes along an' she signals it. She gets in an' the cab goes off.

"After that cab," I tell the driver, "an' don't lose it."

We drive for about five minutes an' we don't go to no bus stop. Finally I see her get outa the cab at the end of some alley down near the Embarcadero, an' it looks to me like she has driven all round the place to get there.

I get outa my cab an' tell the driver to wait, an' I go after her. She turns down the alley an' she walks along till she comes to some dump that looks like a Chinese flop shop. She goes inta a door at the side. When I get to the door I give it a push. It ain't locked an' I go in. In front of me is a dark flight of stairs. I go up, an' see that there is a long dirty passage in front of me. At the end of the passage I can see a crack of light comin' from under a door. I gumshoe along the passage an' listen. Inside I can hear the dame talkin' to some guy. I kick the door open. The room is a dirty sorta place with a truckle bed in the corner.

Lyin' on the bed is a guy, a big guy with a face that looks as if it's been in contact with a steam roller some time. Standin' in the middle of the floor with her back to me, her hands on her hips talkin' to him good an' plenty is Blondie. She spins around as I come in.

"Well, I'll be sugared," she says.

"You bet you will be, baby," I tell her. "You didn't think I was goin' to fall for any of that punk stuff you told me about where your friend Mitzler lives, didya? An'," I go on, "I bet you were givin' me a big horse laugh when I gave you the twenty-five bucks to get outa San Francisco so's somebody wouldn't shoot you up, eh? Listen, Toots," I tell her, "what do you think I am? Have a heart."

I turn to the guy on the bed.

"An' this is Joe Mitzler," I say, "the guy who was supposed to live in California Street."

"What the hell?" he says. "Who in hell are you an' what do you want?"

"Pipe down, angel face," I tell him. "I'll get round to you in a minute."

I hold out my hand.

"Just slip back that twenty-five bucks, will you?" I tell her, "less the cab fare around here."

She pulls a face but she hands back the twenty.

"Now look. Toots," I tell her. "Scram outa here an' keep goin' because to-morrow mornin' we'll have your description out an' if you are around San Francisco I'll have you pinched, see? So long, sister."

She gives me a look like a snake an' she scrams.

I light a cigarette. "Well, Joe," I tell him.

This guy heaves himself off the bed. He sits there with his hands hangin' down in front of him. Lookin' at this guy I get to think' that whoever it was said that we was descended from gorillas musta had Joe in mind. I tell you his face was bust about plenty, an' besides this he's gotta couple old knife wounds in his neck, an' where his shirt is hangin' open I can see a bullet scar across his chest. I reckon Joe is plenty tough.

"What the hell?" he says. "What d'ya think you're doin' bustin' around here? Who are you?"

"Didn't blondie tell you anythin' about me?" I ask him. "Now listen, Joe, my name's Caution. I'm a Federal officer an' I'm plenty interested in the fact that some guys around here have ironed out Mrs. Marella Thorensen to-night, after which they proceed to bust her face in with a chunk of ice, a business which I think was done for the purpose of gettin' a bullet outa her skull.

"O.K. Well, when I go down to the morgue to have a look at this dame, blondie was doin' a big look-out act outside. Later to-night some guys tried to rub me out. They got blondie along with 'em an' I reckon she was there so that she could identify me. What do you know about it, Joe?"

He looks at me an' he grins. When I said he looked like a gorilla I was insultin' the gorilla. I never saw any animal look like this guy. When he opens his mouth to grin I see that all his teeth are broken an' black an' jagged.

"I don't know nothin'," he says.

He heaves himself up to his feet. "An' what the hell, supposin' I did? D'ya think I'd tell you, copper?"

"Look, Joe," I tell him, "you're goin' to talk, see, because I wanta know."

"Yeah," he says, "blondie told me you gotta big idea about lockin' her in the morgue till she came across. Well, that might be a swell idea with a dame, but it don't go with me. Me—I ain't afraid of corpses."

I go over to him.

"Look, Joe," I tell him. "Here's the way it is."

I pull back my right arm an' I smack him across the jaw with my right elbow, bringin' my wrist down as I do it. He goes back across the bed. Then he sits up again lookin' at me, an' I can see this job is goin' to be plenty tough because I ain't even hurt this guy. He sits there waitin' for a minute, an' then he takes a jump at me with his head down. I reckon if he'd hit me he'd have knocked my guts out, but he don't, because I've seen this act comin' an' as he comes forward I bring my knee up an' it connects with his face an' this jolts him plenty. Before he can get his head up again I sock him alongside the jaw. He goes over.

I pull his head up while he is still on the floor an' bang it back on the floorboards. He hits the floor with a noise that you coulda heard a block away, but this guy is still tough. He starts gettin' up again. I have to hit him twice more an' just to make certain of this job I pull the Luger an' smack him one across the dome with the butt. He goes out.

I drag this guy on to the bed. In the corner on the wash-hand stand I find a bottle of water. I pour a little of this over his face. He starts comin' round. Then he opens his eyes an' looks at me an' believe me he wasn't sendin' me no love messages neither.

"Look, Joe," I say, "whether you like it or not you're goin' to talk. You ain't feelin' so well right now, an' I don't wanta get really busy with you. The last time I had a guy who was really tough an' who wouldn't talk, I had to persuade him by holdin' my cigarette lighter between his fingers, right down under the soft skin between the knuckles. I believe it hurts plenty. Now you get a load of this, if you don't talk. I'm goin' to get tough. What are you goin' to do?"

He struggles up an' sticks his head back against the back of the bed. I reckon this guy has gotta headache.

"What the hell?" he says. "Me—I don't know nothin' about this business except there was fifty bucks in it for me, an' I reckon like most other palookas I'm goin' to do a lot for fifty bucks."

He puts his hand out for the water bottle an' I can see that he is runnin' his tongue over his lips. I reckon this guy is thirsty. I hand him the water bottle, an' as I do this he tries to swing me across the head with it. I've got an idea that he may be tryin' something funny like this, so I bust him another one, knockin' two of the remainin' teeth that he has got down his throat. After he has managed to swallow these teeth successfully, we get back to business.

"I wouldn't try anythin' else, Joe," I tell him.

"You're tellin' me," he says. "I won't. They was the only two good teeth I had. What I'm goin' to do now for eatin' purposes I don't know."

He starts talkin'. He tells me that he has had a ring through from a friend of his. This friend is a guy who works along at a dance joint in Chinatown. This guy tells Joe that blondie the girl has been doin' a job of work for a friend of his, a guy by the name of Spigla, an' that somebody has asked Spigla to send some boys out to give some other guy (meanin' me) a good beatin' up, an' he reckons that blondie had better come along too for the purpose of pointin' me out. He says that if Joe will fix this he is on fifty bucks.

"An' that's all I know," he says, "an' if I'd known that I was goin' to get bust over the dome with a gun butt I'd have wanted seventy-five."

"O.K. Joe," I tell him, "an' where does this guy Spigla hang out?"

He tells me that this guy Spigla is to be found hangin' out at some joint called the Two Moons Club in Chinatown, that he is a very nice guy, an' that he probably has not got anythin' against me at all, but that he is the sorta guy who is always ready to take care of anybody for two three hundred bucks, an' that probably somebody has paid him to get tough with me.

I take out my cigarette pack, give myself one an' throw one over to him.

"Look, Joe," I tell him. "Maybe that's the truth, an' maybe it ain't. But I'm goin' to give you a tip-off. For the sake of the argument, as the professors say, I'm goin' to believe your story. But you take a tip from me an' keep your nose clean from now on, because if there is any more nonsense from you or that blonde dame of yours I'm goin' to make it plenty hot for you.

"You gotta realise that you two can be pulled in on an accessory charge to first degree murder. Well, I ain't goin' to do it because I think you are a pair of saps kickin' around tryin' to earn yourselves a few dollars. So just keep quiet an' keep outa my way."

"That's O.K. by me," he says. "Me—I'm through with this business."

He rubs the top of his head.

"All right, Joe," I tell him. "I think you're the wise guy, an' if you're still wiser I reckon that you're goin' out right now to pick up that blonde jane of yours—because I reckon she is waitin' just around the corner some place for you—an' scram outa this man's town, an' if you wanta know why, I'm tellin' you this:

"I got an idea that there's goin' to be plenty trouble for you an' blondie if you stick here. The guys who wanted to rub me out to-night don't seem to me to be very particular sorta fellers about what they do. I reckon they won't be so pleased with you an' blondie for sayin' as much as you've said. Maybe they'll call you a squealer an' present you two with a few ounces of hot lead right in the place where you digest your dinner, see?"

He stretches himself an' grins. "I reckon you're right, stranger," he says. "Me—I'm for the highway. This town looks to me like it is goin' to get hot."

"O.K. Joe." I tell him. "So long."

I scram. I go back to the Sir Francis Drake an' go up to my room. On my dressin' table is a note from O'Halloran, by which it looks as if he has been gettin' a move on. The note says:

Dear Lemmy,—Your idea about contacting Nellie the cook was a good one. I sent a motor cycle cop out there to knock the dame up and she spills some interesting stuff. Such as:

That hand-printed note supposed to be from Marella about not being back until nine o'clock was a lot of boloney. Marella fired Nellie the cook this morning, the reason being that Marella was going to do her own cooking in the future and just have a hired girl in for a few hours a week.

The cop took Nellie back to the Villa Rosalito so's she could look around and notice anything that was different. Well, Nellie says that nothing's different. In fact she says that every article of Marella's clothing is still there—there ain't even a hat or a glove missing. Nellie knows all about Marella's clothes.

This looks plenty screwy to me. It looks as if Marella never meant to leave that place to-night; that she meant to be there when you got there. It looks like somebody snatched this dame.

So get to work on that, muggsy!

So long,

Terry.

I take a shower an' start undressin'. I smoke a cigarette an' play with a few ideas. Here's how they go:

1. Marella is waiting to see me when she gets a telephone call from somebody or other in the neighbourhood. This call is a phoney call for the purpose of getting her out of the way when I arrive.

2. I arrive at the Villa and take a look around and leave. Berenice Lee Sam arrives and waits. She waits because she knows about the phoney telephone call. She has seen me come out of the house and she watches me go. She knows that Marella will be back.

3. Marella comes back. Berenice says they should go upstairs to talk. On the way up the stairs she flips the telephone receiver off the hook so's nobody can contact the house while she is there.

4. Marella talks and Berenice sees that she knows a durn sight too much about something or other.

5. Somebody (it might have been Berenice) grabs Marella, sticks her in a car and runs over to San Francisco and shoots her. They chuck her in the harbour.

6. They remember about the bullet and work the act with the ice.

7. They realise that they have made a mistake somewhere so they try to rub me out. I reckon they would not have tried to bump me if they hadn't thought that I know something that I don't know.

8. The story about these guys having followed me from the Sir Francis Drake up to the Lee Sam house is bunk. If the blonde dame had been telling the truth she would have said that they'd followed me up to Thorensen's place first and then on to the Lee Sam house. She didn't say this because they didn't know I had been to Thorensen's place because they wasn't following me then.

9. They wasn't following me because they didn't know I was up there till I got to Lee Sam's. Then somebody in the Lee Sam house saw me gumshoein' about the place and put a call through to the gun boys in the car. They came up and stuck around until I left.

10. So it looks like I have to find the connection between the guy Spigla who was responsible for the attempted rubbing out of me, and Lee Sam or Berenice Lee Sam because it was somebody from that house who did the telephoning for the murder car.

11. It looks like Very Deep and Very Beautiful Stream is plenty deep. I must talk to this dame some more.

Chapter Four
THE SMART DOLL

AT FOUR o'clock in the afternoon I am still sleepin' like a log, when a bell hop comes in, wakes me up an' gives me a wire from headquarters at Washington.

I sit up in bed with this wire in my hand an' I get a sorta feelin' that the Director is goin' to recall me because Marella havin' been bumped the Federal Government has sorta lost interest in this business. I get a strange feelin' of disappointment that I can't quite work out. Then I bust open the envelope an' I am very glad to find out that I am wrong. The wire says:

District Attorney San Francisco reports Mrs. Marella Thorensen murdered last night stop Chief of Police suggests motive was to prevent information regarding Federal offences reaching you stop He agrees investigation of death of Marella Thorensen and alleged Federal offences known to her be carried out by you stop Has appointed Police Captain Brendy Police Lieutenant O'Halloran to co-operate with you stop Necessary funds available at G office Kearney Street Director.

This is swell, an' I reckon I can see the hand of O'Halloran an' Brendy behind this business, these two guys knowin' that gettin' themselves taken off routine duties in order to co-operate with me probably means a sweet rest an' plenty liquor.

I get up, give myself a shower an' start dressin'. I ring down to the desk for some coffee an' a big shot of bourbon which is a favourite breakfast of mine at this time of the afternoon. Whilst I am dressin' I am doing a little ruminatin' about this Marella job, but all the time my mind keeps comin' back to the Lee Sam doll.

I have told you guys before that it is always the swell dame who starts the trouble, an' I reckon this Berenice is too beautiful not to have started plenty in her time. Anyhow I reckon she started something between Marella an' Aylmar Thorensen, something that didn't please Marella very much.

Lookin' back this case has been screwy from the start. It was a mysterious sorta letter that Marella wrote to the Director in the first place, the sorta letter that a dame would write if she was gettin' the jitters about somethin' that concerned her husband an' didn't want him to know what she was gettin' up to. I start wonderin' if Marella wrote that letter because she was frightened; because she thought that things would be comin' to a head on or about the 10th January an' that it would be a good thing if there was a "G" man hangin' around—even if he didn't know what he was hangin' around for.

Even if he didn't know what he was hangin' around for! Boy, is that an idea or is it?

Looky, supposin' for the sake of the argument that Marella is havin' one helluva row with her husband or somebody, an' she tells 'em that she is fed up with something or other an' that unless something stops she is goin' to inform the Federal Government. Well, if she says that they can stop her, can't they? They just take her for a ride or bump her nice an' quiet. That's sense ain't it? Then she can't talk.

But supposin' instead of sayin' anything at all she just writes a letter to the Bureau askin' for an operative to be sent down but not sayin' for what. Well, then she's in a strong position, ain't she? She can then do a bit of threatenin' herself. She can say to all concerned that she has written a letter to the Bureau; that she has spilled all the beans an' that if anything happens to her the Bureau will know who has done it. What she don't say is that although she has written the letter she has only suggested that something or other is goin' on; she hasn't spilled anything that matters.

So it looks to me that Marella was hopin' that something would happen between the time she wrote that letter an' the 10th January. Then, if the thing she wants happens, she just don't say a word to the Federal operative when he turns up. She says that she has made a mistake an' that she was wrong in supposin' that any Federal offence has been committed. The "G" man is goin' to be sore but that's all he can be. He just goes back to Washington an' says she is nuts.

But supposin' the thing she wants to happen don't happen, why then she can carry out the threat she has made an' shoot the whole works to the "G" man who will be stickin' around to protect her if anybody tries to start somethin' with her.

So it looks to me that by writin' that letter in the way she did Marella was tryin' to have it both ways at once, which is a thing that you cannot very often get away with an' which she certainly didn't get away with. All she got was what was comin' to her.

I am just in the middle of these deep thoughts when the door busts open an' O'Halloran comes in. He is lookin' plenty pleased with himself.

"Hi'yah, Lemmy!" he says. "You heard the good news, bozo? The Chief says you're to be top-sergeant in this Marella Thorensen business, an' Brendy an' I are goin' to be side-kickers for you. Did you get my note about Nellie the cook?"

I tell him yes, an' I ask him to tell me what happened last night when he got old man Lee Sam an' Berenice down to the Precinct Office. I don't say a word about the attempt that the three guys in the Chevrolet made to rub me out, or anythin' about blondie or any of that stuff, because I have always found it a very good thing not to say too much to guys who are helpin' you, otherwise these guys will know as much as you do, which is often very bad for them.

Terry parks himself in a lounge chair an' brings out a pipe that he fills up an' lights. By the smell of this pipe you would think he was smokin' a dead squirrel.

"Here's the way it is, Lemmy," he says. "Last night at the time you said I sent a police car up to Nob Hill. I told the sergeant that I sent up there to grab old Lee Sam an' the girl an' to bring them straight down, so's not to give 'em a chance to tell anybody anything, in case they get sorta suspicious that we was goin' to pull somethin'. O.K. Well, he brings 'em down."

He takes his pipe outa his mouth.

"Say, feller," he says, "is this Berenice a honey or is she? I'm tellin' you that when that dame came inta the Precinct Office I nearly had a coupla fits, an' I've seen ritzy dames before. Has that dame got class? Listen," he goes on, leanin' back in the chair an' lettin' his ideas run easy, "she was wearin' a black lace evenin' gown that looked like she'd been poured inta it, an' she had on a chinchilla cape that woulda kept a soft drink bar goin' in straight whisky all the while prohibition was on. She was wearin' some jewels that woulda knocked your eye out. I've seen some ice in my time but the rocks that jane was showin' was an eyeful. An' has she got personality? Boy, that dame coulda shot a coupla wicked looks at a ninety year old miser an' he woulda give out one big shriek an' started rushin' around lookin' for the key of the safe deposit."

"So what," I tell him. "Listen, Terry, has this dame got you bulldozed? Why don't you keep your mind on your business an' when swell dolls get around just think of your wife?"

"What the hell," he says. "Me, I'm always thinkin' of my wife, but there ain't any law against hopin', is there? He settles down to business.

"O.K." he says. "Well, I start askin' 'em a lotta phoney questions that I've made up about this Marella Thorensen business. I just go on talkin' plenty so as to keep 'em down there like you said. Well, Lee Sam don't say anything at all. He just sits there in a chair with his arms folded across his chest lookin' like a Chinese idol. Whenever I look at him he just nods. I reckon this old bird is a pretty deep guy, an'

reckon that behind that face of his is a helluva brain.

"I go on talkin' plenty. Then I close down, an' I ask Berenice if she would like to make a statement about anything. She says no. She ain't got any statements to make, but that she has been havin' a conversation with her father this evenin' an' that he has asked her to say a few words about something not connected with this case that he thinks the law officers around here oughta know.

"Right then she stops talkin' to me an' she turns around to the old boy an' says something to him in Chinese. Believe it or not I never thought that language was so pretty. The way she spoke it it sounded like spillin' cream on a velvet bed-spread. When they've finished this pow-wow she turns around to me an' says here's the thing: She says that Lee Sam feels that the Customs Officers in the port of San Francisco oughta know that during the last year or so he has been doin' a little bit of quiet smugglin'.

"Well, this don't surprise me any, Lemmy, because you know as well as I do that there's plenty silk importers around here who try to slip a fast one across the Customs now an' then. It's human nature, ain't it? However, I make out that I am very interested in this an' I start makin' notes. I ask her to tell me about this smugglin'.

"She then says that besides the usual regular cargoes of silk that is delivered an' that goes properly through the Customs before they go into Lee Sam's warehouses on the other side of the slot, bales of swell Chinese silks have been dropped overboard at night from some of the smaller boats; picked up in row boats an' landed way down along the Embarcadero, so it looks as if they got some night watchman grafted down there.

"After this stuff has been landed it is taken around by car to Lee Sam's warehouses.

"I get a bright idea. I get the idea that maybe whoever it is does Lee Sam's truckin' for him is the same guy who is pickin' up the silk from the waterfront. So I ask her who this is an' she tells me that Lee Sam's truckin' contractor is a guy named Jack Rocca.

"Now I get a kick outa this, because I know plenty about this Jack Rocca, but I don't say nothin'. I just make a note of the name. Now take a look at this because I reckon it is goin' to interest you."

He gets up an' he brings over to me a typewritten foolscap sheet which I can see is a police report on Jack Rocca, an' believe me it's a honey. This guy was one of the original mobsters who went from Chicago to New York an' back again during the tough days that followed the prohibition. Rocca has done everythin'. He's been a beer runner an' high-jacker. He was in the snatch game. There isn't anythin' he hasn't had a cut at an' he's done all his business in a big way too.

Besides which this guy is clever. He keeps his nose clean. The police suspected him of plenty includin' bein' concerned in the St. Valentine's Day massacre, but they ain't got anythin' on this baby. He just gets away with everything.

Two years ago the report says Rocca comes inta San Francisco. I suppose he thinks that New York an' Chicago are gettin' a bit too hot for him. The San Francisco cops suspect him of bein' behind two or three protection rackets that was goin' on at that time. Finally it looks as if Rocca decides to behave himself a bit. He starts a big truckin' business, an' eventually he gets the Lee Sam contract to truck, silk which believe me is a pretty big one.

I give the paper back to Terry. "Very interestin'," I tell him.

"That's what I think," he says, "an' I'll tellya somethin' else I think, Lemmy. Why is it that this dame wants to blow this stuff about Lee Sam havin' done a bitta smugglin'? Wasn't that a funny thing for her to do?"

"Not so strange, bozo," I tell him. "Listen. Maybe Berenice thought that if she shoots the works about this smugglin', it is goin' to take our minds off the connection between herself, Lee Sam an' the Marella Thorensen murder. Another thing," I go on, "is that this dame is tryin' a very deep an' very fast one on us. See the idea? She knows durn well that if she says Lee Sam has been doin' a bitta smugglin' an' tells you that the stuff was landed on the Embarcadero, one of the first things we're goin' to try an' find out is who it was carried that stuff from the waterfront to the warehouses. This is goin' to bring us to Rocca, ain't it? So it looks to me like Berenice was bein' very clever an' tryin' to concentrate our attention on Rocca somehow. What else do you know about this guy Rocca, Terry?" I ask him.

"He's a nice guy, Lemmy," he says. "He's a big laughin' feller an' the guys who work for him seem satisfied. He owns a lotta property in San Francisco, two or three night clubs, a bunch of

flop houses, an' he's also been runnin' a number racket in Chinatown in conjunction with Lee Sam. That's breakin' the law too,
but who worries about that? If the Chinks don't gamble one way
they'll do it another."

He goes on to say that once or twice during the last year or so
there's been a bit of trouble—complaints from Chinese eats houses
that Rocca has been screwin' dough outa them for protection an'
stuff like that, but he says that every time somethin' like this has
come out it ain't ever got to court, because Thorensen, who is the
Lee Sam lawyer, gets hold of the job an' squares the complaints
before they ever get near the Hall of Justice.

Altogether; judgin' by what Terry says, this Rocca is a nice
clever feller who is plenty tough, an' who is tryin' not to be tough in
San Francisco, but runnin' his business nice an' sweet an' keepin'
his nose clean with the help of Aylmar Thorensen.

"You see, Lemmy," says O'Halloran, "it would be durned easy
for Rocca to make plenty dough in Chinatown, These Chinks stick
together. They all know Lee Sam an' they all like him. He's one of
the first guys to contribute to Chinese charities. So the fact that
the Chinks know that Rocca is workin' in with Lee Sam is goin' to
make Rocca tops with them all the time, so I reckon if they wanta
gamble an' if they wanta pay for protection, an' if they wanta do
anything that ain't strictly legal, they're goin' to do it through
Rocca, ain't they, because if things don't go quite right they can
always go an' grouse to Lee Sam."

"O.K." I tell him. "So what then, Terry?"

"Well," he says, "I write all this stuff down, an' it looks to me
as if you've had plenty time to do what you want, so I say I will
report this business to the Chief, an' that if they ain't got anythin'
further to tell me about this Marella Thorensen business they
can scram back home, but they've both got to hold themselves
in readiness to be brought down to the Hall of Justice if anybody
wants to ask 'em any more questions.

"After which," he says, "Berenice gives me a sweet smile an'
says good mornin'. She also asks if they can be taken back in the
police car, otherwise perhaps somebody will telephone up for one

of their own, an' when I say this ain't necessary they go off. The sergeant drops them back at this place on Nob Hill, an' that's that."

"Swell, Terry," I tell him. "Say, did you see anythin' of Thorensen last night?"

"Yeah," he says, "he came into the Precinct Office. He was lookin' all shot to hell. He said that you'd been up to his place an' had an interview with him; that he'd told you he was scrammin' outa San Francisco an' transferrin' his head office to Los Angeles an' that you said that was O.K. but that he was to leave his address at the Precinct. So he just left it an' scrammed. Was that O.K.?"

"Swell, Terry," I tell him. "Say listen, I suppose this guy Rocca has got two three fellers who help him with his organisation, ain't he. The truckin' business an' the night club business—they're things that gotta have a feller to look after 'em. You get around an' let me know who these guys are, an' if you can ring through some time this evenin' I'll be glad."

He says O.K. He says he'll start doin' some leg work an' will try an' let me know who the guys are who are playin' along with Rocca. He also tells me that Brendy is makin' a check-up of all the guys whose guns have been tested out as havin' fired bullets taken outa stiffs during the last year. He then bids me a fond farewell an' scrams.

Maybe you are wise as to why I have asked him to check up on the guys who are helpin' Rocca. I wanta see if I can get any line on this Spigla guy, the guy who blondie told me last night was runnin' The Two Moons Club, because the way I look at it is this. Supposin' for the sake of argument that this guy Spigla is workin' for Rocca. Well then the whole thing would match up just like this:

Berenice Lee Sam when she goes down to the Precinct house an' starts spillin' a lotta stuff about old Lee Sam havin' done a bit of smugglin', knows very well that the police will start worryin' about who carried the stuff. That dame is a wise dame an' she probably thinks that by doin' this she is goin' to concentrate attention on Rocco without actually sayin' anything about him. In other words the police will start gettin' after Rocca from an entirely new angle independent of the Marella Thorensen killin'.

Swell. Well, supposin', for the sake of argument that, like blondie said, it was Spigla who got those guys to try an' rub me out, then Spigla might have got his instructions from Rocca. But Rocca don't know me, so then again it looks as if Rocca was tipped off by somebody in the Lee Sam house or maybe by Berenice herself that it would be a good thing to get me outa the way. Having done this she is clever enough to concentrate attention on this guy Rocca in connection with a Federal offence—smuggling.

By doin' this maybe she thinks she is puttin' inta my head the idea that what Marella Thorensen wanted to talk to me about—the Federal offences that she mentioned when she wrote to the Director of the Bureau—was this smugglin' business. Maybe this Berenice baby thinks that once I get this idea in my head I will come to the conclusion that it was Rocca who was responsible for bumpin' off Marella, just because she was goin' to blow the works on the smugglin' racket.

Which business if you follow me closely will show you just how clever this dame can be.

I have met up with plenty dames in my time, an' I have found that quite a lot of 'em are inclined to get jumpy when somethin' breaks or when some copper starts stickin' his nose inta their private affairs. But it ain't like this with Berenice. That baby is as cool as a couple of icebergs.

Figure it out for yourself. Here is a dame mixed up in a killin', who, for all she knows, may be facin' a murder rap any time from now on. That letter Marella wrote to her husband, the one I read up in Berenice's bedroom, would make a fine motive for bumpin' Marella. Any District Attorney would pull her in on that letter an' there's plenty janes gone to the chair or got themselves stuck in the cooler for life on less evidence than that.

But still Berenice don't get steamed up. She just sticks around lookin' like a million dollars, bein' fresh in a quiet sorta way an' yet all the time goin' on with some scheme she has got in her head.

Me, I respect a jane who is like this because she don't get excited an' she is likely to hand you out a nice swell kick in the pants at any moment without notice.

I am very fond of dames. They have got something that is very attractive. I like the way they walk an' I can go nuts about a doll who is as swell-lookin' as Berenice is, but I still got enough sense to allow that a jane can have brains too, an' I have found that it is the quiet, cool an' polite ones who produce grief for all concerned at a moment's notice.

When I was over in Mexico after a dago who shot up a mail cart in Arizona I was stickin' around at his place waitin' for him to show up.

His wife was a nice woman. She was smart, smilin' an' very polite. She told me that she would be very glad if somebody would pinch her husband an' either cut his head off right away or lock him up for ever. She said that this guy was so bad that every time she went to bed she expected to wake up dead.

After which she gave me a sweet smile an' went upstairs to turn down my bed because she said she sorta liked the way I talked about things, an' she liked to look after her guests properly.

An' if I hadn't seen the whip snake she stuck in the bed before I got inta it I should be playin' a harp in the place where "G" men go with a couple snake punctures followin' me around all day. Which shows you somethin', don't it?

After these great thoughts I finish tyin' my tie an' I think I will try a fast one.

I ring down to the desk an' ask 'em if they will get me Mr. Lee Sam's house on Nob Hill. Five minutes afterwards I am through to this dump. Some guy—a Chinese house-boy I should think—answers the telephone an' I tell him that I am Mr. Caution an' that I would like to have a few words with Miss Lee Sam. He tells me to hang on an' after a minute he comes back an' says that he is puttin' me through to her. I can imagine this dame pickin' up the ivory telephone receiver that I saw up in that bedroom of hers, with her brain workin' as fast as a rip-saw, wonderin' what I am goin' to say to her an' what she is goin' to say back. I hear her say hulloa.

"Good-evenin'," I tell her. "I hope you wasn't inconvenienced last night by havin' to go down to the Precinct an' answer a few questions. How'ya feelin' this afternoon?"

She gives a little soft laugh.

"Quite well, thank you very much, Mr. Caution," she says. "Incidentally I had an idea that our being asked to go down to see Police Lieutenant O'Halloran last night was in the nature of what you would call a plant.

"Anyhow," she goes on, "it gave you ample opportunity to look around my bedroom didn't it?"

She gives another little laugh. This dame has certainly got her nerve.

"You don't say, Berenice," I tell her, "an' how did you know that?"

"The Chinese are a very quiet race, Mr. Caution," she says, "and my personal maid is *very* soft-footed. I have no doubt that you noticed the small room leading off my bedroom, the one which has no door but which is covered by a silk fringe. She was in there when you came into my room. Naturally she was very interested, although a little bit frightened."

She laughs again. "She says you were very interested in the letter which she saw you reading," she goes on, "the letter from Mrs. Thorensen to her husband."

"You're tellin' me," I tell her. "I certainly was interested in that letter. As a matter of fact, I think you an' me oughta have a little talk about that letter.

"I suppose it hasn't struck you, Berenice," I go on, "that there are a lotta people, includin' the District Attorney around here, an' maybe a jury on a murder trial, who would come to the conclusion that that letter might make a very good motive for you having been the cause, some way or another, for Marella Thorensen's death? I reckon you wanted that dame outa the way pretty badly, didn't you? She coulda made things pretty hot for you."

"Do you think so, Mr. Caution?" she says. "I must admit that it is a very interesting theory."

"You don't say?" I tell her.

You gotta realise that this dame is beginnin' to annoy me. This baby is givin' me prickly heat.

"Maybe there are some more interestin' things."

"Yes, Mr. Caution," she says, "such as . . ."

"Such as that story you put up when you was talkin' to O'Halloran at the Precinct last night. Listen, Berenice," I go on, "why don't you shoot the works? Tell me this little thing. Why did you wanta tell O'Halloran that your father had been mixed up in runnin' some silk through the Customs here without payin' any duty on it, hey?

"We all know that ain't a very terrible offence an' that it just costs him double if he's caught at it, an' we all know that there is a lotta guys try that game on an' that some of 'em get away with it, but why did you suddenly come to the conclusion that you oughta make this confession for your father? What was it made you so moral all of a sudden?"

I hear her pause for a minute, then:

"Mr. Caution," she says. "I think this is a most interesting conversation. I suppose it is a new idea, a sort of third degree over the telephone. But don't you think I ought to be very careful about what I say to you. Somebody might be listening on another line, mightn't they, and a girl has to be so careful."

"They might, but they ain't, Clever," I tell her. "I'm talkin' from the Sir Francis Drake, an' I'll tell you somethin' else, baby. I don't have to have guys listenin' in on the telephone when I'm talkin'. I can do all the remembering I want myself. It might interest you to know that I got an idea about that confession you made last night."

"That interests me very much, Mr. Caution," she says. "Do you think that you and I are sufficiently friendly for you to tell me what your idea is?"

"Sure I will," I tell her, "an' I'll also tell you why I'm tellin' you. I got a very funny theory about crime detection, Berenice. Me—I'm one of those guys who don't believe in detectives who go around with magnifyin' glasses lookin' for clues under the corner of the carpet. I am not one of those guys who line up a lotta people an' say what was you doin' at one o'clock, because no real lady is goin' to answer a question like that—well, not often.

"I never yet knew a detective who went out to look for clues an' found one. I have got a different system. I just wait till somethin' hits me in the eye nice an' hard, an' then I go an' talk about it with those concerned, because I have found that if you talk to crooks for long enough they've gotta give themselves away sometime, just because they ain't tellin' the truth."

"Mr. Caution," she says, "it seems to me that not only do you possess a certain rugged beauty, but that you are also something of a psychologist. I think you should go very far in your profession. At the same time I would be very interested to know what you thought I was trying to do when I told Mr. O'Halloran last night about the smuggling."

By this time I am very nearly frothin' at the mouth because it looks like this dame is playin' me for a mug.

"I'll tell you what I thought you was tryin' to do, baby," I tell her. "Smugglin's a Federal offence, ain't it? You knew durn well that if you put the idea into my head that your old man had been doin' some smugglin', I should immediately wonder who had been carryin' the stuff. O.K. Well, that brings me to Jack Rocca, don't it? It also brings me to the fact that smugglin' is a Federal offence an' havin' regard to the fact that Marella Thorensen contacted the Director of the Bureau of Investigation with some story of Federal offences goin' on around here, I might very easily come to the conclusion that that's what she was talkin' about.

"Maybe you wanted me to come to that conclusion. Maybe you wanted me to believe that it was Rocca who thought it would be a good thing to get Marella out of the way.

"If you can get me to think this then maybe I ain't goin' to take so much notice of that letter I read up in your bedroom last night, an' you don't have to say anythin', because whatever you did say I don't think I'd believe it, and also because there is another little point which I wanta talk to you about."

"Do tell me, Mr. Caution," she says, an' I can almost feel her laughin' while she is talkin'. "I find your theories most interesting."

"O.K., Berenice," I say. "Then maybe this might interest you because you seemta be takin' a lot of interest in what happens to me. So maybe I don't have to tell you that when I come out of your house last night three guys in a Chevrolet tried to iron me out. I suppose you didn't know anythin' about that, or maybe it was that maid of yours who was hidin' in the other room who scrammed down to the hall telephone an' got through to somebody an' said it would be better if I was put outa the way nice an' quick.

"Maybe she even got through to somebody who knew Mr. Rocca, an' maybe he wouldn't be quite so pleased if I was to tell him that you are tryin' to hand everythin' on to him, an' what do you know about that?"

She don't say a thing. There is a sorta pause. I think that maybe I have hit the bull this time. I go on quick.

"You better do some quick thinkin', Berenice. Maybe you're in as big a jam as Marella was. Maybe if you was in this thing with Rocca an' he thinks that you're double-crossin' him he's goin' to get very excited about it an' hire some guy to punch a lotta little holes in that swell shape of yours with a spray that never come out of no perfume factory.

"Get wise to yourself, Berenice. Take a tip from me, an' come clean with the whole story of this business, after which I will stick around an' see that nobody gets at you."

She don't say anything for a bit. I reckon that I have got this dame where I want her. Then:

"Mr. Caution," she says. "I think you're wonderful. One day you must come up and tell me all about yourself, but right now I have to go to my hairdresser.

"Good-afternoon, Mr. Caution. *Do* ring up again . . ."

Believe it or not she hangs up.

I read in a book one time about some guy who was so steamed up that he just naturally died through not bein' able to think up new cuss words quick enough.

This guy has got nothin' on me. Because I am so steamed up with this Berenice baby that words ain't no good to me at all.

I light myself a cigarette an' do a little ruminatin'. It certainly looks to me that Berenice is not gettin' herself very excited about the fact that somebody has tried to get rid of me by shootin' me full of holes, an' this makes me think that she believes that she's plenty safe; that the guy who was responsible for bumping Marella is big enough to look after her.

This bein' so the idea strikes me that maybe Joe Mitzler an' that blonde dame of his will be thinkin' the same thing; that these two guys instead of scrammin' out of San Francisco are still hangin' around under cover. Maybe I will put these two on ice.

I grab off the telephone an' get through to Brendy at the Hall of Justice. I tell him to put a quiet police net out an' pull in Joe Mitzler an' the blonde dame if they are still around. After which I relax.

Chapter Five
NICE WORK

I STICK around. After dinner I ring through to O'Halloran an' ask him if he has got any news about Joe Mitzler an' the blonde girl. He says no but that if I will keep my hair on he will let me know when he gets his hooks on these babies.

I take the elevator downstairs an' get the low-down on The Two Moons Club from the night guy at the Sir Francis Drake. He reckons this Two Moons dump is one of them show places where visitors get around an' see what Chinatown is like. He says that the guy who is runnin' the dump is a smart alec by the name of Spigla.

I ask him if this place has got any sorta speciality. He says no, but that a guy can get most of the things he is lookin' for any time, an' that sometimes he can also get a coupla things that he ain't got on his schedule. He says that the liquor is all right sometimes, but that there is still a lotta home-made stuff kickin' around there, an' that one of the waiters who is a scientific sorta cuss has got a sweet line in synthetic gin that he makes up in a tin tub which is guaranteed to take the linin' off the stomach of a battleship. He also says that there is a very nice line in dames around at The Two Moons; that these babies are very accommodatin'; that they take a deep interest in such bozos as are seekin' love, an' anything else they can grab off.

Once or twice, says the janitor, there has been some real trouble, but it has got itself squared out before it ever got near the cops. One time some dame with red hair got herself drowned in a bath up on the third floor, an' owin' to the fact that this dame had gotta reputation for keepin' away from water the fact was regarded as bein' somewhat mysterious, especially as this doll has also been socked on the dome with what the police doctors call a blunt instrument before she decided to take a bath. However, it seems that Aylmar Thorensen was able to show the coroner that the unfortunate lady had banged herself on the head accidentally the day before whilst openin' a door an' that she had told seven hundred an' forty-five people during the past year that one day she just knew she would drown herself in a bath, so that was that.

At twelve o'clock I buy myself a cab an' I go down there. Whilst we are drivin' through Chinatown I get to thinkin' just how many nights of my life I have spent hangin' around night clubs. I get to thinkin' that maybe if there wasn't any night clubs there wouldn't be so much crime, but still I suppose that don't really matter because if people didn't talk over mayhem an' murder in one place they'd do it in another.

An' there is another angle. A guy who is not so brave gets along to one of these dumps for the purposes of havin' a little liquor an' lookin' over the women. Down there he meets some other guy who suggests that it would be a good thing to stick-up the all-night cigar store around the corner next Thursday. The first guy says that he thinks the idea ain't so keen. He then goes off an' gives himself a couple of long shots of some rot-gut callin' itself liquor an' has a few dances with a dizzy dame who has got a kink in her hair like he likes it. This baby tells him that she has seen a sweet bracelet around at the jeweller's an' that if he was the sorta guy who could hand her a bracelet like that she reckons that she is the sorta dame who could show him such a good time that he would consider rewriting *What Every Man Should Know* in Spanish with a special glossary for Eskimos.

He then sets brave an' goes back to the first guy an' says why wait till next Thursday when the cigar stand is just around the corner, after which the cigar guy who thought he was goin' to make a sale finds that he has got three bullet holes in his waist-coat; that he is quite dead while the two killin' guys are sittin' up a back alley workin' out a sweet alibi that they was flyin' airplanes in Wisconsin at the time of the stick-up. So you can work out the moral for yourself.

But this dump is a swell dump. When I go in I see that the place is all red an' gold. I leave my hat at the cloakroom on the right, an' I go on through some big swing doors an' get on to the main floor. The place is a fairly big sorta place with the dance floor in the middle an' a bar at each end. The bars an' the tables are on a sorta balcony that runs around the dance floor four five feet from the floor, an' the place is packed. There are plenty guys there an' a lotta dames. They are strugglin' about the floor either lookin' like they was enjoyin' it or as if they wish they was dead.

I go in an' sit myself down at a table an' order myself a high-ball. I stick around an' wait.

After a bit I take a look across the dance floor. On the other side of the room sittin' by herself is a Chinese dame. She is a good-lookin' kid, an' well-dressed. She is drinkin' a gin fizz, but the way she is makin' that drink last, an' the way she keeps lookin' over at me when she thinks I ain't lookin', gives me the idea that this baby is keepin' her eye on me.

Presently down some steps that lead from an office at the top end of the floor comes a guy. Right away I get the idea that this is Rudy Spigla. He is a middle-sized slim well-made feller, an' he looks strong. He is wearin' a swell suit an' his hair is plastered down. His face is thin but very intelligent—not a bad-lookin' sorta guy and also a very determined lookin' cuss who looks as if he would stick at nothin' very much.

I look around until I see some wop waiter leanin' up against the wall. I signal to this guy an' I tell him to go over an' tell Mr. Spigla—if it is Mr. Spigla—that I would like to have a few words with him. The waiter who looks as if he ain't been to bed for about ten years takes a pull at himself an' goes over. I see him give the message to Spigla an' I see Spigla look across at me in a fresh sorta way almost as if he expected to see me around. After a minute he comes over.

"Can I help?" he says with a grin.

He stands there with one hand in his pocket lookin' down at me. I've told you that this Spigla is a well-shaped sorta cuss, but he has also got a lotta character in his face. It ain't the usual sorta face that you see on a guy who spends his time runnin' a second-class night dump in the Chinatown quarter in 'Frisco. He has gotta forehead that looks plenty intelligent, a good jaw an' clever eyes. I reckon this Spigla could be pretty good at anythin' he set his hand to.

"Yes, you can help," I tell him. "Sit down. I wanta talk to you."

He sits down. Then he takes a cigarette case outa his pocket an' gives himself a cigarette. It is a nice case made of gold with some initials on the front.

"Look, Spigla," I tell him, "my name's Caution. I am a Federal Officer. Maybe you heard about me.'

He grins again—a silly sorta grin.

"I ain't heard of you," he says, "but then I'm not particularly interested in Federal Officers. They are a type of guy who leaves me very cold."

"Yeah," I tell him. "Well even if you think that, I wouldn't get fresh about it, otherwise I might like to spoil the shape of that nose of yours."

"You don't say," he says, sittin' back an' lookin' at me through a smoke ring which he has just blown. "Well, I don't know where that would get you. Maybe it wouldn't do me any good but I don't reckon it'd get you any place."

"It would probably get you to the hospital, feller," I crack back. "But take a tip from me an' don't get fresh. Now," I go on, "let's get down to cases. I've got information that you are the guy who sent three thugs after me in a Chevrolet last night an' tried to get me ironed out in the Nob Hill area What have you got to say about that, an' if I was you I'd take a little time before you answer, because if I have one crack outa you I'm goin' to smack you in the can so that you can cool off."

He sorta shrugs his shoulders. "Listen, Caution," he says, "I just wouldn't know what you're talkin' about. I never heard of you before you come here to-night an' why I should want anybody to bump you I don't know. You gotta realise that my business is runnin' this club for Jack Rocca. I ain't interested in arrangin' for Federals to get the heat. It ain't healthy. That's all I've gotta say."

"I get it," I tell him. "Clever stuff, hey? Maybe you never heard of a guy called Joe Mitzler. Maybe you don't even know some blonde dame who gets around with him?"

He looks up.

"You bet I do," he says, "but that don't prove anything. Has that fine pair been tellin' you some fairy stories about me?"

"So you know 'em all right," I say.

"You bet I do," he says. "I hired Joe Mitzler as a bouncer in this place. He worked here for two months. He was the guy who chucked fellers out when they got too fresh. O.K. After he'd been here a coupla weeks he pulled some sob story on me about this blonde dame of his an' I give her a job in the women's cloakroom, an' a couple weeks after that I find that this pair are pinchin' everything they can lay their hands on, so I chuck 'em both out."

He moves his cigarette over to his left hand, grabs another one outa the case an' lights it from the stub of the first one. While he is doin' this he is still lookin' at me. I see that his hands are well-kept an' nicely manicured.

"So you see," he goes on, "if these two have been pullin' some story on you about me it looks as if it might be a lotta hooey, don't it? Neither of those two like me very much."

I grin at him. "I'm not surprised," I tell him. "I don't like you very much either. Listen, Spigla," I go on, "did you hear that some dame called Marella Thorensen was pulled outa the ditch last night by the harbour squad? I suppose you wouldn't know anythin' about that?"

"Yeah," he says, "I heard about it. Why shouldn't I? I don't know this dame, but she is the wife of Thorensen who looks after the big boy's affairs for him."

"The big boy bein' Jack Rocca?" I say.

He nods. "That's the idea," he says. "Say listen, I gotta lot of work to do around here, an' whilst I don't mind answerin' questions any time it looks important to you, that is providin' that they are sensible sorta questions, I haven't got a lotta time to stick around now." He gets up.

"Look," he says, "if you wanta ask questions why don't you ask somebody who knows something about it. All you guys are the same. Somethin' happens an' you never know anythin' about it, so you just get around shootin' off your mouth, standin' up people where you can, just in the hope that you might find somethin' out."

I reckon I'm goin' to keep my temper with this baby, although I feel like givin' him a swell bust in the puss.

"O.K., Spigla," I tell him. "You're feelin' pretty good, ain't you? So good that you think you can get fresh. Where's this boss of yours—Rocca?"

He yawns. "He's around," he says, "but just where he is right now I wouldn't know."

I look at him. "Well," I tell him, "I'm goin' to give you just five minutes to find out. If you ain't back here in five minutes' time so's you can let me know where Rocca is right now you're goin' down to the Precinct an' you're goin' to cool your heels for a few days in a cell. Maybe while you're down there we can find somethin' to hold you on."

I grin. "I reckon you're one of them guys," I tell him, "with a record. I reckon that maybe you have slipped up somewhere durin' that sweet life of yours, an' it might pay me to find out about it. Another thing," I go on, "I'm not in the habit of takin' apple sauce from cheap dance-room sissies like you, so if you don't wanta get grievin' go an' get busy."

He don't say anythin'. He just goes off. I see him cross the floor an' go up the stairs that lead to the club offices. About five minutes later a waiter comes over an' says that Mr. Spigla sends his compliments an' that Mr. Rocca will be down at the Club at one o'clock an' will be very glad to see Mr. Caution.

I get up an' follow the wop across the floor, pickin' my way through a huddle of cheek-to-cheek dancers who are tryin' to solve the problem of how to combine a whole lotta neckin' with as little legitimate dancin' as possible.

On the other side of the floor we go up the stairs, through the swing doors that Rudy Spigla came through an' along another passage. The carpets on the floors are swell an' it looks as if plenty money has been spent on this dump.

At the end of the passage there is a lift. I get in an' the waiter shuts the door. The lift starts goin' up on its own without any help from me, so it looks as if they can run to trick lifts as well around here.

After a few seconds the lift stops, the door opens an' I see Rudy waitin' for me outside. He has got that lousy grin on his face that I don't like an' I have a little bet with myself that before I am through with this bozo I am goin' to smack that happy smile off his pan, because this hombre makes me feel sick in the stomach.

Rudy is one of them smart guys that you meet with when you are gettin' around with the mobs. He is the second man, the lieutenant, the guy who does what the big boy says an' likes it. He is feelin' pretty good an' safe all the time because he is always thinkin' that if somethin' bad breaks the boss will take care of it an' him, that he will get away with everything an' that even if the balloon goes go up a bit too high one day an' somebody gets pinched for somethin' then he still thinks that it will be the boss, an' that he can be clever enough to beat the rap somehow.

I have met plenty fellers like Rudy an' I reckon that they are just pure poison. But I have got to admit that there is something about this guy that is somehow attractive. Whether it is the way he walks or looks, or whether it is something inside him that I sorta can't put my finger on I just don't know, but I do know that there are a whole flock of dames who would go for Rudy in a big way just because he has got that little thing that women always fall for with a bump. You can call it sex-appeal or anything you like, but it's there all right.

Somehow, durin' that moment while I am gettin' out of the lift an' lookin' at this hero, my mind goes back to blondie. I wonder whether this Rudy had got that blonde baby stringin' along after him. Maybe she was just one of the crowd that usta think he was the whole world. An' if this surmise is correct then it would explain her bein' on the lookout outside the morgue when I went down to take a look at Marella. It would also explain why she was in the Chevrolet with the boys who tried to rub me out, an' it would also support the theory that I have got kickin' around in my head that it was Rocca who staged that business with the ice blocks down at the morgue, and that it was some of Rocca's boys who gave Marella the works and threw her in the ditch just because she knew a bit too much.

"This way, Mr. Caution," he says sorta polite, an' leads off down the red an' gold passage.

Down on the left is a door. Rudy knocks on this an' when somebody says to come in he pushes it open an' lets me go in. I step ahead. I hear the door close behind me, so it looks as if Rudy has scrammed an' that this is goin' to be a strictly private interview.

Right opposite the door, on the other side of the big room is a helluva big desk. I reckon that this is one of the biggest desks ever, an' sittin' on the other side of it with a pleasant smile on his face, an' a big cigar stuck in his mouth is a helluva big guy.

He has got a big body an' a big head. He has got a jowl made through good livin' that is hangin' over the side of his silk shirt-collar. His hair is black an' wavy an' kept very nicely—it's a funny thing but mobsters always look after their hair properly, I reckon they musta made fortunes for hairdressers in their time—an' I can see that his chin is powdered so I reckon he has just got up an' been shaved.

He is wearin' a very good tweed suit that cost some dough an' he is restin' his chin on one hand lookin' at me with a sorta pleasant smile like I was an old friend who had blown inta town after bein' away for a coupla years.

I take a quick peek around the room. Everything is swell. The furniture looks like a Metro-Goldwyn set when they was shootin' the palace scene an' the carpets are very pleasant to the soles of the feet. Altogether the set-up is pretty good an' mighta belonged to a millionaire instead of a double-crossin' son of a she-dog like Jack Rocca.

"Glad to meet you, Mr. Caution," he says. "Sit down. Have a cigar,"

I pull up a chair. "Thanks a lot, Rocca," I say, "but I reckon that I will stick to cigarettes."

I sit down. He still sits there lookin' at me smilin' very nicely. He looks like the cat that has swallowed the canary.

He says: "I'll be very glad to do anything I can to help you, because I have always found out that it is a very good thing to render assistance to Federal guys when they are stickin' around lookin' for trouble."

"Like hell you have, Rocca," I tell him. "An' I will also tell you something else an' that is that you can turn that stuff off right away. I have already had plenty apple sauce from that Spigla guy of yours. I don't allow to stand for any more, so supposin' you stop bein' funny an' just keep them windscreens you call ears flappin' an' listen."

"Sure, Mr. Caution," he says, "but you don't have to take any notice of Rudy Spigla, that's just his way. He's O.K. only he sounds sorta fresh. He don't mean a thing.

"You're tellin' me," I crack. "I'll bet he don't—not any more than that bunch of guys you stuck up against a garage wall in Chicago six years ago an' riddled with a tommy gun till they looked like something that the cat had found down a drain. I'm wise to you, Rocca."

"What the hell," he says. "All that stuff is over an' done with. Me, I wouldn't hurt a fly."

"Stop makin' me cry," I tell him. "In a minute you'll be tellin' me that you're just a big boy tryin' to work your way through college an' keep your old mother in comfort."

He grins. This guy has got a sorta big open grin an' in spite of the fact that he has got a record as long as my leg there is somethin' pleasant about him, which, maybe, is the reason that he is still alive an' not full of bullet holes in a bronze casket like most of his friends and colleagues.

This Rocca is just another of them contradictory guys who will smile at you an' make you feel as if you couldn't annoy 'em even if you bit a large lump outa their favourite wife's neck, an' who will, with exactly the same friendly grin, soak your underclothes in petrol an' set fire to 'em, which is just what this guy did to a small-time mobster up Detroit way—an' got away with it too.

"Look, Rocca," I tell him. "There is one or two things I wanta ask you, and if I was you I'd be good an' careful to talk the truth."

"Sure," he cays, "anything you want."

"All right," I tell him. "What do you know about Berenice Lee Sam?"

He spreads his hands.

"What the hell?" he says. "What should I know about Berenice except that she is old Lee Sam's daughter? Don't I look after his truckin' business? She is a nice dame. I have only seen her once or twice, an' I don't know a thing else."

"O.K.," I tell him. "Well, maybe you'd like to know that this Berenice shoots off her mouth last night down at the Precinct an' she sorta suggests that old man Lee Sam has been runnin' silk, an' she sorta suggests that you are the guy who has been carryin' it. What have you gotta say about that?"

He grins some more.

"I ain't goin' to say nothin' except it looks like a whole lotta hooey to me. Maybe the dame's gone nuts. What do I want with runnin' silk?" He laughs.

"Runnin' silk ain't part of my organisation. It don't have to be. Anybody will tellya that I am a straight business man, that I make plenty dough outa my truckin' business, that I have got property around this town an' that I don't have to do anything that is illegal."

I nod. "Right," I tell him, "so Berenice was just talkin' outa her ear. She was just makin' it up. Listen, Rocca," I go on, "what do you know about this Marella Thorensen bump off? Who do you think killed that dame? Have you heard about it?"

"Yeah," he says, "I heard about it, who ain't? But what should I know about that?"

He leans over the table.

"It's a screwy business," he says. "I can't sorta understand this killin'. That dame was a nice dame, quiet an' classy. She never got within a hundred miles of a mobster in her life, an' she wasn't mixed up with anythin' screwy. How that dame comes to get the heat I just don't know."

"Maybe not," I say, "but maybe you can make a guess. After all she was Aylmar Thorensen's wife, wasn't she, an' as far as I can make out it was Aylmar Thorensen who has been lookin' after you an' Lee Sam any time when it looked as if the law might get its hook on you."

He grins some more.

"So what?" he says. "Listen, Caution. You got this thing all wrong. Me an' Lee Sam ain't ever got inta any trouble around here. I don't mind tellin' you that we've been runnin' some number rackets around here in Chinatown. You never met a Chink who didn't wanta gamble, did you? Well, everybody is runnin' number rackets everywhere. There's nothin' extraordinary in that. It's an offence, but what copper ever takes any notice of it? Thorensen just used to straighten out any little bit of trouble that started; but if you're meanin' to suggest that because he looked after Lee Sam's legal affairs there was some reason why somebody should wanta bump his wife off you've got the whole thing wrong. That dame never came inta the picture any time."

"Well, she's come inta it all right this time, an' gone out of it," I tell him. "Say listen, Rocca, do you meanta tell me that you're shootin' straight when you say that you don't know nothin' about this killin'—nothin' at all? Do you mean that you ain't got any ideas?"

He looks at me across the desk. He looks straight in my eyes an' believe it or not for a moment I almost get the idea that this bozo is tellin' the truth, because he has got such a swell personality that he makes you think he wouldn't string you along.

"I don't know a thing," he says, "but you can take it from me that I'm a durned sight too wise to have anythin' to do with any killin' around here."

I grin back at him. "You don't know nothing about the guys in the Chevrolet car who tried to get rid of me last night either, I suppose?" I say.

He looks at me sorta bland. "To tell you the truth," he says, "that's the first I heard about it."

We sit there lookin' at each other, an' it looks to me like I am wastin' my time. I get up.

"O.K., Rocca," I tell him. "I think you an' me understand each other pretty well. Maybe before I am through with you you'll decide to talk plenty. I'll be seein' you."

I walk outa the room. He watches me go. I walk down the corridor an' open the lift door an' get in. I get out at the floor beneath an' walk back onta the dance floor. Way over on the balcony on the other side of the room I can see Rudy Spigla talkin' to some dame. It looks to me like I cannot do any good around this place, but I have got two or three rather swell ideas sizzlin' in my head, an' I think I will blow.

I start walkin' around the balcony so as to get over the other side an' out by the entrance where I have left my hat, when sittin' way down at the table where she was before I see the Chinese girl—the one I saw when I come in. She looks at me an' she slips me a very fast wink. Then she looks at the chair on the other side of the table sorta suggestin' that I should sit down there. As I get to the table I drop in the chair.

"Well, baby," I tell her. "What is it? If you're lookin' for a sugar daddy you got the wrong guy. What's on your mind?"

She looks outa the corner of her eye over towards where Spigla is standin'.

"You pletend you having a dlink with me," she says nice an' quiet. "I like to talk. I got something to tell."

I signal the waiter. I order two highballs an' we wait till he brings them. Whilst we are waitin' she don't say nothin', but when the waiter has brought the drinks she motions with her head towards where Spigla is standin'. I look across an' see that he has seen where I am an' that he is beckonin' to me. I say excuse me an' I get up an' I go over.

"What's eatin' you, Spigla?" I ask him. "You discovered you got somethin' you wanta talk about?"

He smiles. This guy is still pretty fresh.

"No," he says. "I wanted to ask you how you got along with Rocca. I wanted to ask you if the big boy has been able to be any help."

"Ain't that too nice of you?" I tell him. "The next time I want you to ask me something I'll let you know."

I turn around, an' I go back to the table. I sit down and drink the highball. It tastes lousy.

"Well what is it, baby?" I ask the dame.

She looks across at me an' smiles. She is a pretty kid an' her hair is done very nice. In spite of the fact that this baby is Chinese, she has still got something.

"Mlister Caution," she says. "I think it would be a very good thing if you don't go back to your hotel. Maybe it not be so good for you."

"Aw nuts," I tell her. "Say listen, what is this? Has Mr. Rocca got you on to tryin' some sorta psychological stunt on me to get me nervous? You try somethin' else, baby."

I get my hat an' I walk out inta the street. The entrance to The Two Moons Club is in a wide sorta alleyway. This is a pretty dark place an' there is only one light at the end. As I start walkin' along my head begins to go round an' I see the light at the end of the alley goin' round in circles. I get to feelin' that I would pay a million bucks to be sick; yet at the same time I don't wanta be sick.

I get it. While I went over to talk to Spigla some clever guy has hocked my drink. Maybe the Chinese girl or maybe it was done before the waiter brought it. Whatever they have given me is doin' me no good at all. I have got a pain in my guts like snake was livin' there an' not likin' it. My knees feel as if they was made of spaghetti, an' it looks like it is a matter of minutes before the pavement comes up an' hits me.

I lean up against the wall an' try to concentrate so as to take a look around me. Over on the other side of the road, down in a doorway, I can see a guy. I reckon this is the palooka who is waitin' for me to pass out.

I get one of them funny ideas that a guy gets when he is goin' under to a drug. I get the idea that if I can get myself to the street lamp at the end of the alley I might have a chance. So I start concentratin'. I concentrate on walkin', although every time I put one foot in front of the other I feel as if there was a ton weight on the end of it.

I get to the lamp, an' I put my arm around the post. I start to be sick, an' I begin slidin' down the post because I can't hold myself up.

The last thing I see is the guy who was standin' in the doorway comin' towards me. He has got his hand in his coat pocket.

Everything looks like black. I go right out.

CHAPTER SIX
NECKING IS SO NICE

I DO not know if you have ever had knock-out drops, but if you have you will know without my tellin' you that it is not so hot when you start comin' back.

My eyes are heavy and as sore as if they was filled with sand, I have got a taste in my mouth that makes me feel like I have been eatin' bad birds-nest soup, an' every time I try to move I feel like somebody is tryin' to shave a bit off my head with a blunt saw.

I do not know where I am but it smells good to me. There is some perfume or something round about an' I am tryin' to remember where I smelt this stuff before. After doin' a lot of concentratin' I get it. This was the perfume that I sniffed when I was gettin' around Berenice Lee Sam's room, the stuff that made her handbag smell so nice. I get a big idea that it is that goddam hot momma that has given me the knock-out drops. So what?

I open up my eyes for a minute an' I see that I am right. I am in Berenice's room. I am lyin' on a settee an' opposite me I can see the door with the silk fringe screen—the door leadin' to the Chinese maid's room. The room is pretty dark, there is only a standard lamp alight. Sittin' up against the wall opposite me is a big Chinese guy, the guy I saw puttin' his hand inta his pocket just before I flopped.

Between him an' me, sittin' in an armchair, smokin' a cigarette through a jade holder and wearin' a peach coloured wrap with silver snakes worked all over it, is Berenice. She is lookin' at me an' smilin' a slow sorta smile, the sorta look that a cat would bestow on some bird it was goin' to use for hors-d'œuvres.

I look at her under my eyelashes. This dame is a sonsy number I am tellin' you, an' I reckon I know plenty guys who would do more than murder if they could get their hooks on a lovely like this as a result thereof. This dame is the sorta proposition that gets me burned up. She has got looks, figure, class an' that certain something they call allure which is the thing that gets guys goin', but it is her nerve that gets me on the floor.

I watch the light from the standard lamp reflectin' on the ice in the rings on her fingers as she takes the jade cigarette holder outa her mouth. I get a feelin' that I would like to smack this dame so hard that she would be constrained to maintain the perpendicular almost continuously—as the geometry fan said.

I think I will try an' say a few words, but even my tongue is swollen with the hells broth that they have slipped inta me, an' when I talk it sounds like I have got a mouthful of spaghetti.

"O.K., Berenice," I tell her. "I reckon that you pulled one that is just a bit too fast this time. Ain't you the disappointin' dame—an' I thought you was clever? I certainly thought that you was too clever to think that you are goin' to get any place by givin' me a dose of hocked liquor an' bringin' me up here.

"What's the idea? Are you tryin' to snatch me or is it my fatal sex-appeal that has got you down? If it's a snatch I don't reckon that Uncle Sam will be prepared to pay very much for my carcass an' if it's the other thing I give you due notice that I do not intend to fight for my honour, so get busy; only I tell you this much that when I get outa here I'm goin' to make things so tough for you that sittin' on tintacks would feel like wearin' silk underpants after what I'm goin' to do to you some way or another."

She just goes on smilin'. Then she waves her hand an' the Chinese maid comes in with a cup of something an' brings it over. I smell it an' it smells like very good tea. I reckon that all they can do to me now is poison me an' that anyhow even death cannot be very much worse than the way I am feelin' right now, so I drink it, an' it *is* very good tea.

Berenice starts talkin'. She says somethin' in Chinese to the guy who is sittin' up against the wall an' he gets up an' scrams outa it. The maid comes in with a silk towel dipped in ice water an' sticks it around my head. I begin to think that maybe I am goin' nuts in my old age an' that this is all a pipe dream, because if this sorta stuff makes sense then I am Old King Cole.

She looks at me again. The smile sorta wanders off her face an' she is starin' at me like she was some old hen considerin' a tough chicken. I have told you before that this dame has got plenty, an' I wish that I knew enough words just to put over how she looks sittin' there in that peach coloured robe with a diamond an' ruby clasp in her black hair an' a humorous sorta look in them turquoise eyes of hers.

Even although my head is still achin' like I have been tryin' to butt down the Empire State building with it, I start thinkin' that it would be swell if this Berenice was a good girl an' on the side of law an' order instead of rushin' around pullin' all sorts of mayhem like she is doin'. I start wonderin' once again why it is that if a dame has got looks an' class an' that swell wiggle when she walks (you know what I mean), then in nine cases outa ten she is the one who smooths your fevered brow with one hand an' busts you a mean sock in the midriff with an old Samurai knife that one of her ancestors used for shavin' with the other.

But I reckon she is goin' to pull something, an' I reckon it is goin' to be something very swell. I take another gulp of Orange Pekoe just to get my mental motor turnin' over, an' I look at her outa one corner of my eye an' try an' come to a quick conclusion as to what the set-up is goin' to be.

First of all it is a cinch that the Chinese dame in The Two Moons Club is the one who hocked my drink, an' secondly it is a cinch that this baby was workin' for Berenice when she done it. So what does this lovely with the turquoise eyes an' the used car morals want to hand me a bunch of knockout drops for, an' then give me tea with wet towels around my head? Does it make sense to you? I reckon that she is goin' to try an' do a deal.

She starts talkin'. Her voice is soft an' low an' thrillin'. If I hadda voice like that an' looked as swell as Berenice I would start so much trouble that the League of Nations would call a special session to decide whether it wouldn't be cheaper in the long run to build me a palace in Iceland so as to keep the Esquimaux from playin' snowballs durin' the long winter nights.

"Mr. Caution," she says, "Lemmy, what do you think about me?"

I draw a long breath. I reckon that I am goin' to tell this doll just what I do think about her.

"Look, Very Deep an' Very Precious Stream," I tell her. "I will tell you just what I am thinkin' about you. First of all I reckon that you think that I got something outa Jack Rocca to-night, something that was so important that you even took the chance of givin' me knock-out drops an' gettin' me up here so's you can try an' make a deal with me.

"I think that there oughta be a law against dames like you bein' born. Because you are too good-lookin' to stick around without makin' a bundle of trouble for all concerned, an' I think such a lot about your technique that when I get outa here I am goin' to have you pinched an' held as a material witness in the Marella Thorensen case. If you didn't kill that dame then I'm nuts, but before I'm through with you I'm goin' to cause you a whole lot of grief, Berenice, an' that is official, so you can quote me."

She smiles. "First of all," she says. "I suggest that you should lay back on the couch so that your very efficient brain can, more or less comfortably, grasp what I am about to tell you; secondly, I think it would be very much to your advantage if you were to stop regarding me as some sort of low snake crawling about the undergrowth seeking whom I may kill. Thirdly, you will be very foolish if you do not pay due attention to what I am about to tell you.

"It was on my instructions that the little Chinese girl drugged your drink at The Two Moons, but you will remember she did this only after she had asked you not to return to your hotel and you had refused to listen to her. I did not want you to return to your hotel, and had you attempted to do so you would probably not be alive at this moment. You will remember that one attempt has already been made on your life, an attempt which you attributed to me, and it is therefore to my advantage to protect myself from any further accusations of this sort."

"Swell," I tell her. "All of which sounds very nice an' sweet. But maybe you will tell me that somebody or other has appointed you to be my little guardian angel in size three shoes. Why are you so interested in keepin' me alive?"

She smiles some more.

"Shall we say that I am more interested in keeping myself alive?" she says. "It will be quite obvious to you that on the very circumstantial evidence that exists at the moment you, and possibly other people, would consider that there is adequate reason to believe that I am concerned in the death of Marella Thorensen.

Your main reason for believing this is the letter which you read from Marella to Aylmar Thorensen which suggests that there had been an *affaire* between us and that Marella had discovered it. You are probably also interested as to how this letter came into my possession."

She puts another cigarette into her holder an' lights it. She brings another one over to where I am lyin', puts it in my mouth an' lights it with a little gold lighter. I don't say a word. I am just thinkin' that this dame has got the swellest nerve that ever I bumped against ever since I been totin' a "G" identification card.

"I am certainly very interested as to how you got that letter," I tell her. "First of all it is written to Thorensen and it ain't got any date on it so it coulda been written any time. Thorensen mighta given it to you to read, in which case he woulda have to have done this before he left for Los Angeles. Anyhow I suppose you had arranged to give it back to him?"

She looks at me with her eyes wide open.

"Why?" she says. "Why should I have given it back to him?"

"O.K." I tell her, "you've told me just what I wanted to know. So Thorensen gave you that letter to read an' asked you to destroy it, didn't he? Another thing I reckon he gave you that letter some time during the day that Marella got herself bumped off. But the thing that is interestin' me is why you didn't destroy it. Why didya leave it lyin' around here, in this room where any one could read it?"

She laughs—you know, one of them little ripplin' laughs. She shows all her pretty teeth between a pair of lips that are so swell that they woulda made King Solomon senda bell hop to let all his wives know that he was bein' kept at a conference an' that they was not to bother about callin' him in the mornin'.

"That, dear Mr. Lemmy, is the whole point," she says. "And with your usual sharpness of intellect you have put your finger on it. First of all Thorensen did not give me the letter, and therefore he never asked me to destroy it. As a matter of fact I very much doubt whether he has even seen it.

"The reason why I left it lying about, as you so aptly put it, instead of destroying it, was that I was keeping it. . . ."

"For what?" I ask her.

"To give to you," she says. "Isn't it obvious that I was keeping it to give to you? Haven't I made it clear already that I knew perfectly well that my father and I were asked, suddenly, to go down to the Precinct in order that some one—possibly you—could take a look around here. Yet knowing this I leave the letter for you to find. I always intended you to have it."

"Berenice," I tell her, "you listen to me. I am wise to you, ladybird. You are one swell, first-class goddam liar and when you die you will certainly go to Hell an' have the fact tattooed all over your lily-white posterior by blue devils writin' with fountain pens dipped in acid. Say, what do you take me for?"

"There are moments when I take you for the usual thickheaded cop, Lemmy," she says. "Especially when you are rude. There are, however, other moments when I believe that you are a really intelligent person possessing a first-class brain and disguising the fact by the use of language that makes me shudder. Can't you see what is behind this letter?"

"O.K., sweetheart," I tell her. "I'll play along. I'll say what you want me to say, an' it's this. I suppose the idea you want me to fall for is that the letter was never written by Marella Thorensen at all. That it is a forgery planted on you so as to supply a possible motive for you havin' killed her?"

"Correct in one shot," she says. "Isn't it obvious? Isn't it quite clear to you that a woman of my type would find it entirely revolting to have anything at all to do with a gross and impossible person like Aylmar Thorensen?"

"No, honeybunch," I tell her, more in sorrow than in anger, "it is not, because I have often found that swell-looking and classy dames like you do go for gross and impossible guys like Aylmar Thorensen.

"Why," I go on, "I remember a dame up in the silver district in Mexico. She was the cutest little number that you ever saw. She had guys fighting over her like cats. There was two palookas stickin' around there who fought each other to a standstill over that baby. They fought for six hours with ten inch knives and when they was finished they was both so full of holes that they looked like a coupla water biscuits. Finally, one of these guys gives a big sigh an' dies, an' she nurses the other for six weeks. Every day she usta go an' pour eau-de-cologne over that mug's head an' drool sweet hooey inta his ears until the poor guy used to writhe about the bed like he was bein' tickled to death by fairy fingers.

"So what? The day the doctor says that this guy is O.K. an' is fit to get his own back on her, what does she do? Why she goes off an' marries a can manufacturer with a belly so big that it practically made any sort of social contact a sheer impossibility. So laugh that off."

I sit up. I am feelin' better an' dyin' to get action.

"Look, Berenice," I tell her. "You know Marella's handwriting don't ya? You know whether that letter was written by her or not. Tell me somethin', how does the handwritin' of that letter match up with the one she wrote you when you was in Shanghai—the one tellin' you to come back an' see her because she wanted to see you bad?"

"I don't know," she says. "The letter Marella sent to me in Shanghai was typewritten except the signature. She often used to type her letters."

She stubs out her cigarette.

"You must believe me, Lemmy," she says. "I tell you that that letter *must* be a forgery; that it was written in an endeavour to throw suspicion on me."

"Boloney, Princess," I crack back at her. "Say, what do you think I am? You expect me to believe that? An' you expect me to believe that you sent that maid of yours down to The Two Moons to give me knock-out drops, an' that big thug of yours to bring me up here, just so as to stop somebody else takin' a sock at me. O.K. Now you can tell me a few more lies. Tell me where you got that letter from?"

She walks across to the table an' helps herself to another cigarette. All the while I am watchin' her. Every time this dame starts walkin' with that peach coloured gown clingin' to her the way it does I feel my mind slippin' right away from the business in hand, because this dame has got a walk that does things to a guy, if you know what I mean.

"The letter was put in my car after I arrived back here yesterday evening," she says, "that is, before my father and I went to the Precinct.

"After I go up to my room here I remembered that I had left my handbag and gloves in the car. I sent my maid down to the garage which is on the other side of the house to get them.

"She found the letter, enclosed in a plain white envelope, placed on top of my handbag on the seat of the car. She brought it up believing, naturally, that I had left it there with the other things. Immediately I opened the envelope and read the letter I saw that some one was trying to throw suspicion on me. Some one who probably knew that you were already regarding me as a suspect. I made up my mind at once that I would give you the letter at the first opportunity."

"O.K., lady," I tell her. "You can give it to me now."

She goes over to a drawer an' gets the letter, and brings it over to where I am sittin'. I read it once again. I reckon it will be easy to have this handwritin' checked. Lookin' at it I see that the letter is written in a light blue ink—Sea Island Blue they call it—an' I get to wonderin' whether Marella always used this sorta ink. I make a note in my mind to find out.

I look up at her. She is standin' just in front of me, an' as I look at her I can smell a sorta suggestion of the perfume that she is wearin'. She smiles down at me.

"O.K.," I say. "So the set-up is now like this. The idea is that somebody who could get inta your garage planted this letter on the seat of the car. An' who in the name of heck did they think was goin' to find it? Do you mean to tell me that they thought you was goin' to send your maid down an' that she was goin' to find it an' bring it to you an' that you was goin' to let me find it an' finally give it to me like you are doin' now? Anybody who reckoned to do a thing like that must be just plain nuts, an' what do you think?"

She shrugs her shoulders. "That's the truth," she says. "That is all I have to say about it."

"All right," I tell her, "but be your age, Berenice. Don't you see how screwy that story is? If whoever it was planted that letter in your car expected you to find it, wouldn't it have been reasonable for them to believe that the first thing you woulda done would be to burn it?"

"I think that is quite possible," she says. "But it is also possibly that they did not expect me to send my maid down to the garage. Possibly they thought that some one else would go down there and find it."

I start to say something but I stop myself. I have got an idea. I just don't say a word. I get up.

"Well, Berenice," I say. "I am goin' to scram. Me—I have got an entirely open mind about everything with the exception that I think you bumped Marella, an' that you are a brainy little cuss who is holdin' out an' makin' a nice setup so's you can get away with it in the confusion.

"I think that this letter is a fake, an' that you have decided that it would be a good thing for it to get inta my hands just so's it would make it look like it is somebody else tryin' to hang this job onto you. Well, I have known setups like that before. An' this one won't get you any place."

She shrugs her shoulders again, an' the little smile comes across her face.

"In China, there is a proverb," she says, "a proverb which says that nothing is easy to a fool."

I walk across to a table where I see my hat an' grab it.

"Meanin' that I am a fool, an' that nothin' is goin' to come easy to me, hey?" I tell her. "O.K., Berenice, well let me tell you that there are plenty other guys who thought that I was a mug an' learned different before I was through."

She smiles some more. "There is another proverb," she says. She comes a little closer to me. "There is a proverb," she goes on, "which says that it is better to be a fool who is beloved than a wise man who knows not the softness of a woman's mouth."

She is right close to me now, an' her eyes are lookin' up into mine. I get an idea that this dame is tryin' to take me for a ride, an' that she is makin' one big mistake about Lemmy Caution, because I am not that sorta guy an' when a dame starts playin' me I get sorta suspicious.

"O.K., Berenice," I tell her. "You learn some more proverbs, but you'll find that they won't get you no place. I'll be seein' you."

I am just goin' to turn around when she puts her hand on my shoulder. I look down an' see this hand, with the rings glitterin' on it an' the polished finger nails, an' I get to thinkin' that those fingers did a mean job when they squeezed that little .22 gun that sent Marella on the long bump. Maybe this dame thinks she is goin' to play me for a sucker.

"Lemmy," she says, "you must realise that I think you are the most delectable person. You are so very direct that there are occasions on which you omit to see the most obvious facts.

"You attract me strangely. I like to be near you. Also," she goes on, "if and when you succeed in proving that I killed Marella I think it would be very nice if you could be the person who was detailed to execute me. It would be such a charming gesture to be 'fried' (as I believe you call it) by a person like you. Even the electric chair would seem less electric if you were near."

I look down at her. This dame is laughin' at me. There are a thousand lights twinklin' in her turquoise eyes, an' her hand is on my cheek.

Before I know what is happenin' she is in my arms. I can feel her give as my arm goes around her, an' when I say give I mean just that.

What the hell. I know all about it. I know that the Federal Regulations for Special Agents say that Agents must be careful not to get themselves mixed up with dames in the course of their investigations. But the guy who drafted these rules was not thinkin' of dames like Berenice, otherwise he woulda wrote 'em backwards.

Something my old Ma used to say comes rushin' into my head. "Every guy must have his moments," Ma Caution usta say, an' if this ain't one of my moments what is? Regulations is regulations, but a dame who can kiss like this one could slip a stranglehold on a bronze statue of the guy who thought that neckin' was bad for the nerves. Me—I am thorough. When I do something I do it an' like it.

Did I break that goddam regulation or did I?

Downstairs in the hall I find the slit-eyed butler stick in' around waitin' to let me out. He opens the door an' I am just walkin' out when I think of somethin'.

"Hey, you," I tell him. "What's your name?"

He says his name is Hi-Tok.

"O.K.. Hi-Tok," I say. "You tell me somethin', willya?"

He says he will if he can.

"You tell me who is the last guy to go into the garage here at night," I ask him, "the guy who would do the lockin' up an' see that everything was O.K.?"

"Mlister Lee Sam do that," he says. "He velly particular. He always lock up himself. He always do that."

I say thanks a lot an' I scram.

Outside the house I look back an' see the light in Berenice's window. I reckon that dame has got a nerve. Maybe she thinks she can play me for a mug. Maybe she is right an' maybe not.

CHAPTER SEVEN
SLIP-UP FOR BERENICE

I AM layin' on my back on the settee in my sittin'-room at the hotel. It is a pretty swell sorta afternoon, an' there is a bit of late sun still shinin'.

Over on the other side of the room Brendy is sittin' smokin' a cigar an' regarding the ceilin' like he was deep in thought. I reckon that I know what is goin' on in his head.

He is thinkin' to himself why the hell don't this son of a she-dog Lemmy Caution make a pinch? Why don't he pinch Berenice Lee Sam when it is stickin' out like the elephant's ears that this dame is the one who has started all the hey-hey around here?

Me, I am also thinkin' about Berenice. An' I want you guys to get this straight. Don't you think that I would lay off pinchin' that dame just because I had a warm session with her last night. Don't you get the idea inta your heads that just because this Berenice has got a method of kissin' an' a line in cuddlin' that would make a confirmed bachelor of ninety-five shave off his side burns an' start learnin' the rumba, that I wouldn't pinch her if I though that was the angle. I just don't, that's all, an' think what you like Berenice's sex-appeal just don't come inta the picture—well not so much.

I am thinkin' about all the things that everybody else thinks don't matter.

Get a load of this: When Berenice went out to the Villa Rosalito that afternoon to meet Marella she thought that she was goin' out there to discuss some urgent business, didn't she? When I asked her what they was doin' out there she says they just sat an' talked. They was sittin' there talkin' from about five o'clock until seven—two hours that is.

But Berenice don't ever say what they was talkin' about. She just keeps as mum as hell about a conversation that nine outa ten women woulda disclosed to me if it was an innocent sorta conversation.

I reckon that if I knew what those two dames were sittin' talkin' about for two hours in that lonely dump with the mist comin' down, I should know plenty. An' all the while the telephone receiver is flipped off downstairs—Berenice done that I reckon—so that nobody can get through an' disturb 'em.

Well, you're goin' to say that it is natural for Berenice to keep her trap shut about what they was talkin' about because it wasn't an innocent sorta conversation, but just for once I am goin' over to her side an' I am goin' to say this:

If she'da known that she was goin' out to the Villa Rosalito to have a show-down with Marella she'd have slipped back quietly from Shanghai on the China Clipper an' eased out to the Villa an' said nothin' to nobody. She wouldn'ta telephoned her old man through an' said that she was goin' out to see Marella. She'd have just gone an' said nothin' about it.

To which you will maybe reply that old man Lee Sam mighta been in on the job with her. But if you say that then I am goin' to say right away that if that had been the case I reckon Lee Sam wouldn'ta telephoned through to the Precinct when his girl didn't come home. He woulda just kept quiet an' said nothin', because that telephone call of his mighta started something they didn't want started.

The big point is this: All the facts—as I can see 'em—confirm that Marella did write to Berenice an' tell her to come over, because she wants to see her urgently, an' when Berenice appears then Marella has changed her mind for some reason or other. She just don't discuss any urgent business, or if she does it is something that old Lee Sam didn't know about.

An' if I am right, this attitude of Marella's is just the same as the one she took when she wrote that letter to the Director. She says in that letter something like this—I know a helluva lot an' if I don't tell you about it within the next ten days then you send some guy along an' I will tell him plenty.

She does very nearly the same sorta thing with Berenice. She writes to her an' says come over here I want you urgent an' then—accordin' to Berenice—when she gets there the urgency is all gone an' they just have an ordinary sorta powwow.

Maybe this don't seem very important to you, but it does to me, because I am tryin' to get inside that dame Marella Thorensen's mind, an' until I do I reckon I ain't goin' to get any place.

O.K. I light myself a cigarette, an' I proceed to tell Brendy all about this letter business an' the show-down I had last night with Berenice. Needless to say I do not tell him about the love stuff that went on afterwards, because Brendy would not know that I am a guy who will kiss a woman with one hand an' smack a pair of steel bracelets on her with the other so to speak. He will proceed to think to himself that I have got one big letch on the Berenice dame an' am layin' off her for that reason.

As it is directly he starts talkin' I can see that he has got somethin' like this in his head.

"What is the matter with you, Lemmy?" he says. "Has this dame got you on the floor or what? This is an open an' shut case, an' I will now proceed to give you the works, because it is all so plain that even a blind guy would get it."

"Yeah," I tell him. "Wise guy, heh? All right, spill it, Sherlock."

"Here's the way it goes," he says. "This dame Berenice is gettin' around with Aylmar Thorensen. O.K. Thorensen knows that if her old man Lee Sam finds out what is goin' on an' that his daughter is havin' fun an' games with his attorney, there will be plenty trouble an' probably the old boy will stick him with a blunt knife or give him an old-fashioned Chinese pill that will make his eyelids turn inside out.

"So he tells the dame to lay off an' take a holiday in Shanghai, an' he then fixes that he will move his office outa San Francisco an' get along to Los Angeles, an' he does this so's it will be easier for him an' Berenice to have some little get-together parties when she comes back. Got me?

"Then he tells Marella that he is goin' to transfer over to Los Angeles an' that she will be seein' less of him than ever, an' Marella starts to smell rats like hell. So she jumps around an' she finds out that Aylmar an' Berenice are just two big sweethearts, an' boy, does she get the needle!

"O.K. So what does she do? She has a show-down with Aylmar. She tells him that he is a pain in the ear, an' that as a husband he is nothin' but a big mistake. She says that she has not minded being neglected when she thought it was business that was keepin' him, but now that she finds out that it is Berenice who is the big attraction she is goin' to get busy.

"She probably knows plenty about Aylmar. She probably knows that he an' old man Lee Sam have been up to plenty of funny business around here an' she tells Aylmar that unless he is goin' to behave himself properly she is goin' to wise up the Federals that he an' Lee Sam have been runnin' silk or whatever they have been doin'.

"Well, Aylmar don't believe her. He tells her that she is talkin' hooey, an' that she can go take fifteen cold baths, an' he goes off an' starts makin' arrangements to move.

"Then Marella gets all steamed up. So she thinks of one big idea. She sits down an' she writes that letter to the Director of the Federal Bureau but she don't actually say anything in it. She only sorta suggests that something is goin' on. Why does she do this? Well, it's stickin' out a foot that she plays it this way so that if Aylmar decides to change his mind she can say that she was mistaken when she wrote the letter an' he can still keep his nose clean. She says that if the Bureau don't hear from her durin' the next ten days they are to send an operative along. Well, you got the idea, ain't you? The idea is that she is givin' Aylmar an' Berenice that much time to agree to what she wants an' if they don't she is goin' to blow the works.

"Right. Well, just so's to fix things she types out a letter to Berenice an' sends it over to Shanghai by air mail, an' she tells Berenice that she has gotta be at the Villa Burlingame about four—five o'clock on the tenth day.

"Then she's all set, ain't she? She knows that on that day at the time Berenice an' the Federal agent will arrive at the Villa at about the same time. Marella aims to stall the agent who is arriving in the afternoon by leavin' a phoney note to Nellie the cook which will make this guy come back after nine o'clock.

"When Berenice gets there Marella tells her plenty. She tells her what she has done. She says that a Federal agent will be along any minute an' that if Berenice don't agree to lay off Aylmar, an' that if he don't agree to stick around an' be a proper husband she is goin' to blow the works to the agent which will put both Thorensen and old man Lee Sam well in the dirt.

"She also tells her that she has written a letter to Thorensen tellin' him what she is goin' to do. O.K. Berenice, who is a tough baby, realises that the time has come for action. So she makes up her mind quick. She says O.K. an' that they will go over an' see Aylmar an' straighten everything out.

"She gets Marella in the car an' she bumps her off with that little gun she's got. By this time the fog has come down an' she drives along to the dock an' shoves Marella in. Then she goes back to Thorensen an' tells him what she has done.

"Thorensen gets the breeze up. After a bit he takes a pull at himself an' gets around an' tells Rocca about the bump off. He tells Rocca about the letter that Marella wrote to the Federals an' says that they can all look out for some trouble when it is discovered that Marella is missin'.

"Later some guy sees Marella floatin' about the dock an' wises up the harbour squad. Rocca gets to hear about this and tells Spigla or somebody to fix things by smashin' Marella's face in so that the body can't be identified an' so that they can get the bullet outa Marella's head, because that bullet would have sent Berenice to the chair. Rocca reckons that if he does this he will have a stranglehold on Lee Sam that will make him plenty dough. He will also have Thorensen where he wants him.

"Well, the big act with the ice block comes off. They get inta the morgue an' they get the bullet out. Thorensen hears about this an' thinks that Berenice is now safe, that nobody will tie her up with the murder, so when he goes down to the morgue he don't mind sayin' that the body is Marella's.

"Meanwhiles Berenice has got the letter that Marella wrote to Thorensen. She is all worked up, an' when she drives the car back home instead of burnin' it she leaves it on the seat with her gloves an' bag. The maid finds it an' takes it up to her room an', after O'Halloran has got Lee Sam an' Berenice down at the Precinct for questioning, sees you readin' it.

"So Berenice knows that she has gotta pull a phoney story on you about that letter. She says it's a fake because that's the only thing she can say."

Brendy gets up an' stretches himself.

"Me, I would pinch that dame Berenice like that," he says, snappin' his fingers. "Because she is the baby that done this job."

I give myself another drink.

"Swell," I tell him, "but that still don't tell us what the story was that Marella was goin' to spill. Do you think that Berenice or Thorensen or Rocca or Lee Sam woulda got frightened just because this Marella dame was goin' to blow the works that they had been runnin' silk? Not on your life. There was somethin' else—somethin' much more important, an' that is the thing I am after."

"O.K., Lemmy," he says. "You're the boss, but I gotta tell you one thing an' that is the D.A. ain't too pleased with the way things are goin'. The newspapers are playin' this Marella Thorensen killin' up like hell an' he wants a pinch made. He reckons, like everybody else, that Berenice done it. We gotta get action on that murder."

I nod. Me—I am goin' to do a little playin' for time, I think, because something he has said has put an idea inta my head.

"Look, Brendy," I tell him. "One thing is stickin' out a foot an' that is that we have gotta get this handwritin' identified." I throw the letter across the table an' he picks it up.

"Get somebody in Thorensen's office—some clerk or somebody who knows Marella's handwritin', to say whether that is her writin' or a forgery. That's the first thing to be done, an' the second thing you can do is this. I told O'Halloran that I wanted Joe Mitzler an' that blonde baby Toots pulled in. Well, I don't, see? If they're still stickin' around in San Francisco just give 'em their heads. Let Terry put a tail on 'em an' keep me posted as to what they are doin'—that is if they are still here an' he can find 'em. But I don't want 'em pulled in, see?"

"O.K.," he says. "You're runnin' this business.

He stretches some more.

"You know, Lemmy," he says, "I reckon that this Berenice baby has got all you guys bull-dozed. When she come down to the Precinct the boys tell me that O'Halloran's eyes was poppin' outa his head. He just couldn't take 'em off her ankles, which is a bad thing for a copper, because a copper should never allow himself to think about a dame's legs."

"No," I tell him, "you don't say. An' so you are one of these guys that never thinks about dames' legs. Just thinka that now. Look, Brendy, ain't anybody ever told you that if you was to add up all the time that all the guys in the world spend thinkin' about women's legs, nobody would have any time left. The trouble with you guys is that you don't think enough about dames' legs. Maybe the whole of this case is just based on legs."

"Meanin' what?" he says.

"Meanin' this," I tell him. "Ain't you ever discovered that most bump-offs is because some guy gets comparin' some other jane's legs with the ones that he is legitimately entitled to consider? I reckon that legs is just hell. Don't crime start in night clubs? Sure it does, an' it starts because there are more legs in night clubs than anywhere else. Me—I gotta theory that if you was to cut every woman off short an' issue 'em with a pair of cork legs you could practically do away with all the coppers in the world. Crime would stop dead."

"Yeah," he says, "well, I don't agree because even if every dame had cork legs there would still be some guys would wanta see whether they kept their stockin's up with drawin' pins or glue."

I don't say nothin' because I know that Brendy is a bit sore on the subject of legs, his wife bein' so bow-legged that when she goes swimmin' she looks like a triumphal arch. I relax an' then come back to the main issue.

"O.K., Brendy boy," I tell him. "You just get around an' do a little leg work yourself, willya? Check up on the handwritin' in that letter an' let me know pronto whether Marella really wrote it or whether somebody is tryin' to pull a fast one on the Berenice baby.

"An' another thing," I go on. "You can ask the guy who is goin' to do the identifyin' whether he has ever known Marella to use that Sea Island ink before. It's a funny colour an' we might get a line through it."

He says O.K. an' scrams.

I look at my watch. It is four o'clock an' a swell afternoon. I telephone down to the desk for some coffee, an' I put my feet up on the table an' proceed to do a little quiet thinkin'.

You will realise that this story that Brendy has just issued out is a good one. It sorta goes with all the angles an' it certainly looks as if Berenice would be the baby that pulled this job.

An' if Brendy is right then all that stuff she pulled on me last night about the letter bein' a forgery an' planted so as to give her a motive for killin' Marella, was all bunk, but it was the only thing she could say under the circumstances.

But I know that you are goin' to agree with me that there is somethin' very odd about that story of hers as to how the letter had got inta the house. If she was makin' it all up wouldn't it a been easier for her to say that somebody had sent her the letter through the post or somethin' like that.

The thing that gets me is that her story is what you might call too durned involved to be all lies, an' as I am a guy who likes to look at a thing from all angles I am goin' to take it—just for the sake of talkin'—that Berenice's story about the letter was true.

All right, well why in the name of heck does the guy who wanted to plant the letter leave it with her handbag an' gloves in the car? If the guy can get inta the house so's to put it in the garage why don't he leave it on Berenice's dressin' table or somewhere like that?

Well, there might be a good reason. Hi-Tok the butler told me that the guy who would be the person to go inta the garage last would be Lee Sam. He would go around to lock up, an' therefore he would be the guy who would find the letter.

So if Berenice is tellin' the truth it looks as if the guy who planted the letter meant Lee Sam to find it.

Well, why would they want that? Well, we can answer that one, because Brendy told us the answer.

Supposin' Thorensen had gone to Rocca to get 'em outa the jam like Brendy said. Supposin' Rocca was the guy responsible for smashin' Marella's face in so as to get at that bullet an' hold up identification, an' supposin' by some means or other he had got hold of that letter—never mind whether it was a true one or a forgery—then wouldn't it be a clever thing for him to plant it where old man Lee Sam would find it, an' the old boy would then get the idea inta his head that his daughter was mixed up in the Marella killin'; that she had done it herself.

Once he gets this idea then Rocca has got him where he wants him. An' you gotta remember that Lee Sam has got plenty dough an' would pay plenty so's to keep anybody from sayin' too much about his daughter.

An' there is another angle. The guy who comes along to the Lee Sam house to plant this letter is takin' a chance, ain't he? Supposin' somebody sees him monkeyin' about the garage. This guy musta known plenty about the Lee Sam house to take a chance like that.

But supposin' he didn't haveta take a chance? Supposin' that letter had been planted by some guy who was *in* the Lee Sam house. Why then the whole set-up would sound less like a lotta hooey.

You remember the time when I was givin' the once over to Berenice's room, an' when I come out the three gun boys' in the car tried to bump me. Didn't I have the idea that they, got a tip off from somebody who was in the house? Well who was it knew that I was in the house? Who was it saw me readin' that letter? Wasn't it Berenice's Chinese maid?

O.K. Well supposin' we let our minds wander a bit more an' allow that it was her; that she was the one who telephoned through to somebody an' got 'em to send them thugs up to iron me out.

Maybe the one she would telephone through to would be Toots, Joe Mitzler's blonde baby, who was in the car, an' that means that there is a connection between Toots an' Berenice's Chinese maid.

So now you know the reason why I have told Brendy to lay off pinchin' Toots. I wanta see if that baby is still kickin' around an' if so whether she is goin' to make another contact with the maid. See?

But the big thing right now is whether that letter is a fake or a real one. If it was a real one then we gotta consider this thing from a new set-up. We gotta consider this thing from the angle that Berenice was playin' along with Thorensen an' that she would be the guy who wanted Marella outa the way more than anybody.

An' so far as I am concerned if I find that Marella did write that letter then I reckon that we ain't got to look any further an' that even if Berenice can kiss like a passionate angel she is still the killer.

I light a cigarette an' finish off the coffee. For some reason that I cannot put my finger on I am thinkin' about that Sea Island ink. I reckon that I will take a look around at the Villa Rosalito an' see what ink is used around that dump.

This gets me on to somethin' else. I wonder whether Marella wrote the original letter in this business—the one she sent to the Director—In her own handwritin' or whether she typed it.

You gotta realise that I ain't seen this letter, I only got a typed duplicate in the folder that the Director's office issued out to me when I took the case over.

I get action. I grab off the telephone an' put a priority call through to Washington. I get it in ten minutes an' get right through to the Records Office at the Bureau. I tell 'em that I am doin' very well thank you an' that I want 'em to send me the original letter from Marella Thorensen so that we can do a little bit of checkin' up here, an' the Records guy says O.K. he will send it pronto by air mail an' that I ought to get it to-morrow.

I smoke another cigarette an' order up some more coffee. It looks to me like this goddam case is goin' to be one of the brightest bits of work that has ever come my way, because there don't seem to be any beginnin' or endin' to it an' all I have succeeded in doin' up to the moment is to nearly get myself shot up by three guys who I don't know an' get myself into a swell hot session with Berenice that may have a coupla unforeseen repercussions before I am through.

Dames are funny things. You're tellin' me! There is Berenice who is a swell baby an' who has certainly got something. This dame is as deep as hell. She is the sorta dame who would stick at nothin' to get what she wanted.

I remember her from the night before. So what! Women have necked me before sometimes because they have felt that way an' sometimes because they thought they was goin' to do themselves some good in the process. Well, that's as may be but kissin' is just kissin' an' it really don't affect the situation where I am concerned—well not a lot.

I remember a dame up in Yellow Springs. I went up to pinch this dame for bein' accessory to kidnappin' an' murder an' carryin' over a state line. This dame is a peach to look at. She looks so demure that you woulda thought that her ma hadn't ever told her anything at all about anything that really mattered.

This dame makes a big play for me whilst I am stallin' her around before makin' a pinch so's the Federal boys who are workin' with me can pick up her boy friend who has just gone out to fill the hooch bottle at the local drug store.

After we pinch these two this dame makes a big howl about the fact that when the boys eventually arrived she was in my arms tight an' I was kissin' her, an' eventually I get a letter from the Director askin' me what the hell. To which I replied that I would like to know just what he woulda done under the circumstances because I knew that if I hadda let go of that dame an' let her get at the razor she had got parked inside her shirt front she woulda probably cut me off in the prime of life, an' I reckoned that as I was holdin' her so tight I might as well pass the time away by seein' whether she was wearin' kiss-proof lipstick or the sort that makes suspicious wives go through their husbands' used handkerchiefs with a magnifyin' glass.

These ruminations bring me to all the dames in this case. I sorta wish that I knew a bit more about this Berenice but she is one of these dames that nobody ever gets to know. That's the big attraction about her. She's got mystery.

Then there is Marella.

Well, I don't know much about her either, except that she is nice an' dead. I reckon that she didn't have much of a time with Aylmar Thorensen, because that guy is a bum if ever there was one. He is a fat, frightened guy an' he would get behind a woman or anybody else any time he got windy.

But I reckon that Marella thought she was a deep one. I reckon she thought that she was bein' durn clever when she wrote that letter to the Director, but she wasn't bein' as clever as she thought. If Brendy is right this dame thought she was goin' to be tops of the situation instead of which all she gets is a bullet just to show her where she got off.

I get to thinkin' about Nellie the cook. Maybe Nellie knows somethin'. Anyhow I reckon that I am goin' to have a little talk with that dame. Maybe she knows somethin' about Berenice an' anyhow she will know plenty about Marella an' Thorensen. Right in the middle of these sweet thoughts Brendy comes through.

"Hey, Lemmy," he says. "I got some hot news for you. That letter was written by Marella all right. I got at Thorensen's head clerk. He knows Marella's writin' as well as he knows his own. He says there ain't any shadow of doubt that she wrote that letter. He says he ain't known her to use that ink before, but then she was a dame who used any ink that was around. She was one of them babies who never carried a fountain pen.

"So it looks like little Berenice is the one, hey?"

"An' here's somethin' else. I just been talkin' to the medical examiner down in the D.A.'s Office. This guy is a nosey sorta guy an' he's been givin' himself a treat by doin' a hot post-mortem on what was left of Marella, an' what do you think?

"He's got the bullet. It wasn't in Marella's head at all. That bullet was fired at close range an' hit against a bone an' went right down inta the neck. He's got it all right, an' it's a .22 calibre, an' what do you know about that? A .22 is a woman's gun, ain't it, Lemmy?"

"That's the way it looks, Brendy," I tell him, "but take it easy an' stick around. I want to play things my way for a bit."

"O.K.," he says, "I'll be seein' you, an' I have told O'Halloran to lay off pinchin' Mitzler or Toots if he finds 'em. I told him to put a tail on 'em an' leave it at that."

I hang up. Here's sweet news. So they found the bullet. They musta been cuttin' Marella about plenty. An' it was a .22 bullet, an' the gun I found in Berenice's handbag was a .22 gun.

An' the letter wasn't a phoney. It was the real works. Marella wrote it an' meant it.

It don't look so good for my little playmate Berenice, does it?

CHAPTER EIGHT
NELLIE

BY THE time I have dropped inta the Hall of Justice an' looked up Rocca an' Spigla in the Records Office, got the address of the cottage in Burlingame where Nellie is livin' an' run out there it is six o'clock, an' I am hopin' that maybe to-night I will be able to get myself some sleep instead of rushin' around this piece of America at all hours, gettin' no place at all, an' gettin' more sleepy all the time.

You will have realised that this business of bein' a Federal detective has got its drawbacks. First of all any sorta dick has a lousy time. Detectives ain't so lucky except in books where they always find clues an' things lyin' about the place so's they know just who the guy is that they gotta pull in.

Well, I have never had a case like that yet. It looks to me like every case you have is sorta changin' the whole time, an' directly you come to one conclusion you find you are all wrong an' you can start again from where it all began from.

Anyhow Ma Caution usta say that the greatest thing a guy can have is patience although it is not so hot when I know durn well that the District Attorney is screamin' for me to pinch somebody— he don't mind very much who—probably because he has got the next election in mind an' he wants to keep the news-sheets quiet.

I would not mind pinchin' anybody either—an' my selection would be Berenice—only I have got the idea at the back of my head that pinchin' this dame right now is not goin' to tell me whatever it was that Marella wanted to tell the Federal government about, which is the business that concerns me right now.

Another thing is this: You guys will agree with me that it looks like Berenice has been drawin' some sweet red herrin's all over the place an' that business sorta interests me. If you think the same way as I do it will look to you that it looks like this dame is tryin' hard to prove herself guilty of this Marella killin', an' havin' regard to the fact that this baby is plenty cute I am not goin' to fall for any play like that.

It is an old racket for somebody to do a murder an' then plant a lotta bad clues which, strung together, make lousy evidence that the killer's lawyer can play holy hell with in court, when all the while the real stuff, the real evidence that would get the chair for the murder guy is never produced because the prosecution have missed it through bein' too quick with the case an' choosin' to make a quick pinch on the phoney stuff that was all laid out for 'em to see.

I remember some clever cuss who killed an old range minder in Arizona just so's he could pinch a saddle off him. Well this guy did the old boy in by hittin' him over the dome with a hammer. He then carefully leaves his old hat lyin' in a corner of the shack an' when the Sheriff gets along there an' takes a look round an' sees that hat, he naturally thinks he has got a swell piece of evidence.

So he walked along an' pinches the owner thereof pronto. In the meantime they find some more swell evidence in the corner of the lean-to of the guy they have pinched. Hidden under a lotta stuff they found a hammer with a lotta grey hairs an' some blood on it. So they don't waste any more time, they just send this guy up for trial. They know they have got the murderer.

When the case comes up this guy's lawyer proves that the hat they found, although it belonged to the defendant originally, was one that he had said he was goin' to give to the old boy a week before the killin'. This lawyer also proves that the hairs they found on the hammer was goat's hairs an' the blood was goat's blood. So what?

So the guy gets himself acquitted. But if these fellers had not been in such a helluva hurry an' looked around to get some more evidence they would have found the real hammer he done it with all cleaned up an' buried under the floor, an' he was usin' this hammer, although everybody knows it was the old man's, six months' later. But because they'd tried this guy once an' acquitted him they couldn't try him again, could they?

So it just shows you what a lotta inconvenience can be caused to all an' sundry by law officers tryin' to make a pinch too quick, because in this case for instance a pal of the old range minder's has to go out an' gun for this killer, which took him two weeks an' meant the wastin' of three good shells an' the helluva lotta sweat over somethin that oughta been done by the State.

Nellie is a sweetheart. She is as black as dark brown velvet an' so big that even an Oxford chair is too small for her. She has got a smile like a big slice in a pumpkin an' teeth that shine like the inside of oyster shells.

Sittin' opposite her over a swell little fire an' with a glass of good bootleg liquor in my hand, I open my ears wide an' pray that Nellie is goin' to give me somethin' good.

She has already told me what the copper who came to see her 'phoned through to O'Halloran, that is, that any note that was left for her about Marella not bein' back until after nine o'clock was a lotta hooey because Marella fired her that mornin'.

It looks like Marella had told her that with Thorensen bein' over in Los Angeles there wouldn't even be much weekend cookin' an' that she reckoned she could get through with a daily hired girl that she was goin' to get in.

"I suppose that Mr. an' Mrs. Thorensen got on pretty well together, Nellie?" I ask her.

She grins an' takes a swig of bootleg.

"Nosah," she says. "Them two was rowin' an' quarrellin' fit to bust like a cat an' dog the whole time, yessah. I never done hear her the like o' the way them twoall usta go on at each other. But you gotta understand that it was all that Aylmar Thorensen.

Yessah. A'm tellin' you that dis man was one big bad man an' de way he usta treat dat poor Marella was beyond tellin'."

"You don't say, Nellie," I tell her, "so he was a bad guy, heh? What did he use to do to her? He used to knock her about, hey?"

"Nosah," says Nellie. "I never saw that Mis' Thorensen produce any physical force so to speak, but he wasn' no sorta husban'. Nosah, dat guy only usta come round de Villa at de weekends an' mos' time he wouldn' even talk to poor Mis' Marella at all. He just usta treat her like she was a piece of dirt all de time. He usta sit up in his room writin' an' workin' an' ef he wasn' doin' dat he was drinkin' de whole time like you never saw anybody drink, although Ah never saw dat man drunk. Nosah, Ah never saw Mis' Thorensen drunk. . . ."

"O.K., Nellie," I tell her. "Now you tell me somethin'. Did you usta see Mrs. Thorensen writin' her letters. Did she usta write letters sorta regular. Did she usta write 'em all in the same place—at a desk or somethin', or did she just write 'em around the place any old how?"

"Nosah," says Nellie. "Ah'm tellin' you dat Marella, poor lamb, was jus' about the mos' tidy an' orderly pusson you never saw. Ef she was writin' letters she was writin' em at her desk in de mo'nin'. All de letters she wrote was writ in de mo'nin', an' dat poor lamb would stamp 'em an' seal 'em an' put on de stamp, an' walk along to the post an' post 'em herself. She was de mos' tidy an' orderly pusson. Why ef anythin' was even outa place she would be seein' it befo' you could blink yo' eye."

I grin. "So she was a pretty quick one, hey Nellie?" I say. "I bet she was pretty good at checkin' the grocery list over"

She grins back at me. "Mis' Caution, she sure was," she says. "Ah tell you dat one two times Ah tried to pinch jus' one two little things fo' myself an' Mis' Marella was on it like a bird. Ah reckon you couldn't get away with pinchin' anythin' in dat house. Why ef a pencil was outa place on a writin' table dat lady would be right on to it, an' would wanta know where it was, an' she would raise one big shout till dat pencil was found even ef she had to turn de whole house inside out."

"Swell, Nellie," I tell her. "I reckon it's a treat when you get somebody with a sorta sense of tidiness, ain't it? So she usta write all her letters in the mornin' an' usta post 'em herself. Say listen, Nellie, when you said she usta seal her letters, just what didya mean by that?"

"She usta have a seal," says Nellie. "You know one o' dem things you slap on de back of de envelope. She usta get de wax an' heat de wax an' den she would get out dis seal an' slap it on. Dis seal was on a ring an' it was like two crossed keys an' she usta slap dat on all her letters, yessah, until it done went."

"An' when did it done went?" I ask her.

"'Bout two months ago," she says. "Dat poor Marella lamb usta keep it in de little drawer on de top right hand side of de desk. It was allus dere. One day when I was cleanin' around I notice dat dis seal was gone, an' I tell her, but she don't say nothin'. She jus' says she reckons she mus'a mislaid it, although I never knew Mis' Thorensen lose nothin' befo'."

"Maybe somebody grabbed it off, Nellie?" I tell her.

"Dat's what I say, Mis' Caution, Sah, dat's what I say. I tol' her Mis' Thorensen I sayd youall better be careful I told her. Dere's people hangin' around here all de time. I seen 'em, an' dey'll grab off anything they can get their han's on, I tell her. I tell her that she sh' be careful leavin' anything around an' leavin' the doors open like she does because this is a lonely sorta place an' dere's plenty people hangin' around for no good. I seen 'em with my own eyes, yessah."

I open my ears.

"Tell me about these people who was hangin' around, Nellie. When didya see 'em?"

She leans forward an' starts wavin' her glass at me.

"I seen 'em plenty, Sah," she says. "Mis' Caution, I seen guys two three times hangin' aroun'. Sometimes in de afternoon when I was all set to finish Mis' Thorensen she says you go take a walk befo' you start to cook dinnah she says. You need a walk she says. I usta go off an' sometimes I usta come down here to de cottage for an hour an' sometimes I usta hang around for a walk because the doctor says I oughta walk.

"Two three times I am up on de road behind de house an' I can see around de place an' I see a car hangin' around on de back road behind de house. One time I see some city guy walkin' across de field an' I says to myself I says dat guy can't be up to no good because dat field leads on to de back of de Villa lawn an' dere is Mis' Thorensen with all de doors an' windows off de latch like she usta have 'em in de afternoon. Two three times more I see dis guy hangin' around. Once I seen him down on de road below de Villa an' once I see him right outside. Yessah he wuz right outside de Villa an' lookin' in. I says that I reckon dat dis guy is jus' waitin' for a chance to bust in an' get at de silver. Nex' day Ah says to Mis' Thorensen Ah says Honey what fo' you have de latches off de doors an' de windows like you do? One dese days one of dese no-goods from de city is comin' bustin' around after de silver an' dere'll be plenty trouble. Well dere was plenty trouble fo' dat poor lamb."

Nellie heave one big sigh. "Mis' Caution," she says, "youall hand over yo' glass an' I'll give you jus' a drop more of dis spirit jus' to warm you up, Sah."

"Look Honey," I tell her, "I reckon I'm sorta interested in all this. I'm sorta interested in these guys you saw hangin' around. Say, Nellie, did you ever see Mr. Thorensen talkin' to any of these guys?"

"I sho' did," says Nellie. "I sho' swear dat one day I wuz comin' up de road from dis cottage an' aroun' by de back of de Villa when I see Mis' Aylmar talkin' to some city man, an' I thought to myself I thought that city man looks mighty like de man I see walkin' across de field towards de lawn at de back of de Villa dat afternoon befo' an' I . . ."

"Hold everything, Nellie," I tell her. "Take a look at these an' you tell me if either of 'em is like any of the guys you saw stickin' around here."

I grab the two pictures of Rocco an' Spigla that I got from the San Francisco records. I hand over the print of Rocca. She looks at it.

"I ain't seen dis man," she says. "I don't know nothin' about him. He's too big for de man I see."

I hand over Spigla's picture. She gives a squeak.

"Dis is de man," she says. "Dis is de man Ah'll take my dyin' oath dat I saw walkin' across de fields de afternoon Ah'm tellin' you about. Dis is de man dat I saw Mis' Aylmar talkin' to on de other day when I was comin' up de road."

I think that now we are gettin' some place.

"Are you sure, Nellie?" I say. "You gotta realise that this is pretty important. You're dead certain?"

"Lissen, Mis' Caution," she says. "I don' mak' no mistakes, nosah. Ah'm tellin' you dat I don' ever forget nobody's face no time. Ef I see a man I sorta remember dat man. Jus' like when you walked in here dis evenin' I remembered you right away. I said to myself dat is de man I saw de day befo' yesterday in de afternoon when dat poor lamb Marella was lookin' outa de window."

I jump up. My hair is beginnin' to tingle. What the hell! I sit down again.

"Now listen, Nellie," I tell her. "Let's get this straight. You're tellin' me that you saw me in the afternoon of the day before yesterday. That would be when I pulled up in a car outside the Villa Rosalito an' went up the pathway an', rang the bell. You say you saw me then, an' you say that Marella was lookin' outa the window while I was doin' it?"

I lean over an' pick up Nellie's glass, an' I give her another shot of bootleg. I am prayin' that this coon is goin' to talk an' say plenty.

"Looky, Nellie," I tell her. "You take a quiet drink an' get sorta composed. Then you tell me nice an' easy everything that happened to you the day before yesterday; everything that happened on the day you saw me go up an' ring the bell at the Villa. Understand? I want you to tell me everything that happened—every little thing."

She puts down her glass.

"Yessah," she says. "Ah'll sho' tell youall de whole lot. De day befo' yesterday Ah get up in de mo'nin' from my bed in de Villa an' I take in dat poor lamb Marella's coffee an' she gives me one shock. She says dat I can lay off an' dat dere ain't no need fo' me to stick around cookin' any mo' because she ain't goin' to need me any mo'.

"She says dat Mis' Thorensen is goin' over to Los Angeles an' dat he won' even be at de Villa fo' de week-ends no mo'. She says dat she's goin' to git some daily hired girl in de Villa an' dat she aims she's goin' to do some cookin' herself.

"Me Ah dunno what to say because Ah am all fulla grief through havin' been aroun' at de Villa so long an' havin' to leave de poor lamb lak dat.

"Ah don' think Ah've ever been so surprised in ma life. Nosah. But Ah don' say nothin' much because ef she don' wan' me any mo' there jus' ain't nothin' to be sayd.

"Ah clean up de kitchen an' at eleven o'clock mebbe she pays me off an' I git my bag an' I say good-day Mis' Thorensen an' she says good-day Nellie an' I walk outa de place an' I come down here to de cottage.

"Ah stick aroun' here makin' crullers all de mo'nin', an' in de afternoon about three o'clock I think Ah'll walk along to de Villa an' if she is dere Ah'm goin' to ask her jus' what fo' she laid me off lak dat. Ah think that even ef she ain't dere mebbe de walk is goin' to be good fo' me lak de doctor sayd.

"I git down there by de Villa an' jus' when I am goin' to cross over de boulevard dere I hear a car comin' up de road, an' I look across over at de secon' floor front window of de Villa an' I see Mis' Marella lookin' out de window at de car dat is comin' up de road. Den she goes away. Ah see de car stop at de door an' Ah see youall git out an' walk up to de fron' door an' I think that if Mis' Marella is havin' folks in for visitin' Ah'd better come aroun' some other time.

"Ah start walkin' up de boulevard an' when Ah git opposite de end of de Villa Ah can look right along de path by de side of de Villa an' Ah see Mis' Marella runnin' across de lawn an' goin' into de Chinese summer house on de far corner of de lawn. She goes in an' she shuts de door.

"While Mis' Marella is doin' dis Ah can see youall standin' at de front door ringin' on de bell, an' Ah grin to myself because Ah can see dat Mis' Marella is playin' one big game on you because she has seen you' car comin' an' she reckons to keep you waitin' whiles she is hidin' away in de summer house.

"So Ah jus' git on an' when Ah look back Ah can see you goin' roun' de side of de Villa so Ah know dat you are wise to de game she is playin'.

"Ah walk back here to de cottage an' Ah make myself coffee an' Ah eat crullers till Ah done near bust."

"O.K., Nellie," I tell her. "Hold everything for a minute, baby."

I do some quick thinkin'. I get this set-up. So Marella was in the Villa when I got there. She was lookin' out for my car. She saw it, scrammed away from the window quick an' knocked the things off the dressin' table because she was het up. She dropped the scarf on the floor the same way, because she was in one helluva hurry.

An' she was in a hurry because she had to get down to the kitchen an' write that fake note to Nellie sayin' that she would not be back until nine o'clock, the note that I was supposed to find an' that would keep me outa the way while she had her interview with Berenice Lee Sam.

Then she rushes up from the kitchen an' she hears me playin' tunes on the front door bell. She scrams out through the back livin' room an' she can't get the French window open. So she gives it one helluva push an' busts the handle off it—the way it was when I went round there. Then she eases over to the Chinese pagoda place on the far corner of the lawn an' she hides there an' watches me get in through the French window. She waits there until she sees me come outa the house an' drive off in the car, an' she knows that her scheme has worked; that I won't be back until nine o'clock anyhow.

After which she goes back to the house an' sticks around an' when Berenice Lee Sam rings the bell she opens the door to her.

Then she asks Berenice to come up to the bedroom for this talk they are goin' to have, and as she goes up after Berenice *she* slips the telephone receiver off.

You remember Berenice said that Marella took it off so's they shouldn't be disturbed. Well, I didn't believe her, but I do now. *Marella flipped that receiver off just so's I shouldn't ring on the telephone to check up on if she was comin' back at nine o'clock an' find out that she was there.*

So now I am beginnin' to see why Marella wrote that letter to the Director in such a funny sorta way. She wanted the fact that a "G" man was comin' down to see her to be some sorta threat that she could hold over the head of Berenice Lee Sam, but she ain't quite certain as to what time the "G" man is goin' to arrive. When she gets the telegram she finds out. Then she is in a jam because she knows that Berenice Lee Sam is showin' up some time between four an' five an' she don't want these two guys to synchronise.

She looks outa the window an' she watches for my car, an' when she sees me comin' she leaves that phoney note down in the kitchen, scrams out to the summer house, an' when I am outa the way, an' Berenice has arrived, she is able to tell Berenice that she is expectin' a "G" man to arrive at the house at any moment, *an' produces the telegram from the Director—the one I found lyin' in the hall—to prove that what she says is right.*

All of which will go to show you that Marella is no mug, at least she wasn't over that business. She was only a mug afterwards when she got herself killed.

While I've been indulgin' in these thoughts Nellie has filled my glass up again.

"Nellie," I tell her, "you been swell. I reckon you've been a great help to me, an' there's just one little thing that I wanta ask you, an' then I reckon I'm finished, an' it's this: Do you remember what sorta ink Mrs. Thorensen used to use? Did she always get her ink from one place? Did she use a fountain pen, or did she use different coloured inks?"

Nellie shakes her head.

"Nosah," she says. "Mis' Marella she done always use the same ink. We got de ink down at de stationery shop in Burlingame village, sorta black ink. Ah never knew her to use any other ink, an' she ain't got no fountain pen. Ah know dat because Ah remember Mis' Thorensen usta tell her dat she oughta use a fountain pen, only she wouldn' do it."

I nod. Out of my pocket I bring a little bottle of Sea Island ink, an' show it to her.

"Take a look at this, Nellie," I tell her. "The ink inside that bottle is the same colour as the label—a sorta misty light blue. Did you ever see any ink like that around the Villa? Did you ever know Mrs. Thorensen to use ink like that?"

"Nosah," says Nellie, "Ah never did."

I look at my watch an' I see it is a quarter after seven. I am not feeling so good because I can see that here is another night when I am not goin' to get any sleep. I have got an idea in my head that I have got this case in the bag. Anyhow I hope I have, although I ain't bettin' on anything. I get up.

"Nellie," I tell her, "you been a sweetheart. You been swell. I don't know what I shoulda done without you."

I give her a fifty dollar bill an' it is a treat to see this coon's eyes shine.

"Ah been glad to have been of service, Mis' Caution," she says, "very glad."

I say so long an' I scram. I drive along the road until I find an automobile club call box. I get outa the car an' I put a call through to Brendy at headquarters.

"Look, Brendy," I tell him. "I want an airplane. I wanta go to Los Angeles. I reckon I'll be back in San Francisco at eight o'clock, so I'd like to leave at about nine. Can you fix that for me?"

"Sure I can fix it," he says. "I'll get you the plane from the D.A.'s office. Airplanes, heh?" he goes on, "sounds like you've got somethin' this time, Lemmy."

"Have I got somethin', bozo?" I tell him. "I'm tellin' you I have got somethin', an' this time I don't think it's goin' to be a pain in the neck neither. I'll be seein' you."

I am back in my room at the Sir Francis Drake. It is a quarter to eight. I drop in at the Hall of Justice on my way out here to give 'em back the pictures of Rocca an' Spigla. I see Brendy down there an' he tells me that there is a plane ready for me between half-past eight and nine. I reckon that with a bit of luck I oughta be in Los Angeles somewhere round midnight.

I order up a bottle of bourbon an' give myself a drink. When the bell hop brings in the liquor he brings up a letter from the office. He puts it down on the table. The envelope has been written on a typewriter and it is addressed to Federal Agent Caution at the Sir Francis Drake Hotel, San Francisco, by air mail. I look at the postmark an' I see that this letter has been posted in San Diego. I am just tearin' this letter open when O'Halloran comes in.

"Hey, Lemmy," he says, "Brendy tells me that you're goin' places. Me—I reckon I could do with a trip to Los Angeles too. I'm plenty sick of stickin' around here tryin' to find out where Joe Mitzler an' that blonde baby Toots of his are."

"Ain't you found 'em yet, Terry?" I ask him.

"Not a smell," he says. "Maybe they're in this city an' maybe they ain't. But if they are there are plenty of sweet hide-outs around here, you know. Say, Lemmy," he says, "you got a line on who done this murder, hey? You got some real evidence?"

"I got plenty," I tell him, "although it ain't exactly evidence at the moment, but I reckon it will be. It looks to me like the dame who killed Marella Thorensen was Berenice Lee Sam, an' I want just one or two more little points an' we'll pinch that dame, an' I reckon that when we pinch her she'll talk plenty, an' maybe we'll find out the thing that I wanta find out, an' that is what Marella wanted to talk to me about. But you gotta keep after Mitzler an' Toots, Terry. I wanta find those two."

While I've been talkin' I have got the envelope open, an' I have pulled out the piece of paper that is inside. I look at it. It is a small "throw-out" bill. It is cheap printin' on rotten paper and it looks like the sorta things that runners for flop houses hand out to sailors when they get off their ships at the docks. This is just what it is.

It is an advertisement for Oklahoma Joe's Rooming House on Strawberry Street which is down near the Embarcadero and which place is not exactly a health resort, and it gives the prices an' a lotta other stuff. But the interestin' thing is what is written along the side of this form. There is some very nice clear pencil writin'—a sorta educated hand—an' it says:

So what, fly cop? If you want to find Joe Mitzler why don't you take a peek round this dump. But mind you keep your nose clean because I don't think Joe likes you, an' he's carrying a rod.

Now what do you know about that. Ain't life amusin'? I fold up this bill an' the envelope an' I put 'em in my pocket. I do not say a word to Terry. Some things is too good to share.

CHAPTER NINE
THORENSEN COMES ACROSS

I HAVE had some bum airplane trips in my time but the lousiest ever was the one to Los Angeles. The pilot is a good guy but he is havin' a bitta trouble with his wife an' it seems to sorta get him down. Every time I close my eyes an' try to snatch a coupla winks of sleep this palooka starts talkin' about this dame he has married an' just what he would like to do to her if he could get away with it.

He also says he has got chronic indigestion, an' when I tell him that I do not think that any guy can have two more lousy things than a bum wife an' chronic indigestion he says oh yes they can an' that he has also got an ingrowin' toe-nail, so you will realise that this trip coulda been a bit more cheerful.

We made Los Angeles airport at midnight an' at twelve fifteen I am on my way up in the lift at Thorensen's hotel to talk to this baby. I have pretty well made up my mind that when I get back to San Francisco I am goin' to pull Berenice in on the murder rap, but I reckon that convictin' this dame is goin' to rest on what Thorensen has got to say.

Work it out for yourself. If Thorensen an' Berenice are in love with each other, it is a cinch that after Berenice had that interview with Marella she was goin' along to tell Thorensen about it. When she told me that she was with Marella from five to seven o'clock I thought that was a long time for two women to have a row in. Even a woman can get a row over in less than two hours.

I have got an idea in the back of my head that when Berenice said she was drivin' around seein' friends she was really havin' a big discussion with Thorensen about what had happened out at the Villa.

I am takin' a chance on Thorensen bein' frightened to get a statement outa him. You will have realised by now that Thorensen is not a very brave bozo, which I believe is one of the reasons why he got outa San Francisco in a hurry. I don't think this guy would like to be associated with a murder rap, an' I think that when he sees I know what I do know he is goin' to talk plenty.

When I go up I find him standin' in front of an electric fire in a dressin' gown. He still looks worried but not so worried as he was the last time I saw him. He has also got a sorta bleached look as if he has been hittin' the hooch for plenty. I reckon this guy is too fond of liquor.

"Howya goin', Thorensen?" I ask him. "Sorry to have to disturb you so late, but there's one or two things I wanta talk to you about."

"Sure," he says, "that's all right. You have got to do your job. Will you have a drink?"

"No thanks," I tell him, "not right now."

I throw my coat an' hat on a chair an' look at him.

"Look, Thorensen," I tell him, "you sit down in that big chair over there an' relax. I wanta talk to you pretty straight. I want you to do some very quiet thinkin'. You are a lawyer an' I shouldn't think you needed assistance in comin' to a conclusion about legal angles. But if you think you'd like to ring up an' get some other lawyer around here to represent you, you do it. I don't wanta take any advantage of you."

I see his eyes widen a bit, an' his face flushes. I am gettin' this guy frightened which is exactly what I wanta do. He pulls a cigarette case outa the pocket of his dressin' gown an' lights himself a cigarette. His fingers are tremblin'.

"If you want a cigarette, there's a box near you," he says.

"O.K.," I tell him.

He goes over an' sits down in the chair like I told him.

"Look, Thorensen," I say, "maybe you don't know just what happened the day before yesterday. Well, I'm goin' to tell you. I told you about the fact that your wife wrote a letter to the Director of the Federal Bureau suggestin' there was some screwy business goin' on, an' sayin' that if she didn't make a further contact with him by the 10th he was to send an operative down there.

"O.K. You know that I was the operative. You know that when I got to the house an' rang the bell there wasn't any reply. I went in the house the back way an' downstairs in the kitchen I found a note, hand-printed, addressed to Nellie the cook, sayin' not to worry about dinner an' that Marella would be back after nine o'clock. This note gave me the idea that Marella had gone off some place an' it wasn't any use my stickin' around, but while I was in the house I saw the telephone in the hall an' I noticed that the receiver was *on* it's hook.

"O.K. I scram, intendin' to go back after nine o'clock an' see Marella. Well I was a mug. Marella was in the house the whole time. She'd seen my car comin' up the road. She was lookin' through the bedroom window. She saw me get out. Then she scrammed downstairs an' wrote that note an' went out an' hid in the Chinese pagoda place on the far side of the back lawn.

"Well, I reckon that I know why she did this. She did it because she was expectin' Berenice Lee Sam, an' she didn't want me around while Berenice was there. When she sees me go she feels pretty good. I'll tell you why. She knows she is goin' to have a show-down with Berenice an' if Berenice cuts up rough or gets funny all Marella has gotta do is to tell her that she has already been in touch with the Federal authorities an' that if she has any nonsense she will make plenty trouble for all concerned. Not only can she say this but she can also support it by producing the telegram from the Director sayin' that an operative will be arrivin' between four an' five o'clock.

"So it rather looks by this as if Marella is a little bit frightened of what Berenice might do. She was feelin' a bit scared then, see, but she reckoned she'd got herself protected all right.

"Then Berenice arrives. Marella takes her up to the bedroom, an' on the way up she flips the receiver off the telephone, an' she does this just in case I'm goin' to ring through. In other words she don't want Berenice to find out that I have already been an' left. She wants Berenice to think that I am goin' to arrive at any moment.

"Now, what is the show-down between these two women? Well you know that as well as I do. The show-down is this: Marella has discovered that you an' Berenice Lee Sam are sweeties, that you've been playin' along together for months."

He sits up an' flushes.

"That's a damn' lie," he says, "just an ordinary damn lie. You're making that up, Caution."

"Like hell I am, Thorensen," I tell him, "I'm makin' it up so much that I've gotta letter written by Marella to you, with the handwritin' identified by your chief clerk in San Francisco, accusin' you of bein' Berenice Lee Sam's lover, an' tellin' you that she was goin' to make plenty trouble an' she didn't mean divorce neither. Well, if she don't mean divorce what does she mean? It means she's got somethin' on you two guys, an' she's goin' to blow it, don't it?

"An' that's just why she wanted to see Berenice Lee Sam. O.K. Well, these two women get talkin' an' I reckon this interview gets a bit stormy. Berenice loses her temper an' her head. She forgets about the fact that a 'G' man is supposed to be arrivin' at the place some time. She pulls that little .22 gun she's got an' she gives it to Marella.

"Now maybe she got Marella out inta the car on some excuse or other before she shot her, an' was able to drive off an' down to the docks an' push Marella in herself. Or maybe she left Marella there an' somebody else come along later an' moved the body. I don't know about that an' I'm not particularly interested in it anyway.

"But there is one thing I am durn certain of, Thorensen, an' that is before she went home—an' we know what time she got home because old Lee Sam, who had been worryin' about her, rang through to the Precinct to say that she was all right —she went to see you. She went to see you to tell you what had happened, to ask your advice, to wise you up about things. That would be the only logical sorta thing for her to do an' that is what she did.

"O.K. big boy, well you're goin' to talk an' you're goin' to talk plenty. I'm durn tired of stickin' around on this goddam case talkin' to one an' all an' just gettin' nowhere. The D.A. in San Francisco wants a pinch an' I'm goin' to give him one—an' pronto.

"If you like to come across an' talk maybe you can still keep your nose clean on this job, but if you don't I'm goin' to stick a pair of bracelets on you, Sweetheart, an' I'm goin' to take you back to-night to San Francisco on an accessory to murder rap, an' I shall also probably give you one big smack on the kisser as well just a show there's no ill-feelin', an' how do you like that?"

He sits there lookin' like somebody had just pulled him outa a snow drift. He is tremblin' so much that he would make a shimmy dancer look like she was standin' still. I reckon I have got this guy where I want him.

"Listen, Thorensen," I tell him. "There ain't any real reason for you to be scared unless you start tryin' to hold out on me, in which case I will see you get plenty.

"Now the police have checked on your alibi for the day before yesterday, an' they are satisfied that you was around in San Francisco all day; that you didn't go out to Burlingame. O.K. Then if we can prove that Marella was killed out in Burlingame that lets you out, don't it?

"You admit that Berenice came an' saw you. Now here's where you gotta think hard. You gotta tell me everything that happened at that interview an' I don't want anything missed out, neither. Bein' a lawyer you will know that it is the little things that count. So get busy, you big jelly."

He gets up an' walks over to the drinks table an' pours himself out a stiff one. I see that his fingers are tremblin' more than ever. I reckon that this guy is well on the way to bein' a really bad case of too much hooch.

"I'll tell you what I know," he says. "There isn't any reason why I should hide anything." He sits down again. "First of all," he said, "it's a lot of bunk for anybody to suggest that there was anything goin' on between Berenice Lee Sam and me. The idea is just rubbish. First of all if you take a look at me you'll see that I'm not the sort of person that Berenice would fall for. That girl's got everything. She's got looks, figure, personality and her old man's worth a million if he's worth a cent, so what the hell has she got to fall for me for. Anybody who knows that girl will tell you that she's as cold as ice. She's never looked twice at any man in her life, she just hasn't any use for men."

I nod. But I am doin' a quiet grin to myself. I was just thinkin' about Berenice bein' as cold as ice!

He goes on talkin'.

"I didn't even know that she'd come back from Shanghai. I'd heard that she was taking a holiday there from old Lee Sam. The thing I was concentrating on was to get out of San Francisco as soon as I could . . ."

"Justa minute, Thorensen," I tell him. "What was the hurry about your gettin' out of San Francisco?"

He lights himself a cigarette an' looks at the end of it.

"I wanted to get away from Marella," he said. "She was getting me down. I don't think I can exactly explain what I mean but during the last six months she seemed to change. She got hard. Sometimes I saw her looking at me as if she would have liked to kill me.

"I disliked the atmosphere out at the Villa. Although I used to go there only at week-ends there was something about the place I didn't like. I couldn't explain what I felt—even to myself—but there was something odd.

"I was pretty relieved when I discovered that Marella wasn't going to raise any stringent objections to my shifting over to Los Angeles. She didn't seem to mind very much. She wasn't even particularly interested in the financial arrangements I made for her. The last two or three times that I saw her she seemed quite content with the idea of life by herself.

"At seven o'clock or thereabouts on the day of her death I was in my office sorting out some papers, when Berenice Lee Sam was announced. I was very surprised because she had never been in my office before. I thought for the moment that she had probably brought some message from her father.

"When she was shown into my room she sat down and seemed quite composed. I'm not saying that meant anything because, as you've probably guessed, it would take quite a lot to upset Berenice. She has an amazing coolness of mind and a poise that is seldom experienced in young women.

"She told me a most extraordinary story. She told me that some days before she had received a letter from Marella. The letter was couched in the most urgent language. It said that Marella was in serious trouble, that it was urgently necessary that Berenice returned to San Francisco so as to arrive on the 10th January. It went on to say that it was absolutely necessary, both for the sake of the writer and Berenice herself, that Berenice should be out at the Villa Rosalito about five o'clock on the 10th.

"Berenice went on to say that she had arrived on the China Clipper at four o'clock. She telephoned her father from the airport saying that she was back in San Francisco and that she was going out immediately to see Marella at the Villa Rosalito.

"She took a cab from the airport to Gettlin's Garage at the Burlingame end of Kearney, where she hired a car and drove out to Burlingame. When she arrived at the Villa she rang the doorbell several times over a period of five or six minutes but no one came to answer the door. She was beginning to wonder whether there was anyone at all in the place when the door was opened by Marella.

"Marella, according to Berenice, was not only surprised to see her but positively amazed. She asked Berenice to come in; said that she understood that she was in Shanghai, that she had no idea that she was returning to San Francisco yet awhile.

"Berenice was, naturally, astounded. She told me that she stood there in the hallway looking at Marella in absolute astonishment. Marella was smiling but seemed vaguely perturbed about something, and, as they stood there Marella picked up a telegram that was lying on the hall table and read it through carefully. Then she threw it back on the table and it slipped and fell between the table and the wall. Marella half bent down as if to pick it up and then seemed to change her mind and left it there.

"Berenice stood waiting for Marella to say something. Eventually in a quite casual sort of voice, Marella asked Berenice what she had come out to the Villa for.

"Berenice told her. She said that she had come in response to the letter she had received from Marella, the letter which had said that her presence at this time at the Villa was a necessity. She told me that while she was talking she saw an expression of astonishment cross Marella's face.

"When she had finished Marella laughed and said that they had better go upstairs and talk it over. As she walked past the small telephone table farther down the hall with Berenice following behind Marella took the telephone receiver off the hook, explaining as she did this that she did not want to be disturbed whilst they were talking.

"Berenice told me that they went upstairs into Marella's bedroom—the front room upstairs. She says that the dressing-table was disarranged and that there was a silk scarf lying on the floor. Marella took no notice of this, in fact, she actually walked over it without attempting to pick it up and Berenice thought that this was rather strange.

"She went on to say that by this time she was aware of something very odd about Marella; something she could not quite explain. Marella asked her to sit down and then began to question her about the letter she had received in Shanghai. Berenice asked her point blank why having written the letter and asked her to come to the Villa it was necessary for Marella to inquire what she wanted.

"Marella laughed and said that she had just been having a joke and that it had been sweet to watch the surprise on Berenice's face. Then, Berenice said, the expression on Marella's face changed. She became quite serious. She leaned forward in her chair and said:

"'I want you to understand, Berenice, that if there is any trouble; if you try to make any trouble for Aylmar or myself—if anyone tries to make any trouble—then it will be just as serious for your father as it will be for us. Remember that. If there is any trouble the first person to be involved will be Lee Sam and you wouldn't like that, would you, Berenice?'

"Berenice told me that by this time she was beginning to wonder as to whether Marella had suddenly gone mad. She asked Marella exactly what she meant.

"Marella got up and said that there was no use discussing the situation, that if Berenice knew the truth of the situation well then explanations were unnecessary, and that if she didn't they were not needed. She then repeated the warning about old Lee Sam in the same serious voice, after which she said that she had a great deal to do about the house as she was without a maid, and that as it looked as if there was going to be a fog didn't Berenice think it would be wise to get back to San Francisco before it came down.

"By this time Berenice had come to the conclusion that it was quite useless to continue the discussion. So she said good-bye, left the house, got into her car, drove in to San Francisco and came straight to my office. She asked me if I could give her some explanation of Marella's extraordinary behaviour.

"I told her that I certainly could not. I said that I would telephone Marella immediately and ask what the devil all this nonsense was about. I told my secretary to put a call through to the Villa at once. We waited, and after ten minutes the girl said that she had called the Villa half a dozen times but that there was no reply. Berenice then pointed out that the telephone receiver was probably still off the hook at the Villa, and that was the reason that Marella was not answering.

"All the time that this was going on I felt that Berenice was eyeing me with a certain suspicion. I should point out to you that far from being fond of me Berenice has always treated me with a certain cool disdain. I rather felt that she regarded me as an inferior being, and I know that on one or two occasions she had tried to persuade her father to give his legal business into other hands.

"Now she asked me point blank whether I and her father or either of us had been doing anything that might entitle Marella to speak in the way she had. She asked me how Lee Sam could be involved in any sort of trouble by anyone. She said that she advised me to speak the truth otherwise she would go immediately to her father and insist that he investigated all this mysterious business.

"I thought the matter over for a few minutes and then made up my mind what I would tell her. I said that I did not know how Marella had become possessed of the information but that there was one thing which might cause a little trouble if it came to light."

He stops talkin' an' gulps down his drink. He looks over at the table as if he thinks he will have another one. Then he changes his mind an' goes on:

"Look, Caution," he says. "I'm going to blow the works. I'm going to tell you the truth an' maybe if it helps you any you'll make it as easy for me as you can. Here's the story:

"A couple of years ago Rudy Spigla who, as you know, is Rocca's head manager for the trucking business which handles the Lee

Sam silks came to me and told me that there was some easy money to be made by running contraband silk through the Customs. He said that by using the Rocca trucks for the contraband we could make a considerable sum of money and that there was no possible chance of a slip-up.

"I asked him why it was necessary for me to come into the business and why he hadn't done it on his own. He replied that he wanted me in so that if the silk running were ever discovered I should be able to fix things so far as Lee Sam and Rocca were concerned. Spigla was especially concerned over Rocca because he was the one who would raise hell at being double-crossed because he was being very careful to play straight in San Francisco. If I were in on the job Spigla said it would be easy in case of a show-down for me to discover that someone else was responsible for the silk-running, and as old Lee Sam would be the one to be fined, the amount of danger was practically nil.

"The scheme seemed a watertight one. There certainly was no danger in it for me because I knew that if the matter came to light and Rocca discovered that Spigla had been doing it behind his back he would square accounts very quickly with a blackjack or a bullet, but that would be a matter between Rocca and Spigla—I should be all right in any event.

"I was pressed for money at the time and I agreed to go in the job with Spigla. We've done damn well out of it too.

"Thinking this over I came to the conclusion that it would be the best thing for me to tell Berenice that old Lee Sam and I had been running silk. I knew that even if the old man denied this Berenice probably wouldn't believe him. I also knew that she would keep the business to herself and cover up in order to keep her old father's name out of it.

"So I told her just that. I said that Lee Sam and I had been running silk through the Customs and that the only possible thing I could think of was that Marella had got wind of it in some way or another."

"That was a pretty swell thing to do, wasn't it?" I ask him. "You're a pretty lousy sorta heel, ain't you, Thorensen? But you're clever enough. You know that by sayin' that the old man was in on the job Berenice would keep her mouth well shut. O.K., go on."

"Berenice seemed very surprised," he says. "She said she couldn't understand why her father should be concerned in petty contraband running when he was worth so much money.

"This was a point," Thorensen went on, "that I got over very easily by saying that she knew as well as I did how every China-man loved a gamble and that it was probably that angle and not the money that had made the old man like the idea.

"I got this over. She believed it."

He gets up an' goes over an' gives himself another drink.

"By now it was about twenty minutes to eight," he said. "Beren-ice got up and said good-bye in a cold way and walked out of the office.

"I thought I'd handled the situation pretty well. I thought it more than probable that as I was leaving San Francisco, and as she thought her old father was in on the job she would probably say nothing about the silk running. Anyhow I decided that I had nothing to worry about."

"Well, you was wrong, wasn't you?" I tell him. "Maybe Beren-ice is more of a fly baby than you think. Maybe you'd be surprised to know that she didn't even believe your story."

He looks surprised. "I don't get you," he says. I grin. "Look, mug," I tell him. "Maybe you'd be sorta surprised to hear that when Berenice an' her old man went down to the Precinct for a little questionin' Berenice got her old pa to make a statement about havin' been runnin' silk."

His eyes open.

"I don't get that," he said. "Why old Lee Sam had nothing to do with it. He knew nothing about it!"

"Right," I tell him. "An' that bein' so why does Berenice get him to confess to a business that he had nothin' to do with an' that he didn't know anything about. Well, here's the answer to that one. Berenice didn't believe your story. She believed that you were coverin' up for somethin' worse; but she knows that you'll stick to that story if there is a showdown, an' so she gets her old man to admit that he's been in on the business simply so that there shan't be a further investigation that might bring somethin' worse to light. Got me?"

He looked a bit scared.

"I get you," he says. "But that's the truth. All Spigla an' I were doing was running silk. There wasn't anything else to it."

"Yeah," I tell him. "That's what you think."

I light myself a cigarette an' get up.

"So that's your story, Thorensen, hey?" I tell him. "Well, strange as it sounds I think you're speakin' the truth, an' maybe you've put me on to something.

"O.K. Well after Berenice Lee Sam goes, after she leaves your office, what happens then?"

"You know the rest," he says. "I stayed at my office until I went to my apartment on Nob Hill. The first I heard about Marella was when Brendy sent for me to identify her."

"O.K., Thorensen," I tell him, "an' there wasn't ever anything between you an' Berenice?"

"Nothing," he says. "Not a thing." He looks scared sick.

"I wish I knew what it was that was so funny about Marella," he says. "When I think about it it worries me. Why did she behave so strangely? What was wrong with her? Why did she send that letter to Berenice in Shanghai, and why did she behave the way she did when Berenice went out there?"

I grin. "Look, Thorensen," I tell him. "I ain't goin' to take you back to San Francisco. I'm leavin' you here. But don't try to leave this town, willya? Be on tap, see? I might need you. I'm goin' to advise the cops here to keep an eye on you meanwhiles."

I pick up my hat an' coat.

"All them things that you was wonderin' about Marella," I tell him, "that funny sorta atmosphere out at the Villa, the way she was behavin', the way she fired Nellie, an' the way she behaved when Berenice went out there. Ain't it struck you that there is a swell answer to all that, or are you so soaked up in liquor that your brain ain't workin' properly?"

He looks at me. "You've got brains, Caution," he says. "I'll say you have. Do you know the answer?"

I nod my head. "Sure I do," I tell him. "The answer is that Marella is a dope."

It is four o'clock in the mornin' when we pull back into the airport at San Francisco. Me an' the pilot are both feeling that a little piece of bed is what the doctor ordered. This guy is feelin' so cold that even the idea of meetin' up with his wife again don't seem quite so bad. As for me I am so durn sleepy that I wouldn't even care if somebody tried to murder me. I'd probably let 'em.

I suck down a cup of coffee with the pilot an' then I take the car back to the Sir Francis Drake. I go up to my room.

On the table is a letter. It is from Brendy. He returns me the letter from Marella to Aylmar Thorensen which I gave him to check up on, an' he also encloses me a communication from the Record Office at Washington which has been sent to me at the Hall of Justice.

I bust this open. It is the letter I asked 'em to send me. The original letter written to the Director by Marella Thorensen, dated the 1st January.

I look at it an' I wonder if I am goin' nuts.

I see that this letter was never written by Marella at all. The handwritin' is different, an' I have seen that handwritin' somewhere else!

I throw the packet down on the table, an' I pull open my coat an' pull out the letter I got before I went over to Los Angeles, the one with the Oklahoma Joe throw-out inside.

I look at the pencil handwritin' on the side—the message that tells me to go down there if I wanta find Joe Mitzler.

The handwritin' is the same. Whoever wrote that pencil letter wrote the original letter to the Director an' signed Marella's name to it.

Now I'm gettin' hot. Now I know why Marella was surprised when Berenice arrived out at the Villa.

She was surprised because she never wrote that letter to Berenice in Shanghai. The dame who wrote the pencil note on the Oklahoma Joe throw-out was the dame who wrote the letter to the Director in the first place, an' she wrote the letter to Berenice in Shanghai an' signed Marella's name to it.

An' can I make a guess as to who that dame is or can I?

I put the letters in a drawer an' I go to bed, just as the dawn is breakin'.

Maybe I can see daylight in more senses than one.

CHAPTER TEN
GETTIN' WARM

WHEN I wake up it is three o'clock in the afternoon. On my way to take a shower I ring down to the desk an' I tell the girl to call up Captain Brendy at Police Headquarters an' ask him an' Lieut. O'Halloran to come round an' see me at four o'clock.

I have a swell shower, a swell breakfast an' just one little shot of bourbon. I also send out for a new tie, because I always buy myself a new tie when somethin' is goin' to break, an' I think that the break is due.

I do not know whether you guys have been checkin' along on this business with me, an' I don't know whether you are thinkin' in the same way as I am. You gotta realise that you know just as much about all this hooey that's been goin' on around here as I do. But this is what I think:

First of all it is stickin' out a foot that Marella only wrote one of the three important letters in this case. The letter she did write was the one written in Sea Island ink to Ayl mar Thorensen accusin' him of bein' Berenice Lee Sam's lover, an' sayin' she was goin' to make plenty trouble. So the thing we *know,* apart from the things that we're guessin' at, is that Marella really did write that letter. Whether it was true or not is another proposition. I have got an open mind on this, an' I am goin' to try an' check up on this fact by all the other angles in the case.

O.K. Well there are two other letters, ain't there? There's the letter, signed Marella Thorensen, written to the Director, the letter that starts all this business. That wasn't written by Marella. And the letter written to Berenice Lee Sam tellin' her to come over from Shanghai. That wasn't written by Marella either.

Now maybe you can understand why Marella's behaviour was so funny on that afternoon. She gets a telegram from the Director sayin' that a "G" man will be with her between four an' five, an' she doesn't even know what the hell this means, but she does something about it, because something happens that makes her decide that she don't want to see this operative an' there must be a reason for that, mustn't there?

It is also stickin' out a foot that when Berenice Lee Sam arrived out at the Villa, Marella didn't even know what Berenice was talkin' about. She hadta pump her to find out why she had come out. She hadta pump her to find out about this letter she had received, the letter that was supposed to have come from Marella.

So here is the thing: We know somebody, using Marella's name, wanted to concentrate two people out at the Villa Rosalito between the hours of four an' five on last Wednesday, one of these guys to be the Federal officer an' the other one Berenice Lee Sam.

O.K. Now here is another thing we know. We know that when Berenice gets there, an' when Marella finds out why she has come, Marella tells Berenice that if anybody makes any trouble old Lee Sam will be involved in it. Now this tells us something. It tells us this:

That Marella was frightened at what was happenin'. She was frightened because somebody had tried to concentrate a "G" man an' Berenice Lee Sam at the Villa Rosalito at that time. She is afraid that somebody is goin' to start some trouble an' if she is afraid that somebody is goin' to start some trouble for her an' for Aylmar, then she must know that there is some trouble that *can* be started. That's why she makes the threat to Berenice.

Now see if we can get an idea as to what that trouble that somebody could start might be. Let's look at some more facts. Let's take these things an' put 'em all together an' see how they add up:

First of all I believe that Thorensen was tellin' the truth. I believe he was tellin' the truth about his associations with his own wife an' I believe he was tellin' the truth about the interview he had with Berenice when she came around to his office. O.K. Well where does that get us? It gets us this far.

We know that Rudy Spigla a coupla years ago has been to Thorensen with a big scheme for runnin' contraband silk in under cover of the legitimate Lee Sam silk cargoes an' usin' Rocca's trucks for the purpose of deliverin' it. We know that Rocca didn't know anything about it. We also know that Lee Sam didn't know anything about it. Now get this: Thorensen comes in on this job because he is pressed for money an' he sees an easy way for makin' money an' an easy get-out if they are caught at it. He knows that the only guy who will get hurt if there is a show-down will be Rudy Spigla an' the person who will get out after him an' hurt him will be Rocca, who will be fed up to hell because his second in command has been double-crossin' him.

We know on information supplied by O'Halloran that Rocca has been keepin' his nose clean in San Francisco. He has been runnin' a legitimate truckin' business, he has been runnin' his night clubs an' flop houses an' he has been runnin' his old protection rackets, but Jack Rocca said when I saw him at his Club, an' I believe him, that he was too wise to start any real funny business in San Francisco.

All right. Now let's come to another point. Nellie says she's positive she's seen Spigla hangin' around at the Villa Rosalito at different times. Well now the thing that naturally comes into our heads is that he would be goin' out there to see Thorensen, but this would be wrong because Thorensen was never out there. Spigla could see him much easier in San Francisco. So I reckon Spigla was goin' out there to see Marella Thorensen.

Now it would be a funny thing, wouldn't it, if Rudy Spigla had blown the works about what he was doin' with Thorensen to Marella, an' it looks to me as if he has done this. I'll tell you why. If Rudy Spigla for some reason best known to himself had told Marella that him an' Aylmar had been runnin' silk contraband for some time, then I reckon that when Marella got that telegram sayin' a "G" man was comin' down, and then when Berenice appears an' starts askin' questions, the first thing that flashes into Marella's head is that somebody has got wise to this business. That's why she says to Berenice that if there's any trouble old Lee Sam will be involved in it.

Now you're goin' to admit that the funny thing is that when Berenice goes on afterwards to see Aylmar Thorensen in order to protect himself he tells her that he's been runnin' silk with old Lee Sam, which is a lie. So it would look this way—that there was some plot on between Marella an' Aylmar, wouldn't it? But a little more examination shows us that we're wrong, because if Marella an' Aylmar were workin' together over anything, first of all they would be a little bit more friendly than they are, an' secondly Marella wouldn't have written that letter to Aylmar accusin' him of bein' Berenice's lover, an' the thing we have got to do is to find an explanation which makes all these bits an' pieces dovetail in, an' at the back of my head I think I've got it, but I'm goin' to check up first.

Brendy is sittin' in the big chair with his feet up on the table smokin' a ten cent cigar an' lookin' like an old owl. O'Halloran is lyin' on the settee with a bottle of bourbon by his side, smokin' that goddam pipe of his. The room is so fulla smoke that I feel I would like to put a gas mask on.

I talk to 'em.

"Now look, Brendy," I say, "here's the way it goes: All this business is sorta comin' to a head. We got ideas, but we don't know just how far we're right, or just how far we're wrong, so we've gotta start something. We've gotta get tough. Now here's the angle. The first thing we've gotta do is to have a complete search of Rocca's offices at The Two Moons Club an' of his apartment, an' we've gotta have a search of Rudy Spigla's place, just in case we find somethin'. At the same time we have gotta nose through the offices, garages, trucks an' everything else connected with the Rocca Truckin' Corporation, because I tell you what's in my head.

"This runnin' contraband silk looks like a lotta hooey to me. Everybody's talkin' about runnin' contraband silk so much an' so openly that it looks to me like they're tryin' to cover up something else. All right, there's only one way that we can get this searchin' business done quickly, an' that's by a raid. We got to put a raid up to-night. We gotta raid all the places at once, The Two Moons Club, the offices, the trucks an' the garages. We gotta synchronise that business. I'm goin' to suggest it should take place at twelve o'clock. You can find some excuse for that raid, Brendy, somethin' that won't get 'em thinkin' too much.

"When you've raided these dumps you pull in Rocca an' Spigla, an' anybody else who's kickin' around. You take the whole durn lot of 'em down to the Hall of Justice. We can hold 'em there until to-morrow anyway. We can let 'em out in time for 'em to go to Sunday church if they feel that way.

"Now while you are raidin' these places, Brendy, O'Halloran here an' me are goin' to be searchin' the Rocca an' Spigla apartments. I wanta look around an' see if I can get my hooks on anything.

"After we have done this search O'Halloran will rejoin you at police headquarters, but I am goin' straight along to have a little talk with this Oklahoma Joe who runs this flop house, this place where some mysterious person tells me Joe Mitzler is hangin' out.

"Say, Brendy," I ask him, "what do you know about this Oklahoma Joe?"

"Plenty," he says, "an' it's funny that his name should come inta this business, because he is about the only guy in this man's town who ain't afraid of Jack Rocca. The story is that he an' Rocca had a little argument in the old days. They settled it with guns an' they both got pretty badly hurt, since when they've had a sorta respect for each other.

"The thing I can't understand," says Brendy, "is why Mitzler should choose Oklahoma Joe's place for a hide-out, because if Joe Mitzler has been workin' for Spigla it seems durn funny that he should take some place for a hide-out that is owned by an enemy of Rocca's."

"Maybe that ain't so funny, Brendy," I tell him. "Maybe there's a good reason for that. O.K. Well, that's how it is. You go off an' fix all that business, Brendy, an' you phone through to me here when you've got it straightened out. When the cars go out to raid these dumps O'Halloran'll proceed to give the once over to the other places."

I turn around to Terry.

"Your business, Terry," I say, "will be to fix it so that at twelve o'clock to-night we can somehow get inta the Rocca an' Spigla apartments, do what we wanta do an' get out again without the whole world knowin' about it. Now have you boys got that?"

They nod.

"I get it," says Brendy. "It looks to me like you're goin' to start a small war in this man's town to-night. Do you realise that if we're goin' to raid all the Rocca places together we've gotta put up about thirty raids. I reckon there will be so many police sirens shriekin' their heads off to-night that somebody will think somebody has declared war on somebody." He sighs.

"Still, Lemmy," he says, "I always heard tell you had a whole lotta brains an' you always knew what you was doin', so I suppose I will have to see this job through the way you say."

I grin at him. "O.K., Brendy," I say, "I reckon we're goin' places this time. Now you boys scram outa here an' get busy, because I wanta do some quiet thinkin'."

They scram.

It is just before twelve midnight when we get goin'. Brendy an' O'Halloran have been doin' some sweet staff work an' they have fixed these raids just as good as I coulda done it myself.

At ten minutes to twelve, by an arrangement we have got with the telephone company, all lines connectin' all the Rocca dumps an' offices, an' the truck garages, have been disconnected just so's nobody who does get wise to what we are at can get through on the telephone an' wise up any other guys.

There is just one place we ain't raidin' an' that is Oklahoma Joe's. I reckon that directly the raids are well under way the old underworld grapevine will get to work an' they will know all about what is goin' on at Oklahoma Joe's. That is the time when my little playmate Joe Mitzler is goin' to feel good that he is in an enemy flop house. He will be very happy that he is not at any of the Rocca dumps.

That is supposin' he is at Oklahoma's, but I ain't worryin' very much about this. I reckon that he is there all right, an' just when he is feelin' good about bein' there an' not around at The Two Moons he is goin' to see my sweet-lookin' pan appear-in' round the corner, after which I reckon some sweet fun an' games are goin' to start.

Sittin' in my car are Brendy an' O'Halloran, a police sergeant and four cops. We have got shotguns just in case anybody thinks they wanta start a war but we are not lookin' out for any real trouble because I reckon that Jack Rocca is goin' to come quiet when he sees that we mean business. I make a note at the back of my head to have a few minutes quiet talk with this bozo about one or two things directly I get the chance.

We bust through the entrance of The Two Moons Club before the guy on the door knows what is happenin'. He don't get a chance to give anybody the low-down. In a minute Brendy is standin' in the middle of the dance floor bawlin' his head off. People are scuttlin' like hell for the back way out, but that won't do 'em any good because there are two more police cruisers waitin' round there to collect 'em that end.

"Keep your hair on," says Brendy. "There ain't anything to be scared of—this is a police raid not a hold-up. Now stick around folks an' just give your names an' address to the officers. We'll keep the guys we want an' the others can go home an' explain to their wives how they come here to see a sick friend. Get busy, boys!"

With O'Halloran at my elbow I scram across the floor an' through the doors leadin' to the passage an' lift on the other side. Just as we get there in the passage the lift comes down an' Rudy Spigla gets out.

"Hi'yah, Rudy!" I tell him. "Come along an' have a nice piece of can. I'm goin' to stick you in the cooler for a bit an' how'dya like that?"

He looks at me like I was a bad smell.

"So you're around again, Caution," he says. "I reckon you're goin' to make some trouble for yourself before you get through. You may be a Federal officer but you can't get around doin' this sorta stuff an' get away with it."

"Oh no," I tell him. "Well bozo, I'll proceed to show you some-thin' else I can get away with."

I smack a hearty one across the kisser an' he hits the wall with such a bump that he almost leaves the imprint of his head on it. He gets up. He looks pretty fierce. He puts his hand around to his hip, but Terry pulls a gun on him an' sticks him up. He then frisks him an' produces a .32 Colt outa his hip.

"You gotta permit for this gun?" says Terry.

"Sure I gotta permit," says Spigla.

He pulls the permit outa his coat pocket. Terry looks at it an' then tears it up.

"You ain't got a permit now," he says, "an' I'm pinchin' you for carryin' a gun without a permit."

"This is a lousy frame-up," says Spigla. "There's goin' to be plenty trouble about this. What're you raidin' this club for. There ain't anything illegal goin' on around here an' you. know it."

"We ain't raidin' this club because we think there's anything illegal goin' on, Unconscious," I tell him. "We're raidin' this club on the grounds that (a) the drainage system don't confirm with the city ordinances, (b) that you are sellin' short-weight portions of spaghetti to Eskimos thereby infringing the Federal Weights and Measures Code, an' (c) because we ain't got anything better to do. If you want some more reasons just you ask the D.A. an' maybe he'll give 'em to you in duplicate."

"In the meantime," says Terry, "I am goin' to give you a good poke in the snout for bein' insolent to my colleague," sayin' which he smacks Rudy another one across the pan that you coulda heard on the other side of the Golden Gate.

"Just before you get goin', Mr. Spigla," I tell him, "you can hand over any keys you got about you because I am about to run the rule over your sleepin' apartment at the Mulberry Arms up on the hill, just to see if you are keepin' white mice there."

"Damn you, Caution," he says. "I'm goin' to get you for all this. You can't search my apartment. You haven't got a search warrant."

"Right, Gorgeous," I tell him, bustin' him another one on the ear just to keep this party nice an' sweet. "You are dead right. I ain't gotta search warrant, but I have got adenoids an' a strawberry wen on my left knee owin' to Mrs. Caution bein' fond of fruit just before my first birthday, an' I reckon that them two things entitles me to search your little nest, honeybell, so sew up your mouth an' hand over the keys."

Just as he is handin' 'em over, Jack Rocca with a couple of cops comes down in the lift. Rocca is smilin' like an angel. He is takin' everything nice an' quiet. I reckon Jack has got brains.

He takes a look at Rudy an' sees that there has been a little trouble because Rudy has gotta bruise on one side of his head that looks like a baby pumpkin, an' the last smack across the snoot that I gave him has marked him plenty.

"Why don't you be your age, Rudy?" says Rocca. "What's the good of arguin' with cops? Take it easy."

"That's the stuff, Rocca," I tell him. "You got sense."

He grins. "Look, Caution," he says, "what's behind this raid? I'm not pullin' anything in this city. I told you that an' it was the truth."

"An' I believed you, Rocca," I tell him, "but the trouble with some of you guys is that you cannot even smell something that is goin' on right under your nose. So long, bozo." The cops take him off.

O'Halloran an' I ease upstairs. Outa the window we can hear the police sirens shriekin' as the boys start the raids along California Street, an' down on the back areas on the Embarcadero.

We turn out Rocca's office an' we turn out Spigla's. There is not a durn thing to be seen. Just a lotta innocent business papers an' receipts and what nots.

"O.K., Terry," I tell O'Halloran. "Here's where we split. You get along to Rocca's place an' give it the works. Turn the durn place upside down but get your hooks on anything that looks like something we want. Me, I'm goin' to take a look around Spigla's apartment. When you're through get back to headquarters an' check over the reports from the other raids. Don't forget to check on the trucks. Stick around there until I come back after I been to see my little playmate, Joe Mitzler."

"O.K., Lemmy," he says, "but you be careful of Joe. That palooka don't like you an' he is the type of guy who would take a lot of pleasure in stickin' a hand-gun right into your navel an' pullin' the trigger just to see if you was made of sawdust inside."

"You're tellin' me," I crack back at him. "But if anybody is goin' to be pullin' triggers it is goin' to be Mrs. Caution's little boy Lemmy. I'll be seein' you."

I scram downstairs an' out the front way. Around the block there is a car waitin' for me like I arranged. I get inta it an' shoot off up to the hill. It is one o'clock when I get to the Mulberry Arms.

I flash my card at the night guy an' tell him that I'm goin' to take a look over Mr. Spigla's apartment an' that I do not wanta be disturbed. I go up in the lift an' a coupla minutes afterwards I am inside Rudy's dump.

Is it swell, or is it? I'm tellin' you that this Spigla is not only a neat guy but he has also got so much taste that it almost hurts. Everything is spick an' span. The place is so well laid out that I reckon if Sam Goldwyn had ever met up with Rudy he woulda made him head of the art department right away.

There are two compactums full of clothes. Suits an' suits all on hangers an' stretchers. There are silk shirts an' silk pyjamas, an' there are also half a dozen new ladies' nightdresses which is a thing that causes me much pain to see as it looks as if Rudy has not been concentratin' on business all the time.

Hangin' around the walls, which are painted a sorta primrose colour with pink wall lights, are a lotta pictures of dames. I take a lamp at these frails an' I'm tellin' you that some of 'em is so easy to look at as regards shape that they coulda won the beauty competition down at Bunkbille Pa. with sacks over their faces. Most of these pictures have got lovin' messages written on 'em such as—"To darling Rudy from Annabelle." Another one says—"I am well lost for love," an' a third one says—"To Rudy who has all my heart." This last one was lucky because knowin' Rudy I am wonderin' why he had only pinched the dame's heart.

I get to work. I start goin' over this place most efficiently. I turn everything out an' over. I start lookin' in the most unlikely places leavin' the likely ones till the last.

An' I do not find a durn thing. There is not one little thing that teaches me anything.

I sit down in a big chair an' I relax. I do a little quiet thinkin' an' I get around to considerin' just how funny it is for a guy like

Spigla—who is anyway nothin' but a mobster pretendin' to be a club manager—to have a swell dump like this an' to be so neat an' nice. I get to tryin' to remember other thugs who I have known an' who are inclined to be nice about their apartments an' their clothes. I try to connect these guys up in my mind. I am endeavourin'— if you know what I mean—to find some common denominator that fits all these palookas just to see if I can get a line on Rudy's mentality through usin' that process. The result is nix.

I light myself a cigarette an' get up an' start lookin' around at the pictures of the molls on the walls. I am just lettin' my mind wander nice an' easy because I have always found that it is when you are not really lookin' for somethin' that you discover what you are not lookin' for. Got me?

I'm tellin' you some of these dolls are the icin' on the cocktail glass. Boy, are they honeys or are they honeys? There is one dame with a faraway expression an' a Gainsborough hat who woulda been just what the doctor ordered so far as I was concerned. There is another dame in a bathin' costume with such swell legs that I am half a mind to pinch this picture an' give it to Brendy so that every time he looks at his wife's under-pinnin' he can start singin' "What Might Have Been" in a high falsetto, consistin' of one part rage an' two parts disappointment.

Way down at the end of the wall near the big carved desk that is standin' across one corner of the room there is a big picture. It is evidently the likeness of some baby that Rudy was specially stuck on because there is a little electric light that you switch on just over the picture that illuminates it. I switch this light on an' I look at the picture.

Boy, here is a dame. She has gotta face that you can't forget. There is a faraway look in her eyes that makes her look like she was achin' for some big he-man to give her the big run-around with bells on.

Written at the bottom of the picture I see this:

"To Rudy who gave me such sweet sleep, such sweet dreams."

Now I ask you? I reckon a dame who would write a thing like that ought to be smacked with a hot fryin' pan an' what do you think?

I go on. I take a look at the desk which I have left until the last because it is the most likely place where I will find somethin'. There is a sweet blotter on the top an' another picture of some frail with frills. I try all the drawers an' they are all locked.

I get out Rudy's keys an' start openin' up the drawers. There ain't anythin' much in 'em. Just a lot of letters which I read an' which don't mean anything, an' a lot of old race track cards an' programmes an' things. These drawers look to me to be the most untidy things in this apartment.

I got through the lot an' there ain't anything.

Sittin' at the desk I let me eyes wander around the room. I told you that the room was a swell place with concealed lightin' on the walls. I notice that there is a concealed light just above the picture of the last dame I looked at an' I wonder why, havin' regard to the fact that this light is there, Rudy has had another light fixed over the picture.

I get an idea. I go over an' take the picture down, an' I see I am right. Behind it there is a little wall safe an' the light above is for that.

I open it with a key on Rudy's bunch.

There is only one thing inside. There is a letter. It is an envelope an' the postmark on the stamp is San Francisco Central an' the time stamp is nine o'clock collection.

I open the envelope which has been slit up, an' read the letter inside. It is written in some handwritin' I don't know an' it says:

Rudy,—This is to tell you that I think yon have given me a swell deal. I've been a heel to hound you like I have and I'm going to be good and make a fresh start like you told me. Thanks for the dough.

So long, Rudy. Here's luck.

Effie.

The interestin' thing about this letter is that it is written in Sea Island ink, the same ink that Marella used when she wrote the letter to Thorensen that I got from Berenice.

I put the letter in my pocket an' do a little grin. I reckon that it is funny that letter bein' the only thing in that safe. It looks like the sorta letter that a man would read an' then tear up.

I wonder why Rudy kept it, but I don't wonder for long. I sorta get an idea. He kept that letter because he thought that maybe he'd need it one day. Well, I've got an idea that he won't.

I close up the safe an' put the picture back. My cigarette is just finished an' I look around for somewhere to throw the stub. There is a swell ashtray on the desk. One of them deep things with a hole at the top to throw the butts in an' a little; stand for a lighter at the side.

I put another cigarette in my mouth an' pull out the lighter outa the ashtray. I light my cigarette an' when I go to put the lighter back I find it won't quite fit in. There is something in the bottom of the little holder.

I turn it upside down an' a ring falls out. I look at it an' I get one big kick. The ring is a woman's size signet ring, an' the seal carved on the onyx is two crossed keys.

Well . . . well . . . well. . . . So this is Marella's seal ring. The ring that Nellie said she always usta use. The one that disappeared.

I stand there with the ring in my hand, an' I look over to the picture on the wall, the picture of the dame that is hangin' over the wall safe. I see the writin' quite clear—"To Rudy who gave me such sweet sleep, such sweet dreams."

Well that's that. I got what I wanted. The ring, that writin' an' the letter in the safe, the letter that Rudy was expectin' anybody who searched the place to find, tell me all I wanta know.

A sweet night's work.

I sit down an' finish my cigarette. I look around this swell dump. I get to wonderin' about the mind of a guy like this one, a man who is so neat an' nice. I get to thinkin' of that poor dame Marella an' I get a bit hot under the collar. I can get annoyed too sometimes!

I smoke another cigarette an' I think over everything. I get the set-up in my mind, the bluff that I am goin' to pull on Joe Mitzler.

I reckon I gotta be careful about that bluff. I mustn't make a mistake with Joe.

Chapter Eleven
FADE OUT FOR JOE

I SCRAM downstairs and I start walking down the hall. There are two things in my mind.

One is I am wonderin' whether I am really goin' to find Joe Mitzler stickin' around this Oklahoma Joe's place, an' secondly just how I am goin' to handle this bozo. I am beginnin' to get some sweet slants on this job. Findin' that letter up in Rudy's safe an' comin across that seal ring of Marella's like that, has wised me up to plenty, an' if I wanted another clue justa help me along I got it when I looked at that picture an' saw the words that that dame had written across the bottom: "To Rudy who gave me such sweet sleep, such sweet dreams." But it is one thing havin' ideas, an' another thing to check on 'em an' prove 'em.

One thing I do know an' that is the solution of this case lies in the conversation that I am goin' to have with Joe an' another conversation that I will tell you about presently.

It is half-past two when I find this Oklahoma Joe's dump, and it is a pretty bum lookin' place too, I'm tellin' you. Strawberry Street looks like a place where anythin' can happen; the whole place is full of cat houses; cheap flop houses, Chinese yen shops, an' all that sorta stuff. There is a dirty sign stickin' outa this dump which says Oklahoma Joe's, an' I go down a dirty passage. Right at the end is a door with a piece cut out of it an' "Enquiries" painted on it, but I don't ring the bell. I just give the door a push an' I go in.

On the other side of the door is a little room. There is a wood an' coal fire on one side an' a table stuck in the middle of the room. Behind this table a guy is sittin'. He is a little guy who looks as if he might have been a sailor.

"Listen, bozo, can't you read?" he growls. "It says ring the bell on that door. That's what we got the hole cut outa the door for, so that fellers shouldn't just bust in here. We don't sorta like it."

"You don't say," I tell him. "Well, I don't like ringin' bells neither. Are you Oklahoma Joe, because if you are I'm advisin' you to keep a very sweet tongue in your head. Otherwise I'm goin' to give you a bust in the pan that you're goin' to remember all the days of your life."

"Oh, yeah?" he says. "Tough, hey?"

"You just don't know, Sweetheart," I say.

I show him my badge.

"Now look, Joe," I tell him. "Guys like you should always decide to be wise guys. You should always decide to behave nice an' quiet an' answer questions that you're asked, especially when Lemmy Caution is askin' 'em. Have you got a guy in this place called Joe Mitzler, or maybe he's callin' himself somethin' else? But here's what he looks like."

I give him a description of Joe as near as I can. He looks at me sorta considerin'.

"Well," he says finally, "you gotta realise that this is a difficult proposition. I believe this guy is here. I believe he's the guy in the room on the second floor, but I got an idea about that bozo."

"Such as . . ." I ask him.

"Such as he is lyin' on the bed with a gun nearby," he says. "Me—it is not my business to ask people a lotta questions, but when this guy cashes in here I get the sorta idea in my head that he was on the run. Another thing," says Oklahoma Joe, "I reckon this palooka is one tough *hombre,* an' is liable to start a whole lotta shootin' if he thinks there is anybody stickin' around, such as a guy like you, or any other form of dick."

"That's very nice of you, Oklahoma," I tell him, "to give me this warnin', but the life of a dick is fulla tough spots, an' Joe Mitzler is one of 'em. So if you don't mind I think I'll go up an' have a few words with this baby."

"O.K.," he says, gettin' up. "We'll have to go upstairs. You'd better come along."

"Not on your life," I tell him. "You just sit where you are, an' relax. If you think I'm goin' bangin' up them stairs behind you just so's Joe Mitzler can have the artillery ready by the time the door opens you've got the wrong conception of Mr. Caution. Stick around here an' don't try any funny business of any sort, shape or description, otherwise I'll fill you so fulla holes that you will look just like a sieve. Have you got that?"

He says he's got it.

I walk across the room, an' I open the door. On the other side is another little passage with a dirty flight of wooden steps leadin' up on the right-hand side. I go up. When I get to the first floor landin' I see two doors. They are both open an' they both lead inta rooms where there are guys snorin' hard. I start gum-shoein' very quietly up the second flight.

When I come to the second floor I find another two doors. I try the right hand one. It is open an' empty. I am also very sorry that I have to use the little flash lamp that I have fixed at the end of my fountain pen in order to find the door handle, because I think that maybe some guy in the other room can see this flash. I step over to the other door an' try it. It is locked, an' as I take my fingers off the handle I see under the Crack a light go on. I reach for the Luger, pull it out, step back an' kick the lock off the door. Then I go in.

The room is a dirty sorta room. It is the usual sorta of bum place you get in a sailor's flop house. Lyin' on a bed underneath the window on the other side is Joe Mitzler, an' he is just puttin' his hand under the pillow. I show him the gun.

"Look, Joe," I tell him, "when you take your hand from under that pillow I wanta see that there ain't anythin' in it, otherwise I'm goin' to blow the top of your head off. See, baby?"

He don't say anythin', he just takes his hand away. Then he heaves himself up an' sits there with his hands hangin' down by his sides lookin' more like a man-eatin' gorilla than ever. I shut the door an' I walk over to the wall where there is a chair. I get the chair an' I put it up against the door, an' I sit on it. I have got my gun in my right hand with the muzzle pointin' somewhere in the region of Joe's guts.

With the other hand I get out my cigarette case, grab out a coupla cigarettes an' light 'em both an' throw one over to Joe.

"Now look, Joe," I tell him, "maybe you have heard that life is a very hard proposition. I reckon it can be plenty hard for a guy like you. I reckon it is goin' to be durn hard anyway, but my advice to you is to make it as easy as maybe."

He looks at me an' a sorta odd grin flickers across his face. He don't say nothin'.

"You listen to what I am goin' to say, Joe," I tell him, "an' you try an' be nice an' helpful. Maybe if you are, things will be a little bit easier for you, because if you ain't you're sure goin' to have a tough time."

He grins some more. "I get you, Mr. Caution," he says. "Let's hear the story. Maybe I'll talk an' maybe I won't. Who knows?"

"I do, Joe," I tell him. "You're goin' to talk, baby, an' you're goin' to like it, so let's get that straight before we start.

"First of all," I tell him, "you will probably wanta know just how I knew you was here. This is the sorta thing that would arouse your curiosity, an' I'm goin' to be perfectly straight with you. Somebody sends me a printed throw-out for this dump," I tell him, "an' written along the side of the bill is a little pencil message that if I'm tryin' to find you, maybe I'll find you here. Well, it didn't take me very long to work out who it was would be the most likely person to send me that message. I reckon it would be Toots, the blonde baby."

I feel in my pocket an' I take out the bill. I get up an' I go across to him with the bill held out in my hand.

"Now look, Joe," I tell him, "I want you to take a look at that bill an' tell me if that ain't Toot's handwriting."

I give him the bill an' he looks at it. While I am standin' there I put my hand under the pillow. Sure enough there is an old Colt .45 there loaded up to the brim. I stick it in my coat pocket. He sees me do this, an' he looks a bit regretful. Maybe he was fond of that gun.

"That's O.K.," he says, "it's that blonde dame's hand-writin', an' how did you guess it was her?"

"Work it out for yourself, Joe," I tell him. "The way I figured it out was this: For some reason or other which we do not know at the moment you an' Toots decided to part company. You was both on the run. You knew that the cops were lookin' for both ol you.

"Now I have always found that if there is a time when crooks disagree it is when they are being chased by cops. They get sorta nervy, you know, Joe, they begin to hate each other plenty. So I figured that Toots took a run-out powder on you, but she wasn't content to do just that thing. She was still frightened, see? She was afraid that the next time you came across her you might maybe use that shootin' iron of yours on her, so what does she do? She sends me this throw-out bill, so's I'm goin' to know where you are, so's I will pinch you. Then with you in the cooler she will be safe, won't she?"

He looks across at me an' grins.

"Ain't you clever, fly cop?" he says.

"You're sayin' it, Joe," I tell him. "Me—I am the original brain trust. Now, Joe," I go on, "the question I wanta ask you is this. Why is it that Toots is so frightened of you? She ain't afraid of you just because she took a run-out powder on you. Dames have taken run-outs on guys before, but that don't mean to say the guy wants to shoot 'em. There is something else behind it, ain't there, Joe, an' shall I tell you what I think it is? Ain't it a fact that Toots was stringin' along with you in the first place because she couldn't do anything else? Ain't it a fact that Rudy Spigla had told her she'd gotta string along with you, an' that if she tried to take a run-out powder on you or pull any funny business you'd give her the heat?"

Joe hands me back the bill. I take it an' put it in my pocket.

"Are you askin' me or tellin' me?" he says. "I ain't talkin'."

"Just fancy that now, Joe," I tell him. "So you ain't talkin'. Well, maybe you will feel a bit more like talkin' when they put you in the electric chair an' turn on the sizzler. I've seen tough guys like you before, but they always talk some time."

He looks a little bit more interested. "Yeah?" he says. "Well what I gotta talk about? I ain't bumped anybody. Say," he goes on, "are you tryin' to hang this Marella Thorensen bump-off on to me?"

"Not on your life," I tell him. "I don't believe you ever bumped Marella Thorensen, but you *did* bump Gluck, the morgue attendant, didn't you, Joe? I reckon you was the guy who did that."

"Oh yeah?" he says. "Well, it's your business to prove that, ain't it?"

I can see that this bozo is goin' to be difficult.

"Look, Joe," I tell him, "why don't you have a break? I ain't askin' you to make any statements or confessions. I'm askin' you to tell me if I'm right or wrong on one or two points. Look, tell me this an' it won't do you any harm. When was it that Rudy Spigla first started to go out to the Villa Rosalito? Was it about six months ago?"

He puts on a surprised look.

"So Spigla went out to the Villa, did he?" he says. "Just fancy that now."

"Not only did he got out there, but you knew it, Joe," I tell him. "I reckon there ain't very much that Rudy Spigla has been doin' around this man's town that you don't know about, as for instance," I tell him, "maybe it was you who drove out to the Villa Rosalito after Marella Thorensen was bumped, stuck her body in a car an' chucked it into the harbour, an' that, Joe," I go on, "is usually called bein' an accessory to first degree murder. Another thing," I tell him, "I reckon you are probably the guy who rang through to the Harbour Squad an' told 'em that there was a body floatin' about in the New York dock. Joe, I reckon you know plenty."

He grins. He sits there lookin' like nothin' on earth with a sorta easy smile on his pan that gives me one big pain in the ear.

You gotta realise I ain't got any use for guys like Joe Mitzler. They are all bums. They just string around causin' plenty trouble for one an' all. They are the toughs who do the jobs, the guys who tote guns for the bigger guys. They are just a lousy lotta heels an' they make me sick.

But this palooka has got somethin' up his sleeve, I sorta sense that. I sorta sense that he ain't worryin' too much about me, an' that that is why he is bein' so saucy. Yet this guy knows that if I take him down to the Precinct an' book him the cops down there will give him a rough workin' over that he will never forget if I just give 'em the say so.

Suddenly I get to thinkin' of Oklahoma Joe down stairs. Now it stands to reason that Oklahoma Joe is the guy who has provided Joe Mitzler with a hide-out an' therefore may be considered to be a friend of his. This bein' so, an' knowin' I was a dick, I am wonderin' why Oklahoma was ready an' willin' to give away the fact that Joe Mitzler had gotta gun, especially when he knew that Joe had said he didn't wanta be taken.

I suddenly get the reason. The reason is that Joe has gotta another gun somewhere. The scheme is then a clever one, ain't it, because directly I got the gun from under the pillow I ain't afraid of what Joe may do, am I? The idea is that I will relax an' put my own gun away. After which Joe can produce his other rod an' get busy on me.

This may be the right idea, an' then again it might not. Maybe Joe Mitzler ain't afraid of bein' pinched, an' the only reason that he would have for not bein' afraid of bein' pinched is that he thinks we haven't got any sorta case against him; that he thinks we can't hang either the shootin' of the morgue attendant, Gluck, or the killin' of Marella onta him.

An' Joe is workin' for Rudy Spigla. I am as certain of that as I am that my name's Caution, an' the work he is doin' for Spigla is work that has been done behind Jack Rocca's back, that is another certainty, an' it is for this reason that Joe is hi din' out in the dump of a guy who is not very partial to Rocca.

But there is only one way for me to find out for sure, an' that is for me to put my own gun away, give Joe Mitzler a chance to pull a fast one, an' then see what he does. Well, I reckon I can take a chance as well as any other guy. I lean back in the chair an' I put the Luger back in the holster under my arm, an' I take out my cigarette pack an' get another one out. I am just lightin' it, watchin' Joe outa the corner of my eye, when he pulls it.

He sticks his hand in his shirt an' he pulls out a little .22 automatic that he has got there, an' he sits there lookin' at me an' grinnin' like all the apes in Hell. I grin back at him.

"Me, I'm surprised at you, Joe," I tell him. "I never thought to see you usin' one of them sissy guns that was made for women."

This gives me an idea.

"But maybe, Joe," I go on, "that was the gun you shot Marella with."

"You're a lousy liar, Caution," says Joe. "I never gave it to Marella, an' if I had I certainly wouldn'ta used this gun. Me, I like a big gun like the one you just grabbed from under the pillow. I ain't ever used this little rod before, but I'm goin' to have a lot of pleasure in tryin' it out on you."

He grins some more. He is a tough guy is Joe, an' I reckon he will kill me just as easy as shellin' a pea. It won't even keep him awake for five minutes any night afterwards, either. That baby is a tough as French nails.

"How come, Joe?" I ask him. "Don't you think you're takin' a whole lotta chances when you start aimin' to bump off Federal Officers? They got a nice hot seat for guys who do that."

"Yeah," he says. "Well, here's one guy they ain't goin' to get. How're they goin' to know that I done it, an' they gotta prove it, ain't they? I reckon that Oklahoma downstairs will prove that you never come here to-night, an' that I never been outa this dump, so how're they goin' to know it's me done it?"

"They'll prove it all right," I tell him. "I reckon they know it was you who chucked Marella inta the dock, an' I reckon they know it was you put that phoney telephone call through to the Harbour Squad to say that there was a body floatin' about. They can do a bit more guessin', can't they?"

"Sure they can," he says. "An' I'll tell you somethin', Caution. It was me that chucked Marella in the dock, an' it was me that put the call through, but the information ain't goin' to be any good to you because I am now goin' to give you some hot lead right in the place where it acts just like a sleepin' draught, after which maybe some friends of mine will chuck you in the harbour too. Just so's to keep everything nice an' square."

I am not feelin' so good. Maybe I was a mug to take a chance with a guy like Joe. I watch him as he heaves himself up to his feet. As he does so he turns the little automatic around in his hand an' do I get one big kick or do I, because this big mug has forgot to push the safety catch down. I remember that he has said that he ain't never used an automatic before, an' it looks like he don't know that there is a thumb safety catch on an automatic.

"How're you goin' to have it?" he says. "In the front or the back, an' would you like it through the head or in the guts? They say it hurts plenty there."

I get up. He sticks the gun up a bit higher. It is pointin' at my chest.

"Ain't there goin' to be a lotta trouble when you shoot that gun off, Joe?" I ask him. "Maybe somebody is goin' to hear."

"I should worry," he says. "They are all friends of mine around here."

I drop my head an' take a dive for him. I hear him curse as he squeezes the trigger an' the gun don't fire. Right then I hit him in the stomach with my head, an' I follow it with a left an' right inta his stomach. Then, I step back an' take a kick at him an' my foot arrives. I catch him a beauty right on the bread pan, an' he lets go a helluva whimper an' drops. I reckon I have hurt this guy.

I take the little automatic off him. I was right—the safety catch is on. He just didn't know about it. I slip it in my pocket.

Joe is lyin' on the floor writhin' about. He is not feelin' so good. I reckon he won't cause anythin' to happen for a few minutes so I ease over to the door an' go downstairs, nice an' quiet, with the Luger in my hand. Down at the bottom, I find Oklahoma waitin'. He looks plenty surprised to see me.

"Hi'yah, Oklahoma!" I tell him. "You got a telephone here?"

He says yes. I show him the Luger.

"Get through to Police Headquarters," I tell him, "an' tell 'em Mr. Caution wants a patrol wagon sent around here to pick up Joe Mitzler an' Oklahoma Joe, an' be plenty quick about it."

"What the hell?" he says. "You ain't got nothin' on me. I ain't done a thing."

I prod him inta the room on the ground floor where the telephone is. Just to help things along I smack him one across the snoot that is a honey. All the while he is telephonin' he is tryin' to stop his bleedin' with a handkerchief that never went near a laundry in its life.

While we are waitin' for the wagon I make him go up the stairs in front of me an' bring Joe down. Joe is not at all well. I have kicked this guy so hard that he looks like he is goin' to have a permanent kink in him, an' I gotta admit that this thought gives me a certain amount of pleasure because I am not very partial to guys like Joe Mitzler.

We park Joe on a chair in the corner of the room. He is whinin' a lot an' tryin' to make out that he is goin' to be sick. I light myself a cigarette an' look at Oklahoma.

"Looky, Oklahoma," I tell him. "Why don't you do some quick thinkin'. That patrol wagon is goin' to be here in about ten minutes, an' in the meantime I gotta make up my mind just what I'm goin' to charge you with."

"Yeah," he says, but he don't look so pleased. "What's the choice?"

"I got plenty," I tell him. "First of all there's shelterin' an' harbourin' a crook who is on the run, an' secondly there is bein' accessory to attempt to murder a Federal Officer—meanin' me, an' thirdly there is a whole lot of other charges that I can think up if I let my imagination run a bit. Well, do we deal?"

He takes a look at Joe, an' then decided that he has not got to worry a lot about Joe.

"What's the deal?" he asks.

"Just this," I tell him. "I want the low-down on this bird an' the blonde dame, Toots, that has been runnin' around with him, the frail who tipped me off where he was hidin' out. Well . . .?"

"I don't know a lot," he says. "This guy works for Rudy Spigla an' so does the dame Toots. I gotta idea that the Toots dame got her nose dirty with Spigla an' he handed her over to Joe here just so's Joe could keep a sorta fatherly eye on her an' stop her from openin' her mouth too wide."

"Swell, Oklahoma," I tell him. "You're doin' fine. You're makin' it better for yourself every minute. Now you tell me this little thing. When was it that Rudy Spigla decided that Joe oughta keep an eye on the Toots moll? Wasn't that about the time that Marella Thorensen got herself bumped off?"

"That's right," he says. "That was the time."

"O.K.," I say. "That is very good. Now you tell me another little thing. Just what was it that Toots found out that Rudy Spigla was afraid that she was goin' to spill? Wasn't Rudy afraid that Toots knew who the guy was that bumped off Marella Thorensen?"

He looks at me sorta old-fashioned.

"Maybe that was it, if it was a guy," he says.

"An' what might you mean by that crack," I ask him. "—Was a guy. Are you suggestin' that it was a dame?"

He grins. "That is just what I am suggestin'," he says. "I thought maybe that it was a dame."

"Well, we'll let that go, Oklahoma," I say. "Now you tell me somethin' else. Just how long has Rudy Spigla or Jack Rocca or either or both of 'em been runnin' drugs around here?"

He looks at me some more.

"I don't know what you're talkin' about," he says.

I reckon I have got this guy at last. He was ready to talk about Joe an' Toots, but he won't talk about the thing that he is mixed up in.

"So you don't know nothin' about that?" I ask him.

"That is a thing that I certainly do not know anything about," he says. "I have said my piece an' I don't know no more."

Right then I hear the patrol wagon arrive an' in a coupla minutes the cops come in. One of O'Halloran's sergeants is in charge.

"You can pinch these two," I tell him. "The guy in the corner who looks like he needs some stomach powder is Joe Mitzler an' you can book him on a charge of attempted first-degree murder of a Federal Officer. Maybe there'll be some other raps later. As for this guy," I go on, indicatin' Oklahoma, "well, I reckon you can take him along too."

Joe looked peeved. "You are a dirty son of a so-an'-so," he says. "Didn't you say you was makin' a deal with me. I told you plenty an' now you are havin' me pinched, an' I would like to know what I am bein' pinched for."

"Sure, honeysuckle," I tell him, "and you are entitled to. I was all ready an' willin' to make a deal with you providin' you shot the works, but you didn't. You didn't tell me somethin' I wanted to know an' you are goin' to pay for not havin' done same."

"Book him on a charge of receivin' an' dealin' in narcotic drugs," I tell the sergeant.

I look at Oklahoma.

"That is the little thing you *wouldn't* talk about, bozo," I tell him. "An' you wouldn't talk about it because you have personally been handlin' the stuff an' I reckon when the cops take a look around here they'll find plenty evidence, too. Take 'em along, boys."

I take a long walk an' I do some heavy thinkin'. I walk back to where I left the car up on the hill, an' I drive it down to the Precinct an' park around the corner. Inside I find Brendy an' O'Halloran.

"Did you boys have some nice raids?" I ask 'em. "An' did anybody get hurt?"

"Sure," says O'Halloran. "Brendy here got hurt. He was raidin' some dump off California an' just when they are pinchin' everybody in this place some guy busts Brendy a sweet one right across the dome with a soda-water syphon."

"How come, Brendy?" I ask him. "How come that you allowed yourself to be bust a mean one like that?"

He grins. "I was lookin' outa the window," he says. "Some dame's shadow was on the blind on the other side of the road. This dame had a sweet figure too," he goes on, sorta reminiscent. "I was just thinkin' that my wife could do with a figure like that when some roughneck busts me one. I reckon my love for art is goin' to be my ruin."

He gets serious.

"Lemmy," he says. "I gotta hand it to you. We pinched a lotta people an' we've let most of 'em go. We got Rocca an' Spigla in the cooler in separate cells, an' we got one or two other guys we been lookin' for."

"What didya find in the offices, an' the truckin' garages?" I ask him. "Did you come across anything that looks like what I wanted to find?"

He grins. "Did we, boy?" he asks. "We don't find anything in any of the Rocca dumps or yet down in the garages or offices. Not one little thing. But we check up on the cars that are out an' we find that there are two trucks deliverin' silk.

"I send a coupla cruisers after 'em an' we find 'em. One is full of Lee Sam silk all right, an' the other sorta looks like it was empty; that is, until we took the false bottom outa it."

"Nice work, baby," I tell him, "an' I reckon that that truck was down near the Embarcadero, wasn't it?"

"Right first time," he says. "An' how would you know?"

"I reckon it was either goin' from or comin' to Oklahoma Joe's," I tell him. "An' I can make a guess what you found in it."

He points to the table in the corner. "That's what we found," he says. "All in nice condition too. There is a sweet selection of drugs an' narcotics there. Enough for a factory. Morphia, opium an' cocaine. Who do we pinch for that, Lemmy?"

"Nobody," I tell him. "Not for a while anyhow. I reckon we will spring the boys we don't want kept in the cooler, an' we will just keep Rocca an' Spigla. An' I don't want 'em to see any lawyers either."

"That's O.K. by me," he says. "An' what is the next thing?" he asks.

"Nothin'," I say. "Me, I am goin' to bed because I gotta go places to-morrow."

"You don't say," he cracks. "Where you goin', Lemmy?"

"I am goin' to San Diego," I tell him, "the place that was on the post-mark of that throw-out bill I got. The one that said Joe Mitzler was at Oklahoma Joe's." I grin at 'em both.

"I have got a date with the dame who wrote that message," I tell 'em, "an' when I get back I reckon we will not keep the D.A. waitin' any longer. I reckon we will start pinchin' some real crooks."

CHAPTER TWELVE
BLUE DRAGON STUFF

WHEN I wake up I look outa my window an' I see that it is one of them swell winter days that I like. Nice an' snappy with a touch of that sorta cold-lookin' sunshine that makes the dames snuggle their heads inta their furs an' look wicked.

I stick around an' take a quiet breakfast, after my shower, after which I proceed to doll myself up in a new suit that I ain't worn yet with a snappy silk shirt that some jane give me as a sorta thank offerin' after her husband was machine-gunned inta strips by some thugs who had mistook him for some guy they did not like.

An' I do some heavy thinkin'. One way an' another I am pretty pleased with the way things are goin'.

I have definitely got my mind fixed on one or two things. These are the things that I am certain about. I will tell youse guys what these things are, an' I will also tell you some of the things that I ain't so sure about.

First of all it is pretty easy to see the game that Rudy Spigla has been playin' over the silk contraband. It goes like this:

Rudy Spigla comes inta San Francisco with Jack Rocca who, havin' been a big-time gangster in Chicago, has now made up his mind to lead a fairly quiet an' easy life an' not start anything around town that is goin' to get him in bad with the cops.

Rudy probably sticks around for a bit an' hopes that Rocca will break into somethin' or other that will make the big-time dough, but Rocca don't do this. He is makin' plenty enough jack for himself an' he probably thinks that Rudy is gettin' a fair cut. But this don't satisfy Rudy. He aims to make himself a bit more on the side.

So he gets a big idea. He strings along until he gets the low-down on Thorensen. Rudy, who is very quick in the uptake, an' a guy with plenty brains an' intelligence, pretty soon realises that Thorensen is a discontented sorta cuss who is not gettin' along so well with Marella Thorensen.

Now it has always been my experience—an' it was probably Rudy's too—that when a guy is not gettin' along so well with his legal domestic partner he usually proceeds to get himself all mixed up with several nice an' frilly frails who are an expensive habit. At the same time his wife who is feelin' very lonely an' neglected is also inclined to need more dough as a sorta balm for her feelin's. So the husband needs more dough two ways, don't he?

Rudy gets the big idea that the time has now come to see if he can pull Thorensen in on a little scheme to make Rudy some nice pickin's.

He therefore eases along to Thorensen an' puts the idea up about runnin' silk contraband inta San Francisco in with the *legitimate Lee Sam cargoes,* the idea bein' that it is worth his while to get Thorensen in with him so's to have somebody to put the job straight if ever they are found out.

He is only takin' one chance. He is double-crossin' Jack Rocca who would rub him out as soon as take a look at him if he got wise, but Rudy reckons he has gotta chance something.

But you have all realised by now that the idea of runnin' contraband silk is all boloney, an' this idea is put up just to keep Aylmar Thorensen happy an' to kid him along that they are not doin' anything that will get them in really bad.

Actually—an' it is stickin' out a foot—Rudy has been runnin' drugs inside the contraband silk cargoes which have come over with the legitimate Lee Sam silk cargoes. This narcotic business is big time in San Francisco, an' I reckon that Rudy musta made a whole heap of jack at this game especially if it has been goin' on for two years.

I reckon that Aylmar Thorensen got wise to it when it was too late. An' I reckon that the time he got wise to it was about the time of the Marella killin' or maybe just before. This was one of the reasons why he wanted to bust outa San Francisco, because he was gettin' frightened an' because he wanted to put as much space between himself, Spigla, Rocca an' Lee Sam as possible before anybody got wise to the game.

I got onto this idea directly he told me that he had confessed to Berenice Lee Sam that he had been runnin' silk with Rudy. An' Berenice Lee Sam suspected the truth like I suspected it, an' that was why she got her old pa to make that confession down at the Precinct. Just so that if there was any trouble old Lee, Sam an' Thorensen would be tellin' the same story.

Now the next thing we gotta consider is why it is that Thorensen, who has been stringin' along with what he thinks is a little silk-runnin' racket nice an' happy for two years, should suddenly get scared an' decide to move his head office to Los Angeles. I think we can answer that one. He has realised what the truth is. He has realised that he has been the sucker; that Rudy Spigla has really been bringin' in drugs in the silk cargoes.

Now this might account for Rudy Spigla goin' out to the Villa Rosalito, an' it might not. He mighta been goin' out there to see Thorensen on the quiet, or he mighta been goin' out there for other reasons. One thing we do know an' that is one day when he went out there he got his hooks on Maralla's seal ring, which is a very interestin' bit of business, to which we will return later as the soldier said.

Now let's take another side of this business. Let's take a look at Toots. It is stickin' outa foot that Toots was workin' in along with Rudy, an' his side-kicker Joe Mitzler. She was workin' along with them the night she was on look-out outside the morgue, an' she was probably workin' along with 'em afterwards.

But for some reason or other she takes a run-out powder after I have told her an' Joe to blow outa San Francisco. Now why does she do this? She knew durn well that both these guys an' Rocca wasn't no angels outa heaven, an' you will allow that she has gotta pretty good nerve herself; therefore why is it that this dame hasta get windy an' give Joe Mitzler's hide-out away to me, like she did?

I reckon it is because she has found out somethin' that she didn't know before. Somethin' that has frightened her plenty, an' this must be a pretty tough thing because if a dame has got nerve enough to stand look-out outside a morgue where some thugs are bustin' a dead dame's face in with ice blocks, an' if she has got nerve enough to be in a Chevrolet with three thugs who are out for the express purpose of blastin' me down, then you gotta admit that she ain't likely to be frightened of spiders.

An' that is the thing I have gotta find out. I have gotta find out:
1. How Toots came inta this business.
2. Why she was stringin' along with Spigla an' Joe over the morgue business an' over tryin' to kill me.
3. Why she suddenly took a run-out powder.

But, when we get down to consider this business, we find another funny thing about Toots, an' it is this:

This dame is so burned up with Joe Mitzler that she is prepared to give away where he is hidin' out to me so's I will pull him in, but she don't make any other accusation against this guy. I mean she don't give me a lead on anything that would send this guy to the chair—which would make her really safe in the future—does she? For instance she don't write the note on the throw-out an' say: "This guy Mitzler was the guy who bumped Marella," or "This guy Mitzler was the guy who helped Rudy Spigla or Jack Rocca or whoever it might be kill Marella." She don't say anything like that an' I wonder why not.

The fact that I know that it was Joe who chucked Marella in the harbour, an' that he is the guy who called through to the Harbour Squad an' told 'em about the body, is simply due to the fact that he told me so himself at a time when he thought he was goin' to put me outa the way.

Therefore I am wonderin' if the reason that Toots didn't tell me anything else about any of these things was because she didn't know anything about 'em.

O.K. Now let's go on to somethin' else.

What about the letters in this case. The phoney letter that was written to the Director an' supposed to come from Marella an' the phoney letter that was written to Berenice an' was supposed to come from Marella. Marella didn't write either of these letters, *but some woman did,* an' that dame was the dame who was tryin' for reasons best known to herself to get a Federal Officer an' Berenice out at the Villa Rosalito at the same time. An' the fact that they got out there was something that scared Marella stiff.

So you gotta realise that when I am talkin' to Toots, an' I hope to be doin' that thing very soon, I have gotta lay out my conversation in such a way as will lead that jane to believe that I know what was goin' on that afternoon out at the Villa, so's she will fill in the missin' blanks for me. An' this is not goin' to be so easy.

After I have indulged in these ruminations I give myself a large drink of bourbon just to keep the germs away, an' ring through to the desk an' tell 'em to get me Vale Down House.

When I get through I ask for Berenice an' in about two minutes I hear this dame on the phone.

"Hey, Berenice," I tell her. "This is Lemmy Caution, an' I wanta talk to you."

I can hear her laugh. I have told you about the way she laughs before. It is so swell that there oughta be a law against it.

"Very well, Mr. Caution," she says sorta demure. "I'll wait in for you. Are you going to put me through a third degree once more?"

I grin to myself. "Maybe I am," I tell her, "but you can make up your mind about one thing, Berenice, an' that is that when I get along there I want some hard truth outa you, otherwise I am goin' to get very tough. Also," I continue, "I do not wish to hear you talk about Chinese proverbs like you did on the last time I saw you."

Her voice gets softer than it was.

"Don't you like talking about Chinese proverbs, Lemmy?" she says. "If you don't, then I won't even mention them. But, if you don't mind, there is one that I think you should know about. There is a proverb about the Blue Dragon . . ."

"Listen, Berenice," I tell her, "so far as I am concerned the Blue Dragon can go fry an egg. Me, I have got business to attend to."

"Very well, Lemmy," she says. "I merely wanted to tell you that since I saw you last I have christened you the Blue Dragon, and to me you will always be the Blue Dragon. . . ."

"Looky, lady," I tell her. "I do not care if I am the cat's pyjamas to you or any other sorta animal, but right now I am goin' to hang up an' come along because I am goin' to talk pretty serious to you, an' if I am not satisfied with what I get outa you I am goin' to pinch your old pa Lee Sam as sure as shootin', an' how do you like that?"

She sounds dead serious. "I think that would break my heart, Lemmy," she says.

"O.K., Berenice," I tell her. "If you don't want your heart broken, stick around an' talk plenty when I get up there or else . . ."

I hang up. I do not know what you guys think about Berenice Lee Sam, but I know what I think.

I think plenty.

Has this dame got what it takes? She comes inta the room wearin' a slim sorta navy blue frock that clings to her as if it liked it. She is wearin' tan silk stockin's an' navy blue kid court shoes. She has got red buttons on her frock an' a red silk scarf round her neck.

Her hair has been dressed American fashion an' if you hadn'ta been told you would think that all this dame knew about China was that they usta wear pigtails there an' go in for bangin' on gongs on the slightest provocation. She stands there lookin' at me an' smilin' that slow smile of hers, fingerin' a string of pearls she is wearin' around her throat.

I get up. "Looky, Berenice," I tell her. "You can park yourself right there in that chair an' listen to me. I am goin' to ask you a coupla questions an' you are goin' to answer 'em. If you tell the truth, you're O.K., an' if you don't then I tell you I'm goin' to telephone through for a patrol wagon, an' I'm goin' to pinch old Lee Sam an' smack him in the cooler on a sweet charge."

She sits down. She looks at me in a cold sorta way. "You're very tough, aren't you, Lemmy?" she says. "May I ask exactly which charge you would bring against my father on this occasion?"

"You may," I tell her. "If I pinch the old man I'm goin' to pinch him on somethin' that I can make stick, an' that is a charge of deliberately importin' drugs through the Customs at San Francisco, an' distributin' same in this city, an' you know what the Federal term of imprisonment that indictment can win, don'tya?"

She gets up.

"If you tried to do that, I'd kill you, Lemmy," she says, an' her voice is like ice.

"Maybe you would, an' maybe you wouldn't," I tell her, "but that's what the charge would be, an' it would be durn difficult for the old boy to prove that he didn't know it was goin' on, an' that Rudy Spigla was pullin' a fast one on him and on Thorensen."

She sighs—a sigh of relief. "So you know about that?" she says.

"I know plenty," I tell her. "You gotta realise that you are still in a spot, an' even if you did keep me outa the way of Joe Mitzler that night you got that maid of yours to give me those knock-out drops, I am still goin' to be tough with you if necessary."

She sits down again an' relaxes.

"I'll tell you anything I can, Lemmy," she says. "What do you want to know?"

"I wanta know two things," I tell her. "First of all I wanta know everything that happened out at the Villa Rosalito last Wednesday afternoon when you went out there an' saw Marella, an' the second thing I wanta know is the truth about how you got your hooks on that letter from Marella to Aylmar Thorensen—the one accusin' him of bein' your lover, because I have got an idea in my head that the last story you told me was a lotta bunk."

"You are right, Lemmy," she says, "I didn't tell you the truth then. I was afraid to, but I'll tell it now. Here it is:

"Last Wednesday when I arrived out at the Villa Marella was, apparently, amazed to see me. She pretended that she was not expecting me, asked me why I had come.

"We were standing in the hall and I was absolutely astounded at her behaviour. She looked strange too, and as if she were ill. I simply handed her the typewritten letter I had received from her in Shanghai. She looked at it and read it through, an' then looked down at a telegraph form which had slipped down behind the hall table. She bent as if to pick this form up and then changed her mind and left it lying there."

"Just a minute, Berenice," I say. "You tell me something about that letter you handed to her, the one you got from her in Shanghai. It was typewritten, wasn't it, but was the signature typewritten?"

"No," she says. "The signature was written by hand. It was signed 'Marella'."

"O.K.," I say. "Goon."

"We stood there for a minute an' then she said that we'd better go upstairs to her room. As we passed the telephone table she took off the receiver from its hook. She said that she didn't want us to be disturbed.

"When we were walking along the passage to her room I noticed that there was a silk scarf lying on the floor, an' that, inside the room, her dressing table was badly disarranged.

"Her attitude was extraordinary. It was quite obvious to me that she was trying to pump me, to draw me out about something or other. I realised this and framed my replies in such a way as to tell her nothing—not even that I didn't know what she was trying to get at. I did this because I was intrigued, curious to know what all this was about.

"Then suddenly, she said: 'I want you to understand, Berenice, that if there is any trouble; if you try to make any trouble for Aylmar or myself—if anyone tries to make any, trouble—then it will be just as serious for your father as it will be for us.'

"Needless to say I was even more amazed and a little bit frightened. I sat there and said nothing.

"Then Marella said that there was no use in discussing the situation; that if I knew the truth explanations were unnecessary and that if I didn't they were not needed. She said that she was without a maid and that it looked as if a fog were coming down and didn't I think I ought to be going back?

"I left the Villa and I was glad to leave it. I was definitely scared of the place.

"I came straight back into San Francisco and went immediately to see Aylmar Thorensen. I told him what had happened. I asked him if he could give me an explanation.

"He tried to telephone his wife but there was no reply. I said that possibly the receiver was still off the hook.

"Eventually, he told me that the only thing that he could think of that might in any way implicate my father was the fact that he and my father had been running some contraband silk cargoes through the Customs here.

"I was quite disgusted and, candidly, I did not believe him. However, I left his office and drove straight back here and saw my father. I told him what had happened and he absolutely denied the accusation. He knew nothing about it.

"It seemed to me therefore that Thorensen had deliberately told me a lie, that he had said that to cover up something else, something possibly worse. I made up my mind that I would go out again to the Villa Rosalito, and by some means or other get the truth from Marella."

"Just a minute, Berenice," I tell her. "Tell me something. You told me that when you saw Marella in the afternoon you handed her the letter—the one she sent to you in Shanghai. Did she give you that letter back?"

"No, Lemmy," she says. "I left it with her. I didn't think it mattered."

"O.K., Berenice," I say. "So you went back to the Villa, an' what happened?"

"I arrive there at about twenty minutes to nine," she says. "I rang and rang on the front bell but no one answered. Eventually I went round by the side of the house and went in through the french windows at the back. The whole place was lighted up inside—all the lights were on, but when I called I got no reply. There was, apparently, no one in the house. I went into the hall and saw that the telephone receiver was back on it's hook.

"I went upstairs but there was no one there. Finally, I went down into the kitchen. There, propped up against a tea canister on the table, I found that letter from Marella to Aylmar—the one accusing him and me of having an *affaire*."

I jump up. "Berenice, you big goop," I yell at her, "why in the name of every durn thing didn't you tell me that before? Why did you haveta tell me all that original bunk about how you got the letter?"

She smiles. "I know you suspected me of killing Marella," she says. "I couldn't very well say that I had been out there again. But, Lemmy," she goes on, "why is the fact that I found the letter in the kitchen so important?"

"Listen," I tell her, "earlier in the afternoon a note was left for me to read—a note propped up against that tea canister in the kitchen. O.K. That note was goin' to bring me back to the house at nine o'clock.

"Don't you get it?" I tell her. "When I come back at nine o'clock I was supposed to find that other letter, an' the place where I would go an' look would be the place where I saw the first note, wouldn't it? I musta come out to that place right on your heels; you musta left it not long before I got out there. I went lookin' around an' found nothin' because you'd been there first."

"Then someone faked that letter," says Berenice. "Someone, possibly the person who killed Marella, wrote that letter and left it where you would find it so as to throw suspicion on me."

I shake my head.

"No, lady," I tell her, "it ain't so easy as that. That letter was written by Marella. It was the only letter that was really written by her."

She gives a little gasp. "Then she must have been alive a little while before that?" she says. "Someone forced her to write it before . . ."

"That's what it looks like, Berenice," I tell her. "An' I am wonderin' just who that person coulda been." I give her a long cool look, an' she don't say anything. She just looks back at me.

"Well, after you found the letter what didya do?" I ask her.

"I put it in my glove and drove straight back home," she says. "I said nothing to my father. He is very old and I did not want to worry him. When I took my glove off I threw it down with the letter in it in my room. I did not treat the letter seriously. I thought it must be a fake. Afterwards, while we were at the Precinct you searched my room and found it. My maid saw you reading it."

"And down at the Precinct you advised your old pa to tell the cops that he *had* been runnin' silk. Whadya do that for?"

She shrugs her shoulders.

"I knew there was something worse," she says. "I knew something worse was being covered up. I knew that Thorensen would stick to that story and I thought for the sake of my father that it would be better if he admitted some lesser fault so that the police might possibly let the matter rest there and hot investigate further. But," she goes on with a little smile, "I was reckoning without the Blue Dragon. . . ."

"Meanin' me?" I ask her.

"Meanin' you,' she says.

She gets up an' goes an' looks outa the window. The sun is still shinin' an' I like the way it sorta glints on her hair. After a minute she turns around an' fetches me a cigarette. She brings a lighter an' lights it.

I look up at her. "Listen, Berenice," I tell her, "I reckon that I am goin' to believe you because what you say sorta matches up with what I have got somewhere in the back of my mind, but I am also allowing myself to think that maybe you are still holdin' out on me, just in case of accidents. Take a tip from me an' if you got anything else to spill you spill it, otherwise things may not be so easy for you an' that old mandarin that's you pa."

She looks straight at me. "I have told you all the truth, Lemmy," she says, "whether you believe it or not. I am not afraid of anything. The Lee Sam family are neither fools nor are they afraid."

"O.K.," I tell her, "but speakin' for myself, an' the Caution family we are sometimes mugs an' we are very often scared stiff so that don't prove anything."

She laughs. Then suddenly she goes serious. She gets a big idea.

"Lemmy," she says. "You say that the letter I found when I went back to the Villa *was* written by Marella. That it was in her handwriting and that there is no possibility that it could be a fake. Now can you explain that. Why should Marella write such a letter? Why should she make such an accusation against me who had never done her harm? You, who seem to know most things, can you explain that to me?"

I look at her an' grin.

"It looks to me, Berenice," I tell her, "that you are not very wise to some of the tricks that dames can get up to. I reckon that plenty dames have written letters accusin' their husbands of havin' a joy ride with other dames. Sometimes the letters are true an' sometimes they ain't true. If they are true O.K., an' if they ain't then you can usually look for a very good reason for the letter bein' written."

"I still don't understand," she says.

"I'm tryin' to tell you," I say. "Ain't it ever struck you that if a woman gets an idea inta her head that she's goin' to be accused of somethin' by a woman, that she thinks she will get in first an' do the accusin' herself?"

She is lookin' at me hard tryin' to understand.

"Looky, honey," I tell her. "Marella was scared when you went out to the Villa Rosalito, wasn't she? She was plenty scared. When she read that phoney letter that she was supposed to have written to you she took a look down at the telegram in the hall, the telegram that told her a "G" man would be comin' out to the house an' she was a bit more scared.

"She took you upstairs an' she tried to pump you to find out what you knew about this an' that, an' you didn't let on that you knew anything.

"O.K. Well what does she do after that? We don't know very much about what she did, but we do *know* one thing, an' that is that she wrote that letter. Well that gives us an idea, don't it? She says that if anybody tries to start some trouble she is warnin' you that she will make some trouble for old Lee Sam. In other words she is threatenin' *you,* an' then she goes off an' writes that letter to protect herself."

She sighs.

"Maybe I am very foolish," she says, "but what did Marella desire to protect herself against?"

I grin some more. "Look, honey," I tell her. "I told you just now that dames who think a woman is goin' to pull a fast one on 'em usually try to get in first. Ain't you got it?"

She looks at me. She is beginnin' to get it.

"You mean," she says, "you mean . . ."

"I mean that Marella thought that you were wise to her," I tell her, "an' so she was tryin' to get in first." I stub out my cigarette.

"Me—I am on my way," I say. "An' I am goin' to give you some orders, Berenice. You stick around this house an' you keep your nose inside it, an' don't go out. Maybe this man's town ain't goin' to he quite so safe for a day or so. When I get back I'll be seein' you."

"Are you going away, Lemmy?" she says. "Shall you be long away?"

"Maybe yes, an' maybe no," I tell her. "But I'll be seein' you even if I have gotta pair of handcuffs with me when I cometa call. So long, Berenice."

She stands there smilin'.

"I have yet to tell you the proverb about the Blue Dragon," she says. "I believe that the original Blue Dragon . . ."

"Lady," I tell her, "I am a very busy guy an' the only time that I am interested in blue dragons is when I have been hittin' the rye bottle too hard. Maybe I'll listen to that proverb some other time."

"I see," she says, sorta soft. "You do not like discussing proverbs with me. I understand very well. The only things that you find time to discuss with me are baseless accusations against my character such as the one that I was Aylmar Thorensen's mistress."

She draws herself up, an' I'm tellin' you guys she looks swell. I could eat this dame.

"There are moments when I despise all men," she says.

I grin. "Lady," I tell her, "that is just sweet hooey an' you know it, an' I can prove it."

"I don't understand you," she says, "how can you prove it?"

I don't say a thing. I just walk over to her an' prove it. She wriggles away after a bit.

"That is not the way for a Federal Officer to behave," she says with a little smile. "Now possibly, I may tell you about the Blue Dragon . . ."

I grab my hat. "Some other time, Berenice," I tell her. "Me, I got some work to do."

I scram. I leave her standin' there lookin' after me.

Dames are dizzy. You're tellin' me. Here am I tryin' to find a killer, an' this dame wants to talk about Blue Dragons.

What the hell!

CHAPTER THIRTEEN
SHOW-DOWN FOR TOOTS

I RUN inta San Diego at seven o'clock. This dump is a sailors' town, an' I usta hang around here years ago when I was on a Navy case. The Police Chief is a bozo called Kitlin—a nice guy who I reckon will do what he can for me.

I check in at a little hotel I know an' take a hot bath an' do a little ruminatin', after which I get around to Police Headquarters an' see Kitlin. This guy almost throws a fit when I bust in, an' we get around to a little spot he knows an' proceed to drink some bourbon.

"Here's the way it is," I tell him. "I getta letter from a dame I am lookin' for—a frail by the name of Toots. O.K. Well this Toots sends me a letter with the San Diego postmark on it, an' I reckon she is around here because I reckon that she had just got enough dough to get here an' when she arrives she is goin' to look for a job."

"An' what sorta job will she be lookin' for, Lemmy?" he asks.

"You search me," I tell him. "I do not know what this dame's ideas are, but I know that her shape is not so bad, an' that once on a time she was an actress out in the sticks. I reckon that she is the sorta dame that the Fleet would go for in a big way, an' if you got any dance halls where they use taxi partners around here, the sorta place that the marines use, I reckon that Toots might be stickin' around there. If she ain't there I guess we gotta try any theatre or vaudeville agencies you got here in town, or maybe you got some sorta burlesque show where she might get a job."

"O.K.," he says, "I will proceed to put the boys out on a drag-net act that will not even let a tiddler slip through. Let's get goin'."

We ease back to Headquarters an' he gets the boys to work. I got back to my hotel an' proceed to lay down on the bed an' give my self up to very deep an' serious thought.

I reckon this is one goddam case. I have had some honeys in my time but this one tops the lot. I have gotta lot of things worked out like I told you, but there are still some blanks that need fillin' in, an' whether Toots is goin' to be able to fill 'em in is, another business. After a bit I go off to sleep.

I am wakened up by the telephone goin'. It is Kitlin.

"We got your girl friend, Lemmy," he says. "One of the boys got a line on her. Of course he didn't wise her up to what was goin' on. She's workin' at the Follies Burlesque off Main at Harbour Place. She got herself a job there a coupla days ago bein' a show girl or somethin'. I reckon you can pick the dame up any time you like."

I say thanks a lot an' that I will get around there.

It is eleven o'clock when I get around to this Follies Burlesque. I ease around to the stage entrance an' walk in. I flash my badge at the guy who is lookin' after the office an' he goes an' gets me the stage manager. I tell him what I want an' he don't seem very surprised. Maybe he is usta havin' his show-girls pinched now an' again.

I go along the passage with this guy an' in a minute we are on the side of the stage. Some dame is just finishin' a number an' the curtain comes down as we get inta the prompt corner. I look over on the other side of the stage an' there in a pair of black silk tights is my little friend Toots, the blonde baby.

"Hi'yah, Toots," I tell her. "I been sorta lookin' for you."

She looks at me. Her eyes go sorta heavy an' sad as if she knew that this time the works are bust properly.

"Jeez," she says, "so I couldn't shake you after all. I sorta hoped I'd got you ditched." She gives a big sigh. "An' where do we go from here?" she says.

"You go an' get your street clothes on, Toots," I tell her, "an' draw anything you got comin' from the manager. After which you an' me will go an' take some hot groceries together an' talk a whole lotta sense." .

"O.K.," she says, but she looks kinda wilted.

I stick around while she is changin' an' gettin' her dough from the guy who runs this place. He don't really want to pay her because he says she is walkin' out on him, but after I have explained the difference between a chorine walkin' out an' bein' pinched, an' requested as to whether he would like a smack on the kisser, this guy decides to pay up.

Outside I get a cab an' we drive down to the Arbola Café. Toots don't say a word. When we are inside the café an' sittin' down she looks at me with a mean sorta smile. I told you before that this dame wasn't bad lookin' except that she is tired the whole time.

"So you finally caught up with me," she says. "An' how do we play it from here?"

I order her a man size steak—medium rare with a lotta side dishes an' one for myself. She also manages to suck down a double shot of rye, after which she seems a bit more like her old self.

"Looky, Toots," I tell her. "You're in bad an' you know it. Just how you are goin' to come outa this business I don't know. In fact," I go on, "if anybody was to ask me to lay a bet as to whether you will do not less that two an' not more than five years in the pen, whether they will give you a sweet twenty year stretch, whether they decide to hand you a natural life sentence or whether they will give you the hot seat . . . well, I would not take the bet."

I look at her kinda grim. "You gotta realise," I tell her, "that you are helpin' yourself or otherwise from now on. If I was you I would talk fast an' plenty."

"Yeah," she says, "that's what you say, sailor, but I have had guys tried to stand me up for a big bluff before, although I oughta say that I appreciate this steak which is kinda nice when a girl ain't been eatin' too regular."

"I'm glad you like it," I say. "I usta know a dame in Wichita, when I was stickin' around there in an Investigation Division up there. This dame was plenty smart an' she had a whole lotta brains—just like you. In fact what with her brains an' the fact that she had sweet curves an' was easy to glance at, she thought she was doin' fine. O.K. Well she gets herself mixed up in a murder rap. She didn't do it, but she was sorta stickin' around when it happened—if you get my meanin'.

"Well, to cutta long story off short, this dame gets pulled in an' questioned, an' she starts bein' clever. She sorta deliberately mixes things up an' she thinks she is doin' fine an' keepin' her boy friend—the guy who did the bumpin' off act—outa this business.

"But she don't get no place. This dame is so clever that she manages to build up a fine bunch of circumstantial evidence against herself, which is funny when you come to think of it, especially as the Court sorta accepted it an' sent her to the chair. So the joke was on her."

"Oh boy," she says, "you're gettin' me scared."

She laughs an' grabs off some more french fried.'

"Whadya wanta know?" she says.

She looks over at me in a leery sorta way. I reckon this dame has still got her wits about her an' that if I make a slip-up she will just wriggle outa tellin' me what I wanta know by some way or other. This Toots has got a certain amount of low cunnin'.

"I wanta know plenty, Toots," I tell her. "First of all I'm goin' to ask you one or two questions, an' if you are bein' advised by me you are goin' to answer 'em just as if you was on oath, an' you ain't goin' to make any mistakes neither."

She looks at me an' grins.

"Otherwise I get railroaded for killin' Marella, eh?" she says, "That's the idea, ain't it?"

"Maybe it is, baby," I tell her, "an' maybe it wouldn't be rail-roadin' you either. If you didn't do it you know who did."

I give her the mustard.

"O.K., Toots," I tell her. "Now let's get down to cases. You tell me this: When did you know first of all that Marella was havin' an affair with Rudy Spigla? Was it about six or seven months ago?"

"That's about it," she says, "it was about six months ago. An' how did you know?"

I reckon that Toots is bein' fresh to ask me questions. But I think that I might as well tell her just so's she will know that I am plenty wise about this business.

"Nellie the cook out at the Villa usta see Rudy comin' out there," I tell her. "I knew durn well that he never went out there to see Thorensen. He went out there to see Marella, an' she used to send Nellie out in the afternoons an' leave the french windows open at the back so's Rudy could get in nice an' quiet. Another thing she gave Rudy that seal ring of hers—the one with the crossed keys on it. I knew she *gave* it to him when Nellie told me that she was a dame who usta raise hell if anything was missin', an' that she didn't raise hell about missin' that ring.

"It's a funny thing," I go on, "to think of a swell dame like Marella havin' anythin' to do with a lousy heel like Rudy. But Rudy had got somethin', hadn't he, Toots? That guy had got a certain appeal an' I reckon it went over big with a neglected dame like Marella who was as lonely as any dame could be."

She nods. Her mouth is full of steak.

"Also," I go on, "there was another little thing between Marella an' Rudy. There was that little matter of dope takin' that the dirty heel got her started on. An' afterwards he usta supply her with the stuff. I reckon that Rudy had got Marella where he wanted her all right."

She looks at me again an' grins. "You're a smart dick, ain't you, Lemmy?" she says. "If it ain't rude how didya know that he was givin' her drugs?"

I grin back at her. "Work it out for yourself, Toots," I tell her. "I took a look around his apartment. On the wall there is a picture of some dame an' she had written on it: 'To Rudy who gave me such sweet sleep, such sweet dreams.' Well, I knew the answer to that one. I reckoned that the sweet sleep that Rudy usta give this dame was narcotics an' that he'd been playin' the same game with Marella."

"Dead right," she says, "an' what else didya find out, copper?"

I look at her. "You mean you ain't talkin' until you sorta found out how much I know, hey?" I ask her.

She nods all brightly.

"I ain't puttin' my fanny in the electric chair without bein' pushed there," she says. "I'm talkin' when I see I gotta talk an' not before."

I laugh an' order her some more rye.

"O.K., Toots," I say. "I will now proceed to show you that the best thing you can do is to talk—that is if you wanta save your own carcass.

"About two three months ago some dame gets wise to the Rudy Spigla-Marella set-up," I tell her. "An' this dame thinks out a sweet idea. I reckon she thought she had got Rudy just where she wanted him. She had him all ends up. She knows durn well that he has been runnin' dope inta San Francisco in the contra-band silk cargoes that he has been bringin' in. She knows durn well that he has got Thorensen workin' with him, but that Thorensen didn't know about the drug part of it, an' she knows durn well that if Jack Rocca was to find out that his side-kicker Rudy had been double-crossin' him he would hand Rudy a pay-off outa the end of a hand-gun.

"I'm tellin' you that this dame was as wise as they come. She knows that Thorensen is fed up with his wife, that he wants to get away from her an' that he has fixed to get out to Los Angeles, an' also that he is makin' a financial settlement on Marella, an' she probably makes a sweet guess that Marella bein' so thick with Rudy probably knows about what he has been doin' in the drug importin' line. You got all that?"

She looks at me old-fashioned. "I got it, sailor," she says. "Tell me more. I am just burstin' with a big curiosity."

"O.K.," I tell her. "Well, this dame comes to the conclusion that the time has come when she is goin' to stand Rudy and Marella up for plenty. She reckons that she is goin' to blackmail the pants off those two. But she is plenty scared of Rudy because she knows Rudy would give her the heat as soon as look at her.

"So she thinks of a sweet idea. She probably writes Rudy a letter—this dame is fond of writin' letters—an' tells him that he has got just so long to kick in with a bundle of dough otherwise she is goin' to make plenty trouble for him. Well, it looks as if Rudy don't fall for this, so this dame proceeds to put into action a very swell little scheme. This is what she does:

"She types a letter to Berenice Lee Sam who is in Shanghai an' she tells Berenice that it is essential an' urgent that she should come back to San Francisco an' go out to the Villa Rosalito between four an' five on the 10th January. She signs this letter 'Marella' an' sends it off by air mail.

"Then she gets some notepaper printed with the address of the Villa Rosalito on it, an' she sits down an' writes a letter to the Director of the Bureau of Investigation, an' tells him that she has got some information about some mysterious Federal offences that are goin' on. She says that if he don't hear from her within the next few days he is to send a 'G' man down on the 10th—the same day as Berenice will be arrivin'. She signs this letter 'Marella Thorensen' too.

"Now this is clever stuff, ain't it? This blackmailin' dame knows that the Director will send back a formal acknowledgement form an' that Marella will get it an' will go running to, Rudy Spigla to ask him what it means. The dame reckons that Rudy will start gettin' scared. Maybe though she was wrong there.

"O.K. She is now sittin' pretty, ain't she? She now proceeds to stick around until the mornin' of the 10th January—five days ago—an' then she proceeds to ring up Rudy Spigla an' tell him this:

"That either he comes across with the dough or else . . . She tells him that a 'G' mem will be goin' out to the Villa Rosalito that afternoon, that Berenice Lee Sam will be goin' out there too, an' that unless he comes across with the dough she is goin' to be there too. She says she is goin' to blow the works to the 'G' man about Rudy havin' been runnin' drugs an' contraband for years, an' that she is goin' to tell Berenice Lee Sam that Marella is Rudy Spigla's mistress, that Thorensen her husband knows it an' is afraid to do anything about it, an' that that bein' so he is not the sorta guy who is fit to handle her father's business.

"She asks Rudy just whether he is goin' to stand for all that or whether he is goin' to pay up."

I stop talkin' an' I look at her.

"It is a cinch that the dame who wrote those letters was the dame who rubbed out Marella," I tell her. "Anyhow that is my story an' I'm goin' to make it stick."

She puts down her knife an' fork. "You got any idea who this dame is?" she asks. "The one who wrote them letters?"

"Yeah," I tell her. "I know who the dame is. You are the dame."

She sorta smiles again. "Can you prove it?" she says.

"Sure I can," I tell her. "It was you who sent me that throw-out bill about Oklahoma Joe's flop house, an' it was you who wrote the message along the side of it sayin' that Joe Mitzler was hidin' out there, because Joe Mitzler identified your handwritin'. You been gettin' pretty scared of Joe lately, ain'tya, Toots? I reckon you thought he would fix you plenty if he got his hooks on you so you aimed for me to pinch him, which is just what I have done.

"O.K. Well I checked up that handwritin' with the handwritin' in the original letter that was sent to the Director an' it was the same. You are the dame who wrote that letter, an' I reckon that when I get my hooks on the typewritten letter that Berenice got in Shanghai I shall find that the signature was written by you too."

She grins at me. "Maybe you won't find that letter," she says.

"How do you know?" I ask her. I lean across the table "That is," I go on, "unless you destroyed it when you killed Marella, *because she had that letter last*. Berenice Lee Sam give it to her an' didn't take it back."

She bites her lips. I reckon she thinks she has said a bit too much. She is beginnin' to look pretty scared too.

"Look, Toots," I tell her. "Why don't you be your age? Why don't you come across with the truth. You know that you wrote them letters for somebody else. Somebody else was goin' to have the lion's share of the dough, wasn't they? Ain't you goin' to be the little mug if you let yourself get pinched an' face a murder rap for somethin' that somebody else mighta done?"

"Meanin' who?" she says.

"Meanin' Effie," I tell her, "the dame who wrote a letter to Rudy Spigla that I found in his safe. The dame who said that she was goin' to lay off houndin' him an' thanked him for the dough. . . ."

I am watchin' her like a cat an' I reckon I am on the right line. I see her lips tremble an' her eyes begin to blaze a bit like she was durned angry at somethin' she is thinkin'. I think I will chance my arm.

"Too bad, Toots, wasn't it?" I tell her. When after you done all that dirty work for Effie, the lousy moll collects the dough from Rudy an' gives you the air, an' not only gives you the air but spills the beans about you to Rudy—tells Rudy how you wrote the letters for her an' then scrams off leavin' you to stand up to Rudy Spigla, who proceeds, when he has found all this out, to put Joe Mitzler on your track, which is what made you scram out here to San Diego.

"Be your age, baby," I tell her. "Save as much of your own skin as you can. Talk, Toots!"

She looks up at me an' her eyes are blazin'.

"Jeez, I will!" she says. "That dirty heel Effie took a run-out powder on me an' left me to carry the bag after all I done for her. That was sweet thanks. O.K. Well I'm goin' to get myself out as best I can an' if you catch up with her an' she gets the chair I reckon she's asked for it. Me, I wouldn't squeal on anybody, but I reckon I'm entitled to sing about that yellow twicin' moll."

She swallows her drink at a gulp. "O.K.," she says. "Here's where I blow the works on Effie."

I light myself a cigarette. "Effie who?" I ask her, sorta casual. "How did she spell her second name?" I put it this way, because I am tryin' to make out that I already know what this second name is.

She looks at me with a grin.

"The name is Effie Spigla," she says. "The dame who killed Marella was Rudy Spigla's wife."

I peek up. I reckon we are goin' to get some place now. I call the waiter an' pay the check.

She gets up. This frail don't look so good. She looks just about all in. She looks as if she can already see herself inside the pen an' she don't sorta like the idea.

"What the hell . . ." she says as we walk out. "An' where do we go from here?"

"Let's take a little cab ride," I tell her. "Let's get around to the local 'G' office an' see if we can find a stenographer who can write your language."

Office of the Unit of Investigation,
Bureau of Investigation,
Department of Justice,
San Diego, California.
1.30 a.m. 16th January, 1937.

This is a statement taken from Marian (Toots) Frenzer at the request of Special Agent Lemuel H. Caution of the Bureau of Investigation, Washington, by me, Arthur Clay Meddoes, Stenographer-Agent of the Unit of Investigation, San Diego, and I certify that it is a true transcript of the shorthand notes written by me verbatim from the statement of the said Marian (Toots) Frenzer.

(Signed) Arthur Clay Meddoes, Special Agent.

My name is Marian Frenzer and I have always been called Toots. I was born at Medola near Kansas City and I am thirty three years of age.

When I got the chance I was an actress, other times I worked the dance halls and got around generally. I have had some pretty tough times too I'm telling you.

About twelve months ago I met up with a dame called Effie Spigla in Chicago. She was a hot momma I'm telling you. I reckon that this dame was as tough as they come and I've seen plenty and know.

I was right on the floor at this time not having had a job for four months and I got myself a job as a taxi-dancer at the Lily of Spain Dance Hall, where I met Effie Spigla. I stayed around there working for some time. She was working there too and finally we roomed together at a rooming house near North Clark Street.

We was both not very pleased with life and game for anything that would make us some dough.

One night when Effie had been hittin' the bottle a bit hard she told me that she had got some news and that if I liked to play along with her she could show me how to make a whole bundle of jack for the pair of us. I said that I would try anything once and maybe twice if I liked it, and she told me that she had got a line on her husband—a guy called Rudy Spigla—who was a big-time mobster but who had chucked the rackets and gone out to San Francisco with another mobster that he used to work for called Jack Rocca.

Effie said that this Jack Rocca was running dance clubs and protection rackets in San Francisco but that she had heard that he was not doing anything very big in that way, but was trying to keep his nose clean with the cops and that he also had a big trucking business and that Rudy Spigla was his manager and working on what was for him pretty small time dough.

She said that she knew Rudy better than her foot and that lie couldn't play straight with anybody even if somebody paid him to do it, and that she would bet her only brassière that was right then at the laundry because she couldn't pay for it, that Rudy would get up to some racket in San Francisco and that she reckoned he would do it in a big way.

She told me that one of his games in the old days was to find a classy dame who was at odds with her husband and get this dame sniffing cocaine or taking morphia or heroin, and that when the dame was a sucker for the stuff Rudy would charge her plenty for supplies and would get information from her about her friends or anything else that would put him where he could work the black on anybody. She said that Rudy was the last word in dope peddling but that he never touched the stuff himself. She also said that he was a wow with dames and that he had got something that made them fall for him like a sack of old coke.

She said that if she went to San Francisco and stuck around to see what Rudy was at he would smell a rat and that he would just as soon blow the top of her head off as look at her. She said that he had already taken a shot at her two years before and she showed me where the bullet went in and came out.

She said that the idea was that I ought to go to San Francisco and stick around and get a line on what Rudy was up to. She said that if he was up to his usual games we might be able

to stick him for some dough otherwise we would blow the works
and get him pinched.

I said all right, I would do it, because life was not very happy
at the time for either of us. So the next evening Effie gets a dancing
partner—an old guy—down at the Lily of Spain and takes him to
Sam Slipner's old joint and gives him plenty to drink. She rolls
him afterwards for everything he has got and next morning she
gives me one hundred twenty dollars and tells me to get myself
a suit and a water wave and beat it for San Francisco. That she
will stick around and wait until she hears something from me.

I went to San Francisco and stuck around for a couple of
weeks seeing how things were. After that some guy I met up
with took me along to The Two Moons Club which was owned
by Jack Rocca and introduced me to Rudy Spigla. I asked Rudy
to give me a job and he gave me a job first of all on the floor as
a partner and afterwards in the women's cloakroom.

After a couple of months I got wise to the fact that Rudy was
up to something and that the guy who was working in with him
was a guy called Joe Mitzler, an ugly gorilla, who used to work
around The Two Moons as a bouncer and general strong-arm
man. I made a big play for Joe Mitzler and he fell with a bump.
I got right next to this guy and learned plenty from him. After
a bit he not only trusted me plenty but also told Spigla that I
was all right and Rudy was not so careful when I was around.

After a few months I was wise to the whole set-up and I got
on to Effie on the long-distance and told her that I reckoned that
the time was ripe to pull something. I told her what I knew about
what was going on and she said lay off everything she would
come out to San Francisco and stay under cover and wise me
up to the way we would play it.

Effie blew into San Francisco in the middle of December and
I slipped off one afternoon and saw her in the dump where she
was going to stick under cover. I told her what Rudy was doing
which was this:

Rudy was bringing drugs into San Francisco and doing a
sweet business. He was cleaning up with both hands. He was
able to do this by bringing in the stuff in silk cargoes which were

being handled by the Jack Rocca Trucking Corporation for Lee Sam the silk merchant.

Rudy had also made a big play for Marella Thorensen who was the wife of Lee Sam's attorney. This Marella had fell with a bump for Rudy's line and he had pulled his old dope stuff on her and introduced her to cocaine and morphia. She was mad stuck on him although whether it was all him or him and the dope I don't know.

Thorensen was wise to what was going on but Rudy had got something on him and he had to like it. He didn't care about his wife anyhow and it looked like he was going to move over to Los Angeles. I reckon he was getting scared.

I told Effie that Rudy was going to make a big play. Directly Thorensen was gone he was going to clean up and get out. He had made plenty and Thorensen who was leaving his wife was making a settlement on her. Rudy's idea was to scram out of San Francisco with Marella Thorensen directly Thorensen went, and directly Rudy got his next drug cargo in and distributed. The distribution of this stuff was done by a guy called Oklahoma Joe who was working for Rudy and Joe Mitzler.

Effie done some heavy thinking and then she got a swell set-up. The idea was to make things so hot for Rudy that he would have to pay plenty and yet fix it so that Effie and me were safe. She told me what her idea was.

I was to type a letter to Lee Sam's daughter Berenice and send it to her in Shanghai where she was having a vacation. This letter was supposed to come from Marella and said that it was a matter of life and death that Berenice Lee Sam should come back to San Francisco so as to arrive on the afternoon of the 10th January and go up and see Marella who would be waiting for her. Berenice wasn't to say anything to anybody about this. It had to be kept secret.

I wrote this letter on a typewriter we got and signed it "Marella." We looked up the right words in a dictionary.

I then wrote another letter to the Director of the Bureau of Investigation saying that there was some funny business going on but not saying what it was. Effie's idea was this: That if Rudy didn't agree to pay up we would send the letters and then tell him what had been done.

When I got the letters written Effie called through on the telephone to Rudy at the Club. I was sticking around in his office when she done it. Effie put on a false voice and told Rudy that unless he kicked in with twenty thousand dollars she was going to make plenty trouble for him and she didn't mean perhaps. Rudy told her that people had tried to bluff him like that before and that so far as he was concerned she could go and jump in the lake.

Next day I eased off in the afternoon and saw Effie. She said O.K. we would send the letters. We got them off that afternoon.

On the 10th January I rung through to Joe Mitzler and told him I had got a rotten sore throat and was goin' to see the doctor. He said O.K. I went around to Effie and we got busy.

Effie called through to Rudy at his apartment and told him who she was. He nearly had a fit. Effie told him that she had fixed it that Berenice Lee Sam would be going out to see Marella that afternoon in about an hour's time. She also told him that the Director of the Federal Bureau had had a letter and was sending a "G" man out there to find out what was happening. Effie said that if Rudy didn't kick in right away with the dough she was going out to the Villa to see Marella, Berenice and the "G" man, and she was going to blow the works. She said she was going to tell Berenice what Rudy had been at with Thorensen's wife, that Thorensen and him had been running silk and that Thorensen hadn't got any right to be attorney for her father. She was going to tell the "G" man about Rudy's drug business an' how he had been dopin' Marella so as to make a getaway with her directly she got her hooks on the dough that Thorensen was going to make over to her. In fact Effie told him that she was going to make plenty trouble for him.

Rudy threw his hand in. She said he would kick in with the twenty thousand, but if Effie was speakin' the truth it didn't look as if there was time for him to get the dough to her before Berenice and the Federal man got busy at the Villa.

Effie said she could tell him how to do that. She said that the thing for him to do was to get the money and hand it over to her directly he had got it and that in the meantime Marella could stall the "G" man by going out and leaving a note that she would be back at nine o'clock.

Effie said that Marella could stall off Berenice Lee Sam some way or other, she didn't give a continental how, and that unless Rudy kicked in with the dough she would go out to the Villa Rosalito and blow the works.

Rudy said that he would have the dough by eight o'clock that night, but that it would take him until then to get it. Effie said all right, and that if he handed the dough over to her then she would tell him just how he could still straighten out everything and be O.K.

I will tell you what she meant by this. Her idea was that when she had got the money from Rudy she would tell him that it would be easy for him to show Marella how she could make things O.K. with the "G" man. Effie was going to tell him that if the "G" man would take a look at the handwriting in the letter to the Director he would see that it wasn't in Marella's handwriting at all, and that the letter to Berenice was typed and the signature was in the same phoney handwriting. So Marella could say that somebody had been playing a joke on her and nobody would be any the wiser.

But she wasn't going to tell Rudy this part of the game until she had got the dough.

I stuck around. I wasn't going back to The Two Moons Club for anybody. I reckoned that if Rudy found out that I was the one who had given the low-down about him to Effie he would have bumped me off there and then. Effie said I was right, that I was to stick around, and that when she had collected the dough and wised Rudy up as to how he could keep his nose clean she would come back and give me my cut and I could scram off where I liked. This made me feel plenty happy. The idea of having ten thousand bucks was a very sweet one, but I wanted to put plenty space between me and Rudy, just in case he got any ideas about me.

About seven o'clock Effie gets ready to go. She takes with her a little .22 gun that Spigla give her years ago, just in case of accidents, and she goes off to see Rudy and collect the dough.

She tells me to wait and that she will come back to give me my cut, but at the time I had a sort of idea in my head that she would take a run out on me which is what she did do.

I stick around and I wait and I wait. But she don't come back. At ten o'clock Joe Mitzler comes around and proceeds to bust me about so that I thought I would never sit down again. That guy nearly killed me with a belt that he used on me.

I found out what had happened. Effie turned up and met Rudy and Joe, and Rudy paid over the dough to her. Rudy is a bit steamed up with the way she has done him in the eye, but he is more worried about this "G" man business and about Berenice Lee Sam getting wise. He says that the "G" man will be going back to the Villa at nine o'clock, Marella having been told on the telephone to stall this guy until then, and that there has got to be some story for him that will put things right.

Effie says he shouldn't worry and that she will go out and tell Marella what to say to this guy when he comes back, about the letter to the Director not having been written by Marella at all and proving this by the handwriting.

Rudy is interested and asks who did write the letter, and Effie, who is feeling good at having got the dough, proceeds to tell Rudy how clever she is and that it was me who wrote the letters and who got the low-down on him for her.

Joe Mitzler tells me that then Effie goes off and goes out to the Villa to wise Marella up on the way to handle the situation, and apparently Marella is having one of her dope jags and gets very rude to Effie. Effie who has had a couple of drinks on the way out comes back with some nasty cracks at Marella, and these dames have a right royal set-to, as a result of which Effie pulls the little gun that she has got with her and shoots Marella.

This sobers her up plenty. She then rings through to Rudy and tells him what the set-up is and that he had better find a way out of it for her or else, and Rudy then sends Joe Mitzler out pronto, and Joe brings Marella's body back to San Francisco and throws it in the Harbour like Rudy told him.

Rudy is pretty burned up at having his little ideas messed up like this but there it is.

Joe then tells me to get my things on and takes me round to Rudy's dump, where Rudy is plenty rude to me. He tells me that I have cost him twenty grand and that he is going to make me pay one way or another. He says that I am to stick around with Joe Mitzler all the time, and that Joe has instructions from him to give me a bullet in the dome any time it looks like I am being funny.

Later that night Joe makes me stand look-out outside the morgue while they are doing a big act to try to get the bullet out of Marella's head, because Rudy has remembered that the gun that Effie shot Marella with is one that he gave her himself and he reckons that this gun may sort of make it look as if he did the bumping off.

Later that night Joe sticks me in a Chevrolet that is hanging around tailing after Mr. Caution and tells me that I am to point out this Caution to the boys in the car who will fix him because it looks as if he knows a little bit too much.

Next day, after Caution has told Joe and me to scram out of San Francisco, Joe takes me round to Oklahoma Joe's place to hide out. He tells me that Effie was laughing her head off at having played me for a sucker, and that she has scrammed off to Chicago with Rudy's twenty thousand, and that Rudy is so steamed up at having his idea of taking Marella for her dough all bust up that he will very likely bump me any time he sees me.

I sort of get the idea in my head that Rudy and Joe are only keeping me around until this Marella Thorensen killing blows over and that they will then proceed to give me the works. So I make up my mind that I will scram as soon as I get the chance.

I manage to pinch fifty bucks out of Joe's wallet, and get out of Oklahoma Joe's by the window. I come straight out to San Diego and when I get there it will be a good idea if I get somebody to take care of Joe Mitzler otherwise he will certainly shoot me any time he sees me from now on. So I take a throw-out that I picked up in Oklahoma Joe's place and write a message on it and send

it to the Caution guy, which wasn't so clever really because if I
hadn't done this I would not have been picked up myself.
     This is all I know.

                                    (Signed) Marian Frenzer.

CHAPTER FOURTEEN
RUDY

IT IS a swell evenin'. There is a little breeze an' it is plenty cold,
but me, I never did mind cold. Rain is the thing that I do not like.
Rain is sorta wet.

Brendy an' O'Halloran are sittin' on the other side of my room
at the Sir Francis Drake. They have already finished off one bottle
of rye an' are sorta lookin' at me like they think I might order
up another, but I don't say a word. These babies can drink, but
maybe you have guessed at that.

"What time didya bring the dame over, Lemmy?" says O'Halloran. "Me, I woulda liked to have had another look at Toots
before they slammed her in the can. That baby ain't no chicken
I'm tellin' you. When you told me about her before I got the idea
that the dame had brains."

"Yeah?" says Brendy, "an' how would you know about brains
anyway? Lemmy brought her over from San Diego last night,
an' how he could force himself to travel with such a bad wicked
woman is probably more than I will ever work out. Also," he
goes on, "the language that this dame uses when she finds that
she is goin' to get stuck in the cooler woulda surprised even my
wife. No, Sir, I reckon that baby thought that just because she
had come across with a statement that she was goin' to get away
with it. Hey Lemmy?"

"Listen, brain trust," I tell him, "if some of you guys will just
keep yourselves nice an' quiet I will be very glad, just so's I can
do a little quiet thinkin'."

"An' what the hell do you haveta think about?" says O'Halloran.
"You got this case in the bag. You are the big 'G' man, ain'tya?
You are the guy who solved the Marella Thorensen murder an'

172 | PETER CHEYNEY

all you gotta do now is to write yourself out a long report to the Federal Government all about the wicked Rudy Spigla an' the drug runnin' that has been goin' on, an' you will probably find that they will make you an admiral or somethin', leavin' Brendy an' me here to go find this lousy Effie Spigla wherever that hot pertater may be hidin' herself out."

He lights up that smoke wagon he calls a pipe.

"I wonder what Effie is like?" he says. "I would like to arrest that dame an' find that she was as lovely as a pair of angels. Just as I would be goin' to slam the handcuffs on her she turns to me an' she says to me with tears in her voice—'Terry O'Halloran,' she says, 'you are the only guy for me. I would do anythin' for you. I would even . . .'"

"Yeah," says Brendy. "An' then you would wake up an' find yourself sleepin' on one ear. Any guy who is goin' to pinch Effie will haveta have brains—a guy like me."

"Turn it off, youse two," I tell 'em, "an' listen to me for a minute. Brendy, you tell me somethin'. When you smacked Rudy in the cooler after the raid did that guy know that we had picked up the truck with the drugs in it?"

"He did not," says Brendy, "an' I ain't seen any reason to tell him about same."

"O.K.," I say, "an' he ain't seen anybody since he's been in the cooler—not even a lawyer, hey?"

"He ain't seen a goddam soul," says Brendy. "An' Rocca ain't seen anybody either. I slammed them two babies into a coupla of single cells an' wished 'em a sweet good-evenin', since when they have been communin' with their souls."

"That's fine," I tell him. "Now listen, Brendy," I go on. "Here's what you are goin' to do. If Spigla don't know anything about our havin' found that drug convoy of his, an' he don't know anything about my havin' pinched Toots an' got that statement outa her, then I reckon he is still sorta blissfully unconscious about the things that really matter around here. So here's what you can do. You take yourself down to the Precinct an' spring Rocca—let that baby out."

"What?" shrieks Brendy. "You're goin' to let that hoodlum out after all the trouble we took pinchin' him an' raidin' all them dumps of his?"

"Are you goin' to do what I say or am I goin' to give you a bust on the snozzle?" I ask him. "You scram outa here an' let Rocca out. You tell him that you raided them places of his on false information, an' that you ain't found a thing an' that he can forget about it an' scram. You got that?"

"I got it, Lemmy," he says, "but . . ."

"Button it up," I tell him. "Ain't you silly palookas wise to the fact yet that Rocca didn't know anything about them drugs. Get wise to yourselves, an' you get along to that cooler pronto an' spring Rocca like I said. Me, I will be along in an hour. I wanta talk to my little friend Rudy Spigla. Scram, turtles."

They scram. You will realise by what Brendy has been sayin' that I have not wised these boys up to all that I know. An' why should I?

I call down to the office an' tell them to get me Vale Down House. Pretty soon I get through to Berenice.

"How're you makin' out, Princess?" I ask her. "How is the Very Deep an' Very Beautiful Stream. Me, I am just ringin' up to find out if you are still all in one piece."

"I'm very well, thank you, Lemmy," she says. "I hope you are too. Possibly if you have time, you may decide to come here for dinner one evening."

I grin to myself.

"Maybe the next time you see me I will come up with handcuffs for the whole durn Lee Sam family," I tell her. "Stick around, Berenice, I'll be seein' you." I hang up.

I walk up an' down my room an' I do some nice quiet thinkin'. I am thinkin' that that was a very swell statement that I got from Toots. That statement is goin' to help plenty. But there are one or two things that I can't sorta square up in my mind. I will tell you what they are:

I reckon that if Berenice Lee Sam went into San Francisco to see Thorensen at seven o'clock, after the show-down she had with Marella out at the Villa, an' then went around an' had a chin with her old man about her talk with Thorensen and then went back to the Villa to have another talk with Marella, she musta been out at the Villa the second time at about eight forty-five. I am pretty sure of this because you will remember that I telephoned through to Terry from the Villa when I was out there the second time, an' he told me that Berenice Lee Sam was at home then. It musta taken her a good half-hour to have got home.

O.K. I got out to the Villa at nine o'clock an' the letter from Marella to Thorensen was gone, an' it had been taken by Berenice like she said, so that checks the time from another angle.

O.K. Well it looks like Effie Spigla musta got out to the Villa somewhere about a quarter-past seven if she was to have a helluva row with Marella before she bumped her off. After which she has to ring through to Rudy an' get him to send Joe Mitzler out to pick up Marella's body an' take it off to the Harbour.

It just shows you how funny life can be, don't it? Here are five people rushin' around the Villa Rosalito all tryin' to get the low-down on each other, an' not one of these goddam people see each other at all. Funny, ain't it?

Just get the set-up. An' hold your breath in case you get sorta raddled.

Caution arrives at the Villa Rosalito the first time at about four o'clock. He goes after a bit an' sees Berenice arrive. Berenice has one helluva talk with Marella an' then drives inta San Francisco an' sees Thorensen at seven o'clock.

Thorensen telephones through to the Villa to ask Marella what the hell it is all about an' he can't get no reply because (Berenice says) the telephone receiver is off the hook. Berenice leaves Thorensen an' goes home an' has a pow-wow with her old pa an' then decides to scram out to the Villa an' have another showdown with Marella.

At about the time that Berenice is talkin' to her old man, Effie Spigla is seein' Rudy at his place an' collectin' the dough. She is tellin' him that she will go out an' see Marella an' wise her up about what she is to say to Caution when he goes back. So that hadta be well before nine o'clock, because that is the time that Caution is goin' back there.

So it looks as if the talk that Effie had with Rudy musta been a pretty concentrated sorta affair.

O.K. Well Effie scrams off an' probably drives herself over to the Villa in a hired car. Just about this time Caution is goin' back to the Villa for the second time an' so is Berenice Lee Sam.

O.K. In the meantime Marella has been doin' some heavy thinkin' an' has written that letter to Aylmar Thorensen an' stuck it up against the tea canister in the kitchen just so's she can pull a fast one on Berenice if Berenice knows too much about her. But just how she was to know what Berenice knew or didn't know is something that I can't say, because she ain't seen anybody at all since Berenice Lee Sam left, that is unless she has got through to Rudy or somebody on the telephone. She musta done this.

O.K. So Marella sticks the letter up against the canister an' just about then maybe Effie Spigla arrives, an' these two dames proceed to have a right royal schmozzle. Effie finally pulls her little gun an' gives Marella one in the eye, after which Effie gets the breeze up an' proceeds to telephone through to Rudy Spigla an' tell him that she has mixed things up plenty by killin' Marella an' what the hell is he goin' to do about it?

Rudy says O.K. he will send Joe out an' Joe will collect what is left of Marella an' dump same in the harbour.

Well it is a cinch that Berenice got out there first and grabbed hold of the letter that was stuck against the canister an' then got away before Joe Mitzler arrived. An' she must have also got away before Caution arrived because the letter wasn't there when he got there.

So it looks to me that Caution, Effie, Joe Mitzler an' Berenice Lee Sam was all runnin' around that Villa Rosalito dump, treadin' on each other's toes almost, as you might say, an' just missin' each other by split minutes. Sweet work—you're tellin' me.

O.K. Well after that Berenice goes home, an' gets there by nine fifteen. An' Joe Mitzler gets back in time to show up at The Two Moons Club an' get instructions from Rudy later in the evenin' about lookin' after me an' tryin' to fill me with lead, an' Caution sticks around until about nine fifteen an' then he goes back to his hotel, an' Effie Spigla has got away in time to bust outa San

Francisco an' to write an' post a letter to Rudy from San Francisco Central with the nine-thirty postmark on it before she scrammed inta the railroad depot next door before she took a big run-out powder on the whole durn lot of us—an' I think she was a very wise dame too. An' what do you think?

All this is swell, but even if it does seem a very hot thing to you, I am not takin' too much notice of it. Because it really don't matter. An' the reason that it don't matter so much to me is this; that I have got somethin' which I think is very much more important an' I will tell you what it is.

I believe that Toots was tellin' the truth as much as she knew it when she made that statement at San Diego. O.K. Well if that is so then we have got one big fact that is important.

It is that Marella musta written that letter to Aylmar Thorensen after Berenice had left the Villa the first time. This letter was written in Sea Island ink, wasn't it? The letter that I found in Rudy's safe, the one from Effie sayin' thank you for the dough an' that she would now stop houndin' him, was also written in Sea Island ink. This may be one of them coincidences you read about but I somehow don't believe in coincidences.

Effie Spigla's letter to Rudy was written after she had got the dough, an' after she had left Rudy an' was thinkin' about gettin' out of San Francisco as quick as she could, but even so it looks to me as if them two letters was written in the same place *an' with the same fountain pen.* It's a sweet mystery, ain't it.

Right at the back of my head I have got a slim sorta idea that with a bit of luck I can maybe get to the bottom of this business. I got an idea but if I do it I have gotta take a chance. Well, I have taken chances before. Maybe I will take another one.

Rudy sits in the corner of his cell lookin' at me an' grinnin' like a prize ape. Mind you, I have gotta certain admiration for this guy. He is a cool, deep, calculatin' cuss. He has got brains an' he also knows how to use same. It is always a wonder to me that guys who have gotta lotta brains do not proceed to use these in a legitimate sorta way. No, they just go crooked.

It is very much the same with dames. Some dame is born with a face like the Eiffel Tower in Paris looked at from above. She has got a figure like a mangle, an' every time she opens her month it sounds like a buzz-saw cuttin' through tin.

O.K. You can bet that this dame is goin' to be a credit to the community. You can bet your last nickel that she ain't goin' to do anything that is not very moral or even a bit wrong. You can also bet that she is goin' to be one of the leadin' lights in the Medola an' District United Ladies Knittin' an' Creature Comforts Guild, an' she is goin' to be self-sacrificin' an' good all the time eschewin' all pleasures except lookin' through the keyhole to see if the hired girl is tryin' to vamp the ice-man, an' if so, what technique does she use.

But if the same dame has gotta face that makes you ponder a bit, an' if she has got one of them slinky figures an' a look-me-over-kid-I'm-hard-to-get twinkle in her eye, if she has got them sorta ankles that makes a tired business man wonder whether his wife wasn't put on her feet too soon as a baby, an' if she has also got a lotta ideas about likin' diamonds an' parties an' sable furs an' what-have-you-got, then you can place your last brass button in the kitty an' call a big banco that this baby is goin' to make some sweet trouble before she hands in her dinner pail an' fills in an application for a small size in angel's wings.

I seen plenty guys in my time, but I reckon that Rudy has got somethin'. There is that cool, steady, far-away look in his eyes that makes a dame either go all goofy an' ask herself what she has been doin' all his life or else rush out an' ask the nearest traffic cop to save her from the wicked man.

I ask him if he would like a cigarette, but he says no thank you very much he prefers his own, after which he produces a gold an' platinum striped case an' lights a cigarette that smells like the pasha's sittin'-room after an all-night discussion with the harem committee on what they are goin' to do with Rosy Pearl since she has gone off her Turkish delight an' tried to bite the old boy's ear off every time he tries to get too fatherly.

"Now, Rudy," I tell him, "I am not going to tell you that I have made a big mistake, an' I am not goin' to tell you that I have got myself inta a jam. But the thing is this: Maybe we have made a little bit of a mistake about you an' Jack Rocca, an' maybe if you are sensible an' play things the way I tell you to, it won't be so bad for you."

He looks at me. His smile becomes a little broader. I am watchin' his eyes, an' even he can't stop 'em lightin' up a little bit.

"Yeah," he says, "meanin' what?"

"Meanin' this, Rudy," I tell him. "I came inta this job because Marella Thorensen wrote a letter to the Director sayin' that somebody was committin' Federal offences around here. O.K. But when I come down to investigate it Marella Thorensen gets bumped off, so although her murder ain't really my job I stick around here, because the D.A. asks me to an' investigate the two things together. But really as a Federal Officer my interest is mainly in findin' out what the Federal offences were.

"O.K. Well, I have now discovered that Marella never wrote that letter to the Director. Some other dame wrote it. I have also discovered that the letter that was written to Berenice Lee Sam in Shanghai—the letter that got her over here an' out to the Villa—was also not written by Marella. It was sent by this other dame.

"Well, the great thing is that I have got this other dame in the cooler. The dame who wrote them two letters is Marian Frenzer, otherwise known as Toots, an' this dame has been wise enough to make a full statement."

I see him drawin' hard on his cigarette.

"That's very interestin', Mr. Caution," he says. "So Toots made a statement?"

"Yeah," I tell him, "an' I reckon what she says is the truth, an' I reckon that because her statement very nearly lets you out an' I got reasons to believe that she ain't exactly fond of you."

I'm watchin' him like a cat. I know he is dyin' to ask me what Toots's statement was. I let him boil for a bit, an' then I tell him a sweet one.

"Well, Rudy," I say, "here's what Toots says. She says you gave her a job at The Two Moons Club, an' she says she fell for you like a sack of old coke. It looks like you had too much sex-appeal for that dame.

"O.K. Then you gave her the air because you get a yen on Marella Thorensen, an' Toots says she reckons she got plenty annoyed about this. So she worked out a way she could make some trouble for you two guys.

"In the meantime," I go on, "Toots has also discovered that you an' Aylmar Thorensen an' probably old man Lee Sam too have been runnin' silk contraband inta San Francisco, so Toots thinks of a swell idea for gettin' her own back on you for givin' her the air. She writes them two letters, one to the Director an' one to Berenice Lee Sam. She thinks that way she'll be makin' plenty trouble.

"O.K.," I tell him. "Here it is. I am quite prepared to make a deal with you if you're prepared to listen. I know you didn't have anything' to do with the Marella Thorensen killin', because I know she was killed out in the Villa Rosalito, an' we checked up on you on the night of the killin' an' we know you was never near that place. So here's the deal:

"I am sick of this case. I wanta close it down. I got my own ideas on who killed Marella Thorensen, an' if you ask me who it was, I think it was Toots. She was jealous of Marella an' wanted her outa the way, but I reckon that ain't my business. I reckon that's the business of the police here. I wanta make my report on the Federal offences angle of this case an' scram.

"Here's the trade I'll make with you. If you like to make a statement admittin' the contraband offences, admittin' that you an' Thorensen have been runnin' silk with or without Lee Sam, whatever's the truth, then I'm goin' to give orders for you to be sprung. That means to say that when you make that statement you can walk outa this cell, an' all I reckon you will have will be a civil action from the Customs Authorities. There'll be a big fine, but I should think Thorensen an' Lee Sam can take care of that. Well, do we trade?"

He takes three or four puffs at his cigarette.

"Well," he says, "what's the good of my arguin'? You got the low-down on me, Caution. I was runnin' silk with Thorensen, an' it looks like you know it, so I'd better admit it. I'll make that statement."

"O.K.," I tell him. "Here we go."

I take a big note-book outa my pocket an' I sit down on the bed, an' he makes a full statement about how he an' Thorensen, with the knowledge of old man Lee Sam, have been runnin', silk. He tells me all about it. When I have finished writin' up this statement I hand the note-book over to him.

"Sign that, Rudy," I say, "an' put the date on it. You will have to use your own pen because mine has run out."

He reads through the statement very carefully, an' he feels in his pocket an' takes out his fountain pen an' signs it. He hands the book back to me, an' I see that his signature has been written in Sea Island ink. I grin.

"Swell work, Rudy," I tell him. "Stick around. I'm goin' to see Police Captain Brendy, an' he'll check you out inside half an hour."

"Thanks a lot, Caution," he says. "Maybe I didn't like your face one time, but I don't think you're so bad. You got some sense anyway, an' I think you got the low-down on this job all right. I don't know, but I think it was Toots who bumped Marella."

"So do I," I tell him. "So long, Rudy, I'll be seein' you."

I go out of the cell an' the guard locks the door behind me. I walk along to Brendy's office.

"Look, bozo," I tell him, "do what I tell you an' don't argue. The time is now nine o'clock. At half-past nine you go in an' spring Rudy Spigla. You tell him that while he has been in here he has been held as a material witness in the Marella Thorensen case, but that you're satisfied he ain't had anything to do with it. You tell him that the Customs people here will be bringing civil charges against him in respect of the smugglin' that's been goin' on, an' that you'd like him to come down an' see you in a day or two to amplify the statement he's made here."

I show him the note-book.

"O.K., Brendy," I tell him. "Now when this guy gets outa here, we ain't goin' to lose sight of him. Maybe I've got an idea where he's goin' to. You've gotta have a smart guy at The Two Moons Club to tail him if he goes there. You've gotta have another smart guy at Burlingame waitin' to see if he goes out to the Villa Rosalito, but I don't think he's goin' to either of those places. I think he's goin' up to his apartment. I think he's goin' up there to see if I took that letter from Effie Spigla outa his safe, so I'm goin' to be hangin' around there waitin' for him. I'll look after that end of the job. You got all that?"

He sighs. I believe I told you that Brendy is not a very quick guy when it comes to thinkin'.

"I got it, Lemmy," he says. "You're the boss. I'll have them boys posted an' I'll talk to him like you said. I'll spring him at nine-thirty."

"Sweet work, feller," I tell him. "I'll be seein' you." I scram.

I am standin' in the shadows on the other side of the street opposite Rudy's apartment block on the hill. It is five and twenty to ten. At twenty to ten a car drives up an' Rudy gets out. He goes inside. Directly he goes in I walk to the corner an' look around. I signal the guy who has got my own car waiting for me to bring it up. He brings it up to the corner.

"O.K.," I tell this copper, "you can scram."

He scrams.

I get in the car an' sit there with the engine runnin'. I wait about ten minutes. Then Rudy comes out. He is smokin' a cigarette an' he has changed his overcoat. He gets inta his car an' he goes off. I go after him. We drive for about fifteen minutes. One time I think he is makin' for the Villa Rosalito, but I am wrong. He pulls up at a little hotel just outside the city limits on the Burlingame Road. He waits there for a few minutes and then he drives the car around inta the hotel garage which is round the back.

I stick around. Two three minutes afterwards he comes back an' walks inta the hotel. I leave my car where it is standing by the side of the road, an' I go along to the hotel. It is a little sorta place an' there is an old guy dozin' in the reception office.

I show him my badge. "That guy who just came in," I tell him, "what's his name an' what's his room number?"

He looks in the book.

"The name's Carota," he says, "an' the number's 38. Do you want me to call him for you?"

"No thank you," I say. "I reckon I'm goin' to make a personal call."

I get in the lift an' I go up to the second floor. I get outa the lift an' wait till the bellhop takes it down. I pull out my Luger an' walk along to No. 38 with the gun in my hand. I try the door. It ain't locked. I push it open an' I go in.

Just inside the room, which is a sittin'-room connectin' with the bedroom, takin' his coat off is Rudy. Walkin' towards him is a dame. Rudy spins around on his heel.

"Well, sucker." I tell him, "so you fell for it, an' if I was you I would keep your hands away from your hips otherwise this gun might go off."

I turn to the woman.

"Well, Marella," I tell her, "howya makin' out?"

Chapter Fifteen
CHORD OFF FOR A HEEL

RUDY looks at me. He has gone sorta yellow. His shoulders are sorta droopin'. This guy knows that he has come up against the grand slam.

The woman flops down on the lounge that is against the wall. She is a swell lookin' piece an' even if she has done her hair like a mobster's moll she still looks as if she has class. There are blue rings under her eyes an' her hands are tremblin'. I reckon that maybe Marella has been hittin' the hop again.

"Sit down, Rudy," I tell him. "I wanna talk to you."

He flops inta a chair. I go over to him an' frisk him. He has gotta .32 Mauser pistol in his hip. I take it off him an' put it in my pocket.

"Well, Big-Time," I tell him. "Are you goin' to come clean or am I goin' to spill it for you?"

He pulls himself together an' grins. "Yeah," he says, "I'm wise to you, Caution. I'm wise to your bluffs. I reckon I let you play me for a sucker when you had me down in the can. I suppose you sorta guessed I'd come up here, an' you thought you could tail along afterwards an' make me talk. Well, I ain't talkin'."

"Who cares, punk?" I tell him. "I have got all I want against you in the bag, sweetheart. The only thing you have gotta decide is whether you are goin' to save me some trouble or not."

I turn around to the dame. "Marella," I tell her. "I reckon that you are a mug to have tried to play along with a lousy heel like this. You musta been pretty hard up for a guy to string along with a cheap bozo like this one. Why he ain't even got brains."

Rudy breaks in.

"Say, clever," he says. "Am I in order in askin' you what, you are chargin' me with. You can't arrest me for nothin', you know?" He grins. "You been bustin' around this city talkin' big an' large about findin' who killed Marella Thorensen an' now you find out that nobody killed her, she's alive. So what?"

"I never said you killed Marella, Rudy," I tell him. "But you killed Effie all right, an' I've known you killed her for quite a while."

"Yeah," he says. "An' who told you that?"

"You did, punk," I tell him. "You told me when you left that letter that Effie wrote to you so that I could find it in your wall safe up at your apartment. You was a mug about that. If you'd got that dame to write that letter in ordinary ink you mighta got away with it. But like the big sap you are you forgot that you lent your fountain pen to Effie to write the letter with an' then afterwards you lent it to Marella here to write that letter to Aylmar Thorensen sayin' that he was Berenice Lee Sam's lover. That was not a wise thing to do."

He starts a big sneerin' act.

"You know plenty, don't you, copper?" he says.

"Like hell I do," I tell him. "An' I will show you just what I know, sweetheart, an' then you can have a big think about what you are goin' to do."

I light myself a cigarette. I see Marella watchin' me an' I go over an' give her one. I reckon she needs it too.

"You musta thought I was a big mug," I say. "What you forget to think was this—that directly I knew that Marella wasn't expectin' Berenice, an' directly I knew that Marella didn't know what the hell that telegram from the Director was about, that I would also know that she would call through to you to ask what she should do.

"O.K. Well you have already stalled Effie inta waitin' until about seven-thirty for the dough that you say you are goin' to give her, so you reckon you gotta stall everybody else too, don'tya? You tell Marella on the telephone to leave that phoney note for Nellie down in the kitchen where the 'G' man will see it when he comes so that he will not come back till nine o'clock an' you tell her to stall Berenice Lee Sam any way she likes because you ain't afraid of Berenice because you think you can hang a smugglin' rap on her pa.

"An' that, sweetheart, is why the telephone was back on the hook when I went back to the Villa at nine o'clock, because Marella had called through to you. The fact that she did not answer when Thorensen rang through to her when he was seein' Berenice just after seven was not because the receiver was off the hook. It was because Marella was already on the way out to see you in San Francisco to ask you what the hell all the mystery was about.

"Effie had a sweet scheme for blackmailin' you but she hadn't got enough brains to see it through an' look after herself. The poor mutt was mug enough to let you know that she had got somebody else to write those letters. She told you this after you had given her the dough an' she was feelin' good. She was explainin' to you how Marella could stall off the 'G' man by saying that the letter was not in her handwritin', that somebody was playin' a big joke. The same thing went for the Berenice letter."

He is lookin' at me hard. This guy is gettin' more scared every minute.

"I'll tell you what happened, Big Time," I tell him. "You made a date with Effie to hand over that dough to her in your apartment, an' you had the dough waitin' for her. When she come up you did a big act with her. You pretended that you thought she had pulled a clever one on you. You handed over the dough, an' you told her that you didn't mind payin' it out because you was goin' to take Marella for the dough that Thorensen had made over to her, in a day or so, so you was feelin' generous.

"The mug Effie falls for this line of talk, an' you then ask her how you can put the Berenice Lee Sam business an' the 'G' man business right, an' she tells you that, too.

"O.K. Then you pulla fast one on her. You say you don't mind givin' her the dough, but that this business is goin' to make things pretty tough for you with Marella; that Marella goin' to be plenty steamed up with you over this all business, an' that she will be afraid that there might be some more of it. You ask Effie to write you a letter sayin' thank you for the dough, an' that she will not hound you any more. You tell her that this letter is to show Marella. Effie writes the letter an' the envelope an' gives it to you.

"All right. You then get hold of her an' give her the works. You snatch the little .22 gun she has brought with her outa her hand-bag an' you shoot her. I reckon that you told her plenty first too.

"I reckon that you had Joe Mitzler around an' that the pair of you parked Effie in the next room or somewhere.

"Just when you have done this Marella blows in. She is all steamed up to hell. She wants to know what all this palooka about 'G' men is about, an' what the visit from Berenice is about an' just how much about her an' you Berenice knows. You pull some story on her an' while you are tellin' it to her you get one helluva idea. You tell Marella that Berenice Lee Sam is goin' to make things plenty hot for the pair of you an' that she will probably blow the story about your bein' tops with Marella, an' you tell Marella to write a letter accusin' her husband of stringin' around with Berenice Lee Sam an' to blow back to the Villa an' leave it up against the canister in the kitchen where the 'G' man will find it.

"An' you lend her your fountain pen to write the letter with. This poor mug Marella who is plenty fond of you does what you tell her.

"An' boy while she is writin' that letter you get the swellest idea of all. Nobody in San Francisco knows Effie an' so nobody will miss her. You reckon that she is about the same size as Marella, so you get Marella to take her clothes an' her rings off an' you take the clothes off Effie an' you change 'em. So Marella is Effie an' Effie is Marella. O.K.?

"Marella then goes back off to the Villa pronto to leave the letter she has written where I will find it when I go back. But I don't find it because Berenice gets there first an' grabs it.

"Directly Marella has gone off you send Joe Mitzler to throw Effie's body in the harbour. Nobody ain't goin' to see this because there is a helluva fog on.

"You think that you are now sittin' pretty; that everything is O.K. All right, pretty soon Marella comes back an', when she comes back an' starts talkin' to you she shows you the typewritten letter that Berenice got in Shanghai, the one she, gave Marella an' forgot to take back afterwards. Probably about this time Joe Mitzler comes back. You show him the letter an' he recognises the handwritin' of the signature. He knows that Toots signed that letter, an' so you are wise to the fact that it is Toots who has been workin' in with Effie.

"So you gotta find Toots. The thing is can you get your hooks on her an' shut her mouth before she starts talkin'. I reckon that you had Effie's handbag, an' I reckon that inside was some letter or somethin' that gave away the address where she had been stayin'. You send Joe Mitzler round there to pick up Toots an' to tell her one helluva story about Effie havin' taken a run-out powder on her with the dough, an' also given away where Toots is hidin' out.

"Then you get another sweet idea. You reckon that if somebody finds Effie's body there is just a chance that Toots might get a fit of bravery an' identify it. So you get Joe to run around an' telephone to the harbour an' you know that they will take it to the morgue an' that there will only be one guy on duty at the morgue at that time of night. You reckon you can pull a fast one an' bust Effie's face in so that *nobody* could identify her.

"But you tell Toots that you are doin' this because Effie has shot Marella with the gun you gave her an' that you are afraid the cops will identify the bullet if they find it.

"So you make Toots stand look-out outside the morgue while you are workin' that big act with the ice block, an' you also make her go out in that car with the thugs who tried to iron me out, not because you really wanted to get me outa the way bad but because you wanted to get Toots so tied up in your lousy killin's that she would haveta keep her mouth shut. I reckon that Joe Mitzler woulda shot her too, but you reckoned it wouldn't be wise to have another killin' on your hands right then.

"Also the attempt made on me is goin' to make me think that this has been done by the same person who hadda motive for bumpin' Marella, accordin' to the letter that I was supposed to find, an' that would be Berenice Lee Sam, an' if it is any satisfaction to you that is exactly what I did think until I found one or two other little things that smelt durn funny.

"You made one or two bum mistakes, Rudy. That ring Marella gave you, the one with the crossed keys on it, you oughta have chucked that away, because I found it an' I knew she'd given it to you. I suppose you hadta have it around so's she could see it until you'd got the Thorensen dough off of her.

"You made a mistake when you left that letter that you got Effie to write. I reckon you sent Joe around to the San Francisco Central Post Office to post that letter so that if anybody suspected you of bumpin' Effie they would think that she had posted that letter just before she caught a train outa town.

"But men don't keep envelopes. They always throw 'em away, an' I knew you kept that envelope an' that letter an' left 'em in the safe so that there would be evidence to help you over Effie if anybody was gettin' wise to you.

"The last thing of all is that you oughta use ordinary ink in your fountain pen instead of Sea Island ink, but then you are a smart an' original guy an' you like to be snappy—even about your ink.

"Well, Rudy . . . how does it go?"

I light myself another cigarette.

"Listen," I tell him. "Why don't you make a statement an' get Marella outa this. She is a poor dame an' she has only made the mistake of fallin' for a lousy son of a dog like you. If you make a statement you can put her in the clear an' she can scram outa here an' maybe get a break somewhere. I reckon she ain't had a very good time anyhow."

I look over at Marella. She has got her head down on the lounge an' she is sobbin' like she would bust.

"Hooey," says Rudy with a grin. "You gotta hang this killin' on me. Well . . . I never done it. I never bumped Effie. Maybe I gotta story as good as yours."

"Such as?" I ask him.

He leans over towards me an' he looks like all the devils in hell. He has just thought of another sweet one.

"My story is that Marella killed Effie out at the Villa Rosalito when she went out there, an' that Marella got Joe to chuck her in the lake. An'," he goes on with a smart look, "Toots's statement will support that story." He grins. "Don't you get that, fly cop?" he sneers. "Toots's statement will support that story an' I'll still get an acquittal on it."

I look over at Marella. She is sittin' up starin' at him. She is just realisin' the sorta guy he is—the sorta guy she got a yen for an' went all out for.

"Ain't you the lousy heel?" I say. "So you will still try to get out on a dame that was mug enough to fall for you."

He laughs. "That's my story," he says. "An' I reckon it's a good one."

I don't say anything. I am thinkin' hard. An' if you think it out you will see that he has got some sense. Toots is a witness for us but her statement that Effie went out to the Villa an' bumped Marella has now gotta look like the reverse. I reckon that statement in the hands of a clever lawyer might even win this dog an acquittal an' get Marella in the dirt. You never know with juries. Maybe this punk could even pull that one off.

I get up. "Have you got dough?" I ask Marella.

She nods.

"Get your things on, baby," I tell her.

She don't say anything. She just gets up an' goes inta the bedroom an' puts on her things. Pretty soon she comes out with a little suitcase in her hand.

I walk over to the sideboard an' pour her out a drink. I give it to her an' she swallows it.

"Scram, Marella," I tell her. "Blow outa San Francisco. Get outa this town pronto. Maybe you got friends some place. Well, go an' find 'em. So long, baby. I'm givin' you a break."

She looks at me. She is tremblin' all over.

"Thank you for that," she says.

She scrams.

I give myself a drink an' while I am sinkin' it I look at Rudy over the top of the glass. I am still holdin' the gun on him an' I see that he is beginnin' to look sorta puzzled.

"O.K., Rudy," I tell him. "So you're still goin' to be tough, hey? You're still goin' to be the bad man, an' you're goin' to tell the court an' the jury that Marella killed Effie; you're goin' to rely on Toots's statement backin' that stuff up. You think that you can get out by puttin' Marella in, an'"—I go on—"I got an idea that you might get away with it which would be a funny thing, wouldn't it?"

He grins some more. He is beginnin' to feel good.

"Maybe I can at that," he says. "Maybe I will get away with it!"

I give him a sweet smile. "Like hell you will, heel," I tell him. "So you wanta be tough, hey? O.K. Well, if you want it tough— here it is!"

I go over to the telephone an' call the desk downstairs. I tell 'em to put me through to The Two Moons Club; to say that somebody wantsta speak to Jack Rocca very urgent. While I am waitin' I put my handkerchief over the mouthpiece of the transmitter so that Rocca cannot guess who is speakin' to him. After a bit I hear him come on the wire. I speak sorta hoarse.

"Listen, Rocca," I tell him. "I am a guy who lives on a gun an' I been doin' work for Rudy Spigla. Well, I reckon I know a lousy heel when I see one an' this guy Spigla is tops in that line.

"I'm givin' you the low down. Right now this he dog is with a guy—a Federal dick—named Caution at the Four Star Hotel on the Burlingame Road. An' he is talkin' plenty. He is tryin' to save his own bum carcass by hangin' everythin' he can think of on to you. He reckons that if he puts you in bad enough he might get out.

"O.K. Well, what are you goin' to do about it? This guy Spigla is gettin' dangerous for all of us. He knows plenty. I thought that maybe you'd like to take care of him."

"Thanks, pal," he says. "I reckon I'll stop that baby's mouth before he gets a chance to get on any witness stand. Say, who is that talkin'?"

"Nobody very much," I tell him. "Just a pal. I don't reckon you'd know my name. But I reckon if one or two of your boys liked to drive around here an' stick around in about half an hour's time this Spigla would be leavin'. An' it's very quiet around here. It would be just too bad if somethin' happened to that guy, wouldn't it?"

"You're tellin' me . . ." he says. I hear him hang up. I look across at Rudy. He is sweatin'.

"I reckon you an' me is goin' to sit around for a bit, Rudy," I tell him. "We just sit around here until we hear that car with Rocca's boys in it pull up on the other side of the highway. Then you are goin' to take a little walk, but I am afraid that I shall haveta sorta part company at the doorway. You will be walkin' out, but me—well, I am goin' to stick around inside until the Rocca boys' tommy gun has sorta stopped squealin' . . . understand?"

I ease out of the Four Star Hotel nice an' quiet just after some highway cops had packed Spigla's body away in a patrol wagon. Rocca's boys had certainly given that guy plenty. I drive down the road until I find an all night drug store. I go in an' buy myself a nickel's worth of telephone. I get through to Vale Down House.

Pretty soon I hear somebody answerin'. It is that husky voice of that swell dame Berenice.

"Very Deep an' Very Beautiful Stream," I tell her. "I am stuck out here on the Burlingame Road, an' I reckon that I have now got time to listen to this big story you gotta tell me, about this Blue Dragon of yours."

I hear her laugh. It sounds like pourin' cream on a velvet carpet.

"It is not a story for the telephone, Lemmy," she says. "It is a story that should be told personally. Otherwise it may lose a great deal of its charm."

"That would be all wrong," I tell her. "Maybe I will come along an' take some more statements from you. Till soon. Sugar!"

I hang up. I wait for just a minute an' then I ring through to the Hall of Justice an' ask if Brendy is there. They say yes an' put him on the line.

"Looky, Brendy," I tell him. "You know a lot about these Chinese guys an' their proverbs an' things? Well, whatdya know about some Chinese story about some Blue Dragon?"

"Oh, it's one of them things, Lemmy," he says. "There is some story about a Chinese dame who was a swell looker an' she was sorta tied up to some rock by a guy who was nuts about her. This guy tells her that unless she falls for him in a big way he will leave her there an' that at midnight some Blue Dragon will come along an' probably make a meal off her.

"O.K. Well, he goes back at midnight an' finds that instead of bein' frightened of the Blue Dragon the dame has fallen for this animal an' has put a garland of flowers around his head an' is generally pettin' him. The long an' short of it is that the Blue Dragon mauls the other guy after which the beautiful dame can refuse the Dragon nothin'.

"But what the hell," he goes on. "Say, did you know about Spigla. Some thugs have shot this guy to pieces. Me, I think . . ."

But I have already hung up. I get back inta the car an' I step on it plenty. Pretty soon I see the lights on Nob Hill.

Me, I have been a lotta things, but I have never been a Blue Dragon. But if I am goin' to be one—boy, am I goin' to be good or am I?

THE END